Domain
of the
Netherworld

BRIAN LEON LEE

ISBN-13: 978-1494312763

By Brian Leo Lee
(Children's stories)
Just Bouncey
Bouncey the Elf and Friends Meet Again
Bouncey the Elf and Friends Together Again

Mr Tripsy's Trip
Mr Tripsy's Boat Trip

By Brian Leon Lee
Trimefirst

All available as eBooks

www.bounceytheelf.co.uk

For Rita

The Author

The author was born in Manchester. On leaving school, a period in accountancy was followed by a teaching career in Primary Education.
He has published, as Brian Leo Lee, several children's short stories including the popular Bouncey the Elf series.
Trimefirst, a science fiction novella, was published under the name of Brian Leon Lee in 2012.
Now retired and living in South Yorkshire.

1

'Aren't you ready yet!'

A voice called impatiently from the hotel bedroom doorway.

Chaz looked up from tying his trainer lace, then bent down and finished the double knot. 'Sorry! Won't be a sec.'

Standing in the bedroom's half open doorway was his Uncle Bryden. Of medium height, he was dressed for the outdoors. A woollen cap hid his mop of fair hair and he was wearing his all weather anorak and a heavy looking backpack pulled down on one shoulder. His well-dubbined hiking boots creaked as he leaned forward.

'I did say 6.30 didn't I?' he said with a frown.

'Yes… but…'

'The taxi is waiting so get your skates on. OK,' he insisted, this time with a smile.

Chaz looked at his uncle, his Dad's younger brother and said as he turned to pick up his own anorak and backpack, 'I'm ready.'

In the lift, as they went down to the hotel lobby, Chaz thought back to last week. *A phone call from his Dad, an oil rig maintenance engineer and as usual a change of plans. He couldn't get away from the rig. They were short handed again and as senior engineer he had to fill in. Again as usual, his mum was not around to help. The divorce had really split the family up. She was in the States somewhere out of contact.*

His Dad went on to explain that his Uncle Bryden was just about to go on his holidays and would be delighted to have Chaz along. They could meet up at his uncle's flat that weekend.

So that's how he ended up in this lift in the middle of Sofia, Bulgaria.

Bulgaria! Bloody hell!

The taxi skidded to a halt on the forecourt of the Central Station of Sofia. Hurriedly paying the taxi driver, Uncle Bryden grabbed his backpack and urged Chaz to do the same.

'We left it a bit tight,' he said, glancing at his watch and walking quickly towards the main entrance.

'I reckon we have just enough time to get something to eat and drink.' He stopped and said, 'Here, take the tickets and my things and go grab our seats. OK.'

Chaz nodded and began to trudge slowly along a platform, still only half awake, looking blearily at the hurrying throng of other late travellers rushing to catch the train.

It was more by luck than judgment that he found the right one.

(For some reason, the Bulgarians numbered the platforms in Roman numerals 1-V1 and the actual track in Arabic numbers, 1-12. The indicator board showed the track not the platform number. Their Vidin train was on track 8 platform 1V).

Chaz boarded the train, struggling with the two backpacks along the central aisle, squeezing his way past similarly loaded passengers until he reached their reserved seats.

With a big sigh, he lifted up the backpacks onto the luggage rack and sat down. 'Jeez! What a start to the day.'

He then realized he was sweating like a pig. With a loud groan he stood up and took off his anorak, throwing it down onto the seat next to him.

Looking around he noticed most of the other passengers had found their seats and had begun to settle down except for a small child, fortunately further up the carriage, who began to whine for a drink.

Slumping down in his seat, Chaz gave a big yawn and glanced through the train carriage window. The platform was practically deserted now, just a couple of gossiping porters lighting up their cigs after the last minute rush.

—

A whistle sounded and with a jerk the train began to move.

Chaz sat up. 'What the hell... where's Uncle Bryden?'

'Not worried were you?'

Turning round in his seat Chaz saw his Uncle approaching him along the central aisle, carrying two paper bags and a plastic carrier bag.

'Of course not,' replied Chaz, trying unsuccessfully not to show it.

Sitting opposite to him, Uncle Bryden put the bags down on the table between them.

'We were a bit late so most things have been sold out.' He handed Chaz a paper bag. 'I did manage to get a few 'ears' and some drinks though.'

Chaz blinked. *'Ears,'* he thought. *My God it's true. He had read that a favourite delicacy in Bulgaria was fried pigs ears.*

'Er, thanks Uncle but I don't fancy them this early in the morning.'

With a loud laugh Uncle Bryden said, 'Sorry Chaz I couldn't resist it. Go on, open the bag.'

Slowly, Chaz reached out and opened the bag. He sniffed and then a great big grin spread across his face.

'You... You...' he said as he brought out a flat round cake.

It could just, with a lot of imagination look like a squashed ear. It was still warm and covered in sugar. It looked a bit like a doughnut. Taking a bite he found it tasted like one as well.

As a smiling Chaz began to gobble up the remaining three 'ears,' Uncle Bryden said they were actually called Mekitsas.

'I don't care what they're called. They're great,' said Chaz as he took a bottle of water from the plastic bag.

After their early breakfast Chaz learnt a bit more about the trip. His uncle was a museum conservator who worked for a private art museum in London. He and his fellow

—

scientists in the department tried to answer questions that helped with the interpretation of any art object including: How old is it? Where does it come from? What is it made of? How was it made?

'Actually, Chaz,' his uncle went on, 'This trip could lead me to one of the greatest finds in cave art for years.'

He paused as he opened a bottle of water and had a drink.

'Have you heard of the *Belogradchik Rocks?*'

Chaz thought for a moment and then said, 'I read about them in a guidebook. Aren't they the ones that are famous for their funny shapes.'

Uncle Bryden nodded. 'That's right. The hills around there have been eroded into fantastic shapes, many resembling rocky figures. Well, not far from there is the largest cave system in Bulgaria. The Magura Caves. They have a huge number of ancient cave paintings, some dating from the Neolithic times. That's where we are going. A new series of caves have recently been discovered and I've been invited to do a preliminary investigation.'

He looked at Chaz and added, 'This holiday of mine is a cover to keep the press in the dark. If this got out there'd be hundreds, maybe thousands of people trying to get into the caves.'

Chaz tried to hide his disappointment.

What a holiday this is turning out to be.

His uncle stood up and rummaged in his backpack and pulled out a small notebook. Sitting down he began to read.

The train rattled and swayed along the track. Chaz, listening to his iPod, swayed with it until he put his arms and head on the table and nodded off.

A screech of metal wheels skidding on the rails woke Chaz with a start.

'What... Where... Oh...'

He looked around and saw that several passengers were getting their luggage down.

The train had stopped in a station.

10

'Ah, back to the land of the living.' His uncle grinned down at him. 'Come on, we get off here too.'

'Where are we?' he croaked, his throat dry from his sleep. Then he saw the station sign. **Ureshos.**

A one-horse town might just beat it for size. It had the railway station and a handful of small wooden shacks. A battered minibus and a worn looking Dacia taxi were waiting by a ramshackle ticket office. The passengers who had already left the train trooped over to the minibus.

'Come on Chaz. Chop Chop,' Uncle Bryden chivied as he went over to the taxi. 'We haven't all day.'

Dragging his feet, Chaz took his time. *This is getting beyond a joke,* he thought.

As they both sat down on the rear seat of the taxi, the springs twanged in protest.

'Don't vorry my friends,' said the driver as he fixed their backpacks to a precarious looking roof-rack. 'This car could take you to the moon and back with no trouble at all. She has more than 500,000 km on the clock already. Heh. Heh.'

He grinned through a set of blackened and twisted teeth. 'Ve go now, yes?'

After lighting a foul smelling cigarette, he started the engine. With a sickening crunch, he engaged the gears and set off leaving a cloud of stinking diesel smoke to drift over the mini-bus, which had not yet left.

Uncle Bryden winked at Chaz and then rolled his eyes as if to say. *Don't blame me. I didn't order it.*

The taxi took the road towards Belogradchik, the impressive rock formations clearly visible and then veered off onto a side road. A wobbly looking sign said Rabisha 20 km. An hour later they arrived at the village, aching all over.

'Let's take the Lunar rocket next time,' said Uncle Bryden in a rueful voice, rubbing his back. 'Come on Chaz. Let's get something to eat from the Ritz over there.' He was pointing to a shabby, two storey building which had a sign which read OTL, next to a two pump petrol station cum garage.

Chaz tried to forget the next hour or so. The 'meal' was fried pigs ears with cabbage or roasted pig's ears with cabbage. The water glasses were opaque with dirt, so they made do with a couple of bottles of local beer. The urgent visit to the toilet made Chaz's day. *Would you believe it*! *A hole in the floor for Gods sake?* He was nearly sick but he was already feeling sick because of the pig's ears he didn't eat. Staggering back to the table, he made urgent signs to his uncle. LEAVE.

Getting the message, Uncle Bryden paid the bill and half carrying Chaz they left the OTL. He then ordered the taxi to take them to the Magura Caves. Guess what. It was the moon taxi.

'Allo agin, I take you quiic.' The blackened and twisted teeth grimaced like a death mask as a stream of cigarette smoke floated out of wide nostrils.

'Do we have to?' whispered Chaz.

'Lie back in the seat. You'll feel better soon,' his uncle said sympathetically.

The journey was horrendous for Chaz. He thought he was going to die. Stomach cramps, the seat springs trying to bore into his backside and to top it all, the maniac taxi driver began to sing. Well, cats wailing would be more preferable. He didn't even notice the largest lake in Bulgaria as they bounced and rattled by its shore.

 The sound of silence told Chaz his torture was over. They had arrived at the Magura caves. Fortunately there was a decent washroom by the entrance.

So while his uncle was sorting out the paperwork for the visit in the Administrative office, Chaz went in for a wash and brush up. Bliss. He felt human once more. A couple of stomach tablets had done the trick.

Outside he met his uncle who was looking worried. 'The Professor I was supposed to meet here is ill and his replacement hasn't arrived either. We had better wait in the office,' he said grumpily.

They had both just picked up their backpacks when a clapped out car driven by what appeared to be a local bandit, squealed to a halt, missing them by a hairs breadth.

A young woman not much older than Chaz jumped out of the nearside door clutching a leather shoulder bag.

She was wearing traditional peasant dress. It was a colourful arrangement of a long white skirt covered front and back by short red and black striped aprons, which were edged with a broad band of black velvet, and crisscrossed by rows of gold braid to which small coins were attached. A leather belt around the waist was joined by a pafka (a double silver buckle joined by a hook).

A short-sleeved blouse and a dark red short-sleeved waistcoat, both embroidered and a small gaudy headscarf fighting to keep her long dark hair in place, finished off the ensemble. However, a pair of white trainers peeking out from her long skirt marred the desired effect somewhat.

With a large smile she approached them. 'Hi. You must be Mr. Lorimore,' she said to Uncle Bryden in perfect English. 'I'm Iskra Daskalova. The Professor has arranged for me to look after you while you are here. I am one of his students at the Academy of Music and Fine Art. I'm sorry I'm late. We were rehearsing for one of our Saints day fiestas and we overran. I didn't even have time to change.'

Chaz gave a wide grin. *Wow!* He thought. *This might be fun.*

They went into the admin block and Iskra led them through the main entrance into a small office. 'This is the Professor's hidey-hole. Park your bags and take a seat.' She went round a paper-cluttered desk and sat down.

Chaz and his uncle were quite impressed by the confident manner in which Iskra had taken control of the meeting. They settled down on two comfortable looking chairs. *Anything, including a bed of nails,* thought Chaz, *would be comfortable after that taxi ride.*

Iskra rummaged amongst the papers on the desk and then

bent down and opened a drawer. 'Ah, this it it.' She held up a folded map. 'My Professor really is not well. This should be in his safe. Anyway, let's not waste any more time. Yes!'

Opening the map, Iskra laid it on the desktop. It showed the layout of the cave system. Chaz and his uncle stood up and looked at it closely.

'As you can see,' Iskra pointed with a pencil, 'The cave has one main gallery and three minor ones. They total about two and a half kilometres in length.'

Chaz was impressed despite his feigned indifference.

'Excuse me, Iskra,' Uncle Bryden interrupted. He was eager to get on. 'Can you show me where the professor made his new discovery.'

'Of course Mr. Lorimore, I ......'

'Please. Call me Bryden.'

'OK, Bryden.' Iskra gave a quick smile and pointed to the map with her pencil. *(Chaz was not amused by this turn of events).*

'This spot here, the Hall of Stalactites and Stalagmites is immense. It is over 100m long and is covered with them. It was no wonder that no one had noticed a small fissure behind one of the stalagmites next to the cave wall.'

Iskra went on. 'Last month, the Professor decided to measure some of these stalagmites. He had become aware that the records had not been up-dated for some time. To cut the story short, he discovered the fissure and broke through into a new gallery and found the cave paintings.'

'He must have been over the moon,' said Bryden. 'What a find.'

'Yes,' said Iskra. 'However, he knew he had to keep the news private until he verified the paintings as originals. He has only told the Academy Director and a few of us students. That is why he sent for you Bryden.'

'Right!' said Bryden taking command.

'Iskra do you think you could rustle up some food and drink to take with us?'

'What! Now?' A startled Iskra looked at Bryden.

'Of course now! We can't waste a second,' replied Bryden. 'The news could leak any time. You know the media will pay top money for a story like this.'

Iskra nodded in agreement and went for the food and drink.

'Now then Chaz, we need to travel fast and light, so only carry what you really need. OK.'

Chaz was gob-smacked by the change in his uncle. 'Er, right oh then,' and he went over to get his backpack and began to sort out some of his stuff.

He grabbed a compact pouch containing emergency essentials and an ex-army hip water-bottle. He was fixing them to his belt when his uncle looked over and said, 'Good thinking Chaz but don't forget your anorak. It can get quite cool in caves.'

Nodding, Chaz sneaked his iPod and earbuds into one of his cargo pants pockets.

A few minutes later Iskra returned carrying a day-bag. 'I managed to get a few slices of Banitsa and some cans of coke from the café.'

'It will have to do,' answered Bryden. 'I hope we won't be too long down there.' Then he asked, 'Are there any decent torches around, Iskra? Oh and a length of climbing rope if possible?'

Iskra smiled and said, 'This is a cave-site you know,' and went to one of the cupboards along the office wall. Opening one, she revealed an array of torches, ropes, first-aid kits and lots more.

'Great,' said Bryden, going over and helping himself to three large torches and a coil of rope. 'You never know what you might need down a cave and once in it's too late to go back. Oh Chaz, grab a first-aid kit please. Better safe than sorry.'

Bryden made sure that he had his small, specialist equipment kit:

Odds and ends he had found useful in the past; a small

but powerful magnifying glass, half a dozen small jars of different chemicals, a tiny scalpel, a bunch of small, art paint brushes, a small notebook and of course his digital camera. He carefully placed them in a pouch and clipped it to his belt.

Chaz looked across as his uncle packed his stuff. He was keen on photography himself and would have loved to own one of those cameras. They had a focus of what was it, f/1.4.

Iskra suddenly pulled a face. 'I can't go down into the caves dressed like this.' She looked down at her long dress and pulled a face again.

'Look!' said Bryden. 'We just don't have time to piss about while you go back for a change of clothes. OK.'

'Well. I suppose I'd better put my wrap on then,' grumbled Iskra as she pulled a short, black woollen cape from her shoulder bag.

'For Gods sake grab a torch and let's go,' said Bryden in an exasperated voice as he slung the coil of climbing rope over his shoulder.

Iskra glared at Bryden before she slung her shoulder bag on and picked up her torch and the day-bag of food and drink. Then, leading the way out of the office she took them along the path towards the cave entrance. A sheer rock face dotted with scrub trees appeared around a bend. The cave was under the overhanging rock face, about 5m or 6m wide and 3m at it's highest.

'The next guided tour isn't scheduled for nearly an hour,' explained Iskra as they approached the cave. 'So we won't be delayed by groups of tourists blocking the walkway. There are also electric lights all the way to the Hall of the Stalactites.'

Iskra walked into the cave and then called back to them over her shoulder. 'Although they are not very good, I mean bright.'

Bryden had a thought. *Seeing that the way through the caves would be illuminated, it would be better to avoid using their torches now in order to save the batteries for the new cave system.* Calling to Iskra, he explained his idea.

Iskra walking down the passage, half turned and waved to indicate that she had heard.

Chaz nodded to say that he had got the message too. Feeling a little apprehensive now that he was here, he followed Iskra and his uncle into the cave.

2

A few metres inside, the cave began to narrow into a sloping, winding passage. It got steeper as they went down and the rocky floor soon became slick from the dripping water oozing from the walls and roof.

Chaz found that he could hardly see Iskra and his uncle who, though only a metre or two ahead of him were nearly invisible in the gloom of the sparsely spaced lights fixed precariously to the passage walls a few centimetres above the floor.

Jeez, he thought, *What a holiday this is turning out to be.*

Iskra, familiar with the cave layout, pressed on. She was still feeling miffed because she had not been able to change into more suitable clothes. So when she reached the next gallery, (a large open space) she began to walk more quickly through the shadows cast by the low powered light bulbs, to the other side.

Bryden, stumbling out of the narrow passage just managed to keep his footing. 'Careful. Watch your feet Chaz,' he called out in a loud voice. The dark open space had caught him unawares.

'What's up?'

Before Bryden could say anything, out of the darkness came a fluttering mass of … what? Then he realized what was happening. 'Chaz! Cover your face. Now!'

Not knowing what to expect, Chaz raised his hands to his face. The next instant he was being buffeted by what seemed like thousands of bats. 'Jeez! What the hells happening.' *The loud shout his uncle had made must have spooked them.*

Though it seemed like an age, it was actually only a few seconds before the horde of chittering bats flew past Chaz and silence reigned once more in the gallery.

'Did the bats startle you?' the echoing voice of Iskra

called out across the cavern and she smiled to herself in the semi-darkness.

'Hang on Iskra. Don't get too far ahead. Remember it's me and Chaz's first visit and we don't know what to expect.'

'OK but I thought you were in a hurry to get to the new gallery?'

'Not that fast, Iskra. We'll be with you in a few minutes.'

Following his uncle along the dimly lit gallery, Chaz cursed as he slipped and slithered along the walkway covered with a mixture of bat droppings and water oozing from the rock.

'Have we far to go?' asked Chaz hopefully when he reached Iskra.

Squinting through the gloom, Iskra clicked her torch on for a moment and said in reply, 'I think we should reach the Hall of Stalactites in about twenty minutes.'

'Will it get any easier?' Bryden asked her. 'I didn't think it would be as awkward as this.'

'It's the old problem, money,' replied Iskra. 'The Department of Culture and Arts keep promising to upgrade the lighting and improve the walkways but nothing ever happens. Anyway, let's have a drink.'

Iskra opened her day-bag and handed out cans of coke to them. Pausing to have a drink herself, she sighed and said, 'I'm sorry I left you in the Bat Gallery. I acted like a child. It won't happen again.'

Not realizing quite what she meant, Chaz and his uncle mumbled that it was ok.

Feeling refreshed after the short break they set off along the now familiar ill-lit walkway. It continued to go deeper and deeper into the hillside. Soon it became a dank, narrow passage only wide enough for one person and a small one at that.

Shuffling along with his head bent to avoid catching the roof, Chaz at the rear as usual, began to mutter to himself. *Caves in Bulgaria! Why the hell did his uncle have to come here? What's wrong with the one in the south of France? At least it's warm there and I bet it's dry as well.*

Then, without any warning, (Iskra had kept it as a surprise) the passage opened out into a huge gallery.

Chaz and his uncle gasped in amazement. They were standing on a ledge near the very top of the giant cavern. It must have been well over one hundred metres long. A narrow path zigzagged downwards some twenty metres to meet the floor, which was at least fifty metres wide.

A forest of stalactites and stalagmites jutting from the roof and floor, illuminated by several spotlights which were dotted along the gallery, glistened and sparkled like giant jewels as the calcified rock reflected the light.

'Not bad, eh!' said a smiling Iskra. 'Let's go down but take care. The hand rail is a bit wonky.'

Chaz didn't know whether to gawp at the array of stalactites hanging down from the roof or keep an eye on the wobbly rail that stopped him from plunging over the edge of the steep path on which he was descending so slowly.

'Come on Chaz! It's not that bad,' Iskra's voice floated up to him from the bottom of the path.

'It's alright for you two. You're used to caves. I'm not.'

Bryden tried to be patient. They were so near to the new cave system and he wanted to get moving. So he turned towards Iskra and asked her how far it was to the fissure.

'A few minutes that's all,' she replied. Then as Chaz half stumbled off the path and joined them, she opened her shoulder bag and fumbled around in it for a bit before taking out a small key hanging from an equally small fob.

'This will open the security door,' she explained. 'After the Professor had made his discovery he made sure no one without permission could enter the new gallery.'

'Very sensible,' said Bryden. 'If the site got con-taminated by non-professionals, God knows what damage could have been done.'

'Exactly,' Iskra interrupted. 'That is just what the

Professor said.'

'Well, now that our intrepid explorer is with us, let's go,' said Bryden with a friendly grin as he ruffled Chaz's hair.

Chaz was not amused but when he saw Iskra smile at him, he relaxed and gave his uncle a gentle punch on the arm. 'OK then, I'm ready to go.'

Once more Iskra lead the way but this time everyone could see quite clearly where they were going because of the spotlights.

The path wound round and past some of the largest stalagmites that Bryden and Chaz had ever seen. It was awesome.

Chaz couldn't help himself. 'How old are these Iskra. I know they must take years to form but these are massive.'

'Well, we know the caves were first formed about fifteen million years ago by an underground river forcing its way through cracks in the rock. When the river stopped flowing and the caves more or less dried out, rainwater soaked down through cracks in the local rock. Here it is limestone and mixes chemically with it. The water drips coming through the roof and falling to the floor left minute traces of calcium and other minerals hanging on the roof. Over thousands, even millions of years the drips formed into spikes and pillars of the hard rock we see today. The longer or taller it is, the older it is.'

'I see. Thanks Iskra.'

By now Iskra had led them away from the central path and was weaving in and out of a group of slim stalagmites between one and two metres high, towards the cave wall. There, partially hidden by a sturdy looking stalagmite was a padlocked iron gate set into the rock.

'Here we are,' said Iskra quietly as she used her key to opened the lock. She then pulled the gate open. A horrible screech filled the air and Chaz cringed. 'Sorry, I forgot about that. We can't afford the oil you know,' she said, smiling at her own joke.

'The professor found the fissure blocked by small rocks

and boulders so he ordered it to be cleared and then widened enough for him and an assistant to get through,' she explained.

Snapping the padlock back onto the gate, Iskra pushed at a flimsy looking wooden door that blocked the way in. It opened without a sound.

'Time for our torches,' Iskra said as she switched hers on. The beam shone down a narrow passage strewn with small rocks. 'Careful where you put your feet,' she warned. 'We haven't managed to clear up yet as you can see.'

'Don't worry about it,' said Bryden in an excited voice.

'How far to the cave paintings? How far?'

3

Iskra looked closely at Bryden. Even in the torchlight she could see the tension in his face. 'For goodness sake! Calm down!' *Professors,* she thought. *They're all the same. So eager to get into the limelight.*

'It will only take us a few minutes. This passage opens out into a small gallery and then you can start your work.'

Nodding his head, Bryden pointed his torch so that the beam shone down the passage. Like other parts of the cave system it was wet with water droplets dripping and plopping from the roof and walls. The droplets reflected back the light, like myriads of tiny diamonds glinting in the sun.

Taking care not to slip or trip over the loose rocks strewn all over the floor of the narrow passage, Bryden couldn't help but walk as fast as he could towards the newly found gallery.

Chaz, who was also taken up by the unspoken excitement of his uncle, pushed past Iskra in order to get behind his uncle.

'Chaz! You nearly knocked me over.'

'Sorry! I didn't mean to.'

The passage began to drop down like an irregular staircase, some treads small others quite deep. This put paid to any more potential fallouts. They all had to concentrate on where to put their feet.

Then Bryden yelled out.

'My God! Just look at that!' He had reached the end of the passage and his waving torch shone across a small chamber. The new gallery! It was about ten metres wide and looked to be around twenty metres long.

Chaz, easing past his uncle, took a step into the chamber, ducking his head just in time to avoid getting a nasty headache from a jutting piece of rock hanging down from the low roof. 'Jeez!' he exclaimed as he looked across to the far side.

The rocky wall had two flattish areas on which a series of painted animals could be seen. What amazed Chaz was the fact that they looked as though they had just been done. The colours were remarkably fresh and bright.

'Well Bryden! What do you think?' Iskra stood by his side and looked at him, trying to see his face but it was hidden in a shadow. 'Is this worth your long journey?'

Without answering, he dropped the coil of rope and he pulled out his camera and took a series of photos. Then, stumbling over some loose rocks, he went across the chamber for a closer look. 'There's something not quite right about them,' he said in a perplexed voice.

'Chaz, Iskra, point your torches on that animal please, the one that looks like a stag. Yes! That's better!' The concentrated beams of light picked out the particular one Bryden wanted to examine. He flipped open the pouch around his waist again and took out his magnifying glass. Leaning forward, he took a close look at the cave painting.

'Bloody hell!' he exclaimed, taking an involuntary step backwards. 'It's impossible.'

'What do you mean Bryden? You're beginning to worry me.' Iskra shone her torch right into his face.

'This is not a prehistoric cave painting like the ones you have in the other part of the Magura caves. It's quite modern. I would bet my life on it that it can't be more than a few weeks old.'

Iskra was aghast. 'It can't be. The Professor only discovered them two weeks ago. This cave has been blocked for.... well I don't know but the professor was positive this was a new discovery. Are you sure? Really sure.'

Bryden reached out a hand and said, 'I should never do this but ...' He rubbed a finger down one leg of the stag painting and showed it to Iskra and Chaz. It was smudged with red dust.

'How can a prehistoric painting still be pulverulent,' he said quietly. 'There is something very wrong here and I'm going to find out what it is.'

'Say again, uncle.' Chaz was completely clueless as to what he had meant.

'Sorry, Chaz, it sort of slipped out. Lab talk you know.'

Bryden tried again. 'The wall paintings found here in the Magura caves were made with bat guano. Isn't that right Iskra?'

Iskra nodded in agreement.

'Well. When I examined that stag over there, it was not made by an artist using bat guano pigment. I'm absolutely positive about that.'

'How can you be so sure,' asked Chaz who was now beginning to show more interest in the discussion.

Bryden smiled. He was enjoying the way this was developing. He knew Chaz was resentful for being dumped on him for his holidays and that he was not really interested in his work. *Largely,* Bryden thought, *through ignorance about what he actually did. Still, I had better be careful with what I say.*

'Actually Chaz, it's about the pigments used by the artist or artists who painted these wall paintings. That smudge I got when I rubbed the stag's leg was from red ochre. That's a pigment which is made by first hammering a special red rock into very small pieces, then grinding it down into a powder. The powder is mixed with something like say animal fat, anything that would make it into paste.

Voila! You have made a painting medium. The crucial thing is that as it dries it leaves a layer of red dust. Not one of the wall paintings in the Magura Caves is made with red ochre paint. Do you agree Iskra?'

Stunned by what she had just heard, it took a moment or two before she could answer. 'That… That… is absolutely right Bryden. The Professor will be heart broken when he hears about this.'

Chaz broke in. 'Er, do you think we could have

something to eat. I'm starving.'

Bryden looked at his watch. 'God! Is that the time. No wonder you want something to eat. What about you Iskra?'

'Now you mention it I could do with a Banitsa.' She slipped off her day-bag and produced three paper bags, passing one each to Chaz and Bryden.

'Thanks, Iskra. Sorry I forgot about the time, Chaz,' Bryden said, grabbing the bag from her, whilst at the same time placing his camera on the floor and wedging his torch between two rocks.

Chaz just nodded his thanks to Iskra and began to stuff his face with the Banitsa which had a savoury filling that he rather enjoyed.

Watching the way he ate it, Iskra smiled and along with a can of coke gave him another slice.

He realized that now he was her slave forever. Well, at least until the next meal.

Feeling agreeably relaxed after their break, Bryden and Iskra began to talk 'shop' on issues regarding the cave art world.

Meanwhile, Chaz had taken out his iPod and after putting his earbuds in, he began to listen to one of his favourite bands. His uncle didn't seem to notice or was not concerned that he had brought it along.

Nodding along to the beat of the music, he got up from the rock he had been using as a seat. Absent-mindedly rubbing his aching backside with one hand, he shone his torch towards the cave paintings, ambling over for another look. Knowing how they were painted seemed to make them more interesting.

Wandering down to the far end of the cave he found himself looking at a pig. Then he realized that it must be a wild boar. *It's quite realistic*, he thought. The big pair of tusks were very prominently portrayed. *Jeez, I wouldn't like to meet that on a dark night.*

Moving to his left his torch flashed along the wall. He stopped. *Something was different,* he thought. He moved the light back along the wall. There, high up a flash, a glint of something shiny.

Chaz was intrigued. He lifted the torch slightly and gasped in astonishment. He saw a glittering, shimmering shape. A bird. The colours were unusual. Hues of red, yellow and orange twinkled and sparkled in the torchlight. *This was no red ochre painting,* he thought. *What the hell was it?*

'Uncle Bryden! Iskra! Over here! You won't believe what I've found?' Chaz was animated beyond belief. He swung his torch towards his uncle and Iskra who had jumped up at his first shout. They both raised their hands to cover their eyes from the glare.

'Calm down Chaz, calm down,' Bryden said, squinting through his fingers wondering what the hell all the fuss was about. He bent down and picked up the torch he had previously jammed between two rocks and followed Iskra who had already begun to walk over towards Chaz.

'Look! Look up there!' Chaz excitedly pointed upwards.

Three torch beams focused on a recess near the top of the cave. A fold in the rock face had shielded it from direct view, explaining how they had missed seeing it earlier.

The bird seemed to be about 75cm tall. It reflected the concentrated light back like a mirror, a dazzling array of fire-like colours, so strong they hurt the eye. What fascinated Chaz was the fact that he found he could see each and every one of the bird's feathers. *Impossible of course*, he thought.

'It can't be.' Iskra suddenly became very animated and grabbed hold of one of Bryden's arms. 'You'll think I'm mad Bryden but I believe it is a representation of the mythical and fabled Firebird.'

'What the hell is that when it's at home?' scoffed Chaz.

'It's supposed to have magical properties,' replied Iskra in a shaky voice. 'Don't mock what you don't understand Chaz.'

'Hey! Uncle Bryden, you don't believe in all that

twaddle, do you?' he said with a chuckle. To his surprise he heard his uncle say to Iskra in what seemed a strange voice,

'Are there any sacred symbols in here Iskra? If there are, then we could be in danger.'

'It's hard to see something like that in this torchlight,' she replied, 'Though I did notice some bits of what looked like broken pottery in the corner as I went over to Chaz.'

'Come on Uncle. What are you saying? That this place is haunted?'

'Don't joke like that Chaz please.' Iskra's voice came out in a whisper. 'These caves have been known for centuries to be a place of special interest for religious ceremonies and other ritual practices.'

'Why all the whispering? This is ridiculous. We're in the twenty first century for Gods sake,' said Chaz, a little sarcastically.

'Look! I'll prove it,' he said. Before either Bryden or Iskra could move, Chaz jumped onto a biggish boulder resting by the wall of the cave. 'See that feather.' He pointed to a magnificent, radiant tail feather, shimmering with an iridescent glow. It looked so real. 'I bet I can get that one.' Stretching one hand, Chaz reached out for the feather.

'For Gods sake leave it alone,' yelled Bryden at the top of his voice as he grabbed hold of Chaz round the waist just as Iskra grabbed a leg, trying to pull Chaz off the boulder.

By then Chaz had just managed to get a grip on the feather. He had a momentary thought. It was a real feather but it felt both hot and cold at the same time. A terrible feeling of dread flashed through his body. He tried to let go of the feather but it seemed to be stuck to his hand. Then the weight of his uncle and Iskra pulling at his leg proved too much. He fell off the boulder still clutching the now vibrant, gleaming feather, to fall right on top of his uncle and Iskra.

A shimmering halo of light began to emanate from the now pulsating, flashing feather. It swelled into a protective cocoon, which enveloped all three of them in the warm embrace of an ethereal essence.

Then, as they clung together, terrified as to what would happen next, it was gone.

'Is everyone ok?' Bryden's voice verged on the hysterical.

Having just been scared out of his wits, Chaz hesitantly replied, 'I.... I... think so.'

'Iskra! Iskra!' Bryden called out in a worried voice, 'Where are you? If you can hear me say something.'

'If you get off my f....... face,' a muffled voice underneath him said, 'I might be able to answer you.'

'Hell! Sorry Iskra. I can't see a thing.'

'Move over so I can get up. I think I have a spare torch in my bag.'

A few moments later Iskra sat up. 'God! That's better.' After taking a few deep breaths, she pulled her shoulder bag round and rooted for her torch and switched it on.

They all blinked at the sudden brightness. Then Bryden looked at them and said with great relief, 'Thank God you're both alright.' He looked around. The small torch did not spread much light.

'You know, something strange has just happened and I for one am glad it's all over.'

'Uncle! Uncle Bryden!'

'Yeah, Chaz, what is it?' Bryden turned to look at him. *Funny,* he thought. 'Are you sure you're ok? You look a little, er, unsettled. Don't worry Chaz, it's all over. Things will be fine.'

Chaz pointed over his uncle's shoulder.

'Look! Look at the cave paintings! They're not there. They've all gone.'

Bryden turned round. Chaz was right. Not one painting could be seen. It looked as if there had never been any there at all.

4

The silence that followed Chaz's statement went on for at least a couple of minutes as they each tried to comprehend what had just happened.

It was broken when Bryden asked Iskra to shine her torch around the cave gallery. As she did so it became immediately apparent that something momentous had occurred.

The chamber floor was more or less devoid of loose rocks. Just one biggish boulder similar to the one Chaz had climbed on a few minutes ago rested against the now, blank cave wall. There was no sign of Iskra's day-bag, his camera and torch, the empty coke tins and paper food wraps.

'I'm not sure I like the look of this,' said Bryden in a quiet voice.

'I say,' Chaz interrupted, 'Look at my hand, it's all red and puffed up.'

Iskra pointed the torch at his right hand, which they could see was swollen and looked as though it had been too long in the sun. It was also clenched tightly round something.

'Aaahhh! Get it off me,' shouted Chaz in a panicky voice and he tried to flip open his fist. 'Uncle Bryden, I can't feel anything. What's wrong with it?'

'Hang on a minute Chaz while I have a look.' Bryden reached over and gently took hold of it.

Chaz flinched. 'Hey that hurt.'

'Sorry. It looks like a burn but it also appears to be a kind of, well, I know this will sound stupid, frostbite.'

'Frostbite!' Iskra and Chaz chimed together.

Then Chaz remembered the strange feeling of hot and cold when he first grabbed the feather. 'It's that damned feather,' he almost shouted. 'It obviously had some kind of stuff on it that makes your hand swell if you touch it.'

'Be that as it may,' said Bryden, 'We need to treat it.

Fortunately for you Chaz, you picked up that emergency first aid kit back at the Admin office.'

'So I did. Good thinking on your part uncle. It's clipped on my belt. Can you get it? My hand is a bit sore.'

Even Iskra managed a grin at the attempt of a joke.

Before Bryden could apply the antibiotic ointment, he had to prise open the clenched fingers. Fortunately for Chaz, it proved to be painless but they all got a shock when they saw a tiny glittering feather in the middle of the palm.

'What the hell is that?' cried Chaz, knowing full well what it was.

'I have this funny feeling,' said Iskra. 'I think we had better take great care of this... whatever it is and what it represents.' Then she said to Bryden, 'Would you mind holding the torch for me. I'll need both hands for this.'

She touched Chaz on the arm. 'Hold out your hand please.' Reaching into her shoulder bag, Iskra pulled out a small pack of plastic self-sealing bags and took one out. Then, after putting the rest of them back, she got her cosmetic wallet out and removed a pair of tweezers.

'Hold still, please. I don't want to drop it.' And very carefully, Iskra picked up the tiny feather with the tweezers. 'Damn, I forgot to open the bag.'

'Here, hold the torch Chaz while I open the bag for Iskra,' Bryden said. He took the little plastic bag from Iskra and opened it wide enough for her to drop the feather safely into it.

'Good! Now to seal it and put it out of harms way.' From the miraculous shoulder bag, Iskra produced a clamshell sunglasses case. 'I broke the glasses. Fortunately for us, I kept the case,' she explained as she placed the strange feather inside it. 'There, that should do it.'

Now Bryden could get to work on the hand. 'Let the air get to it Chaz,' he said after he had applied some of the ointment. 'I know it feels uncomfortable but it's for the best. After a few hours you should feel a lot better. Just try not to rub it against your clothes. OK.' Then Bryden smiled, 'Oh, I forgot, don't pick your nose with that hand either. The ointment will make it drop off.'

'What!'

'Just kidding, Chaz. Just kidding.'

'Now that we've got Chaz sorted, we had better try to find out what else is different in these caves,' Bryden said seriously. 'We can't stay here.'

'I agree,' said Iskra and immediately stood up. 'Come on, my torch won't last for ever.'

'What's the rush?' asked Chaz. 'It's only a few minutes to that big gallery with the spotlights. We won't need the torch then will we?'

'I wish I had your confidence Chaz,' said Bryden. 'Somehow, I feel that something very odd has happened. Anyway, let's get going. We're doing nothing here.'

Keeping close together they crossed the floor to the exit of the cave gallery and began to climb the narrow passage. With each step the torch wavered to and fro and shadows danced off the walls at every turn. 'I hope you two can see alright,' said Iskra over her shoulder.

Bryden just grunted and Chaz saved his breath, concentrating on keeping his sore hand away from the passage wall.

The 'staircase' seemed easier going up. Then Bryden said, 'Have you noticed that there are no loose rocks lying about the floor of the passage. It seems as though someone has been clearing it up.'

'That's impossible,' said Iskra. 'We've only been down here for a few hours and anyway this passage is out of bounds to all staff until the Professor says so.'

'I say you two,' Chaz interrupted, 'Is that the entrance or what?'

Iskra pointed the torchlight further along the passage and gasped out aloud. 'It c..c.. can't be,' she stuttered. 'The wooden door and the iron gate. They're gone! Even the gap looks different, smaller somehow.'

'What about the spotlights?' asked Chaz in a whisper, 'I

---

can't see any. They're not working or, Jeez! Are they there at all?'

Standing by the edge of the huge gallery amongst the scores of stalagmites that covered the cave floor, Chaz shivered. It was not that cold. He was wearing his anorak thanks to his uncle's advice. It was the thought of being cooped up in this place with only one small torch for light. He remembered the walk down earlier that day. Even with those crappy lights along the passages, it was still spooky. *The spotlights in here were good though. What made them go off? Was it a power failure?*

A flicker of light made Chaz jump. Iskra came round a large fat stalagmite. 'Are you alright?' she asked.

Chaz nodded but of course Iskra couldn't see him nod in the semi-darkness.

'Bryden thinks we should press on as quickly as we can,' Iskra informed him.

'Good! I can't wait to get out of this dump.'

'What was that Chaz?' Bryden appeared from the other side of the stalagmite. It made good cover for a toilet stop.

'I said that I couldn't wait to get out of this dump.'

'Well, I suppose this isn't the best time to ask you to give your review stars for the Magura Caves.'

'Damn right,' said Chaz vehemently.

'OK! Let's leave it at that for now shall we. Iskra will lead off please and Chaz, keep close. The last time there was a power failure it took four days before they got the lights on again. Unfortunately, three tourists went mad. They had taken the wrong turning in the dark and got lost in the side passages. They foolishly tried to drink the water dripping down the walls and got poisoned from the mineral saturated water.'

'My God! I knew it was a crappy place. Jeez.'

Because Bryden was walking behind Iskra, in the shadow of the torch, Chaz didn't see the big grin on his uncle's face.

Up front, Iskra had to put a hand to her mouth to stop

herself from laughing out aloud.

The journey back to the surface seemed easier than on the way down. That surprised Iskra until she noticed that the passage floor was much drier so they made more rapid progress. This information made her feel uneasy. Things *were* definitely different but why?

The torchlight began to dim and Iskra looked hopefully ahead for the twisting passage that indicated the beginning of the ramp leading to the exit.

'Iskra!' The strong voice of Bryden stopped her in her tracks.

'Yes! Bryden. What is it?'

'Switch off the torch, please.'

Not knowing why, Iskra complied.

For a moment or two there was complete blackness. Then Chaz cried out, 'I can see a light in front of us.'

'Actually Chaz,' Bryden said in a relieved voice, 'It's daylight.'

'So it is,' said Iskra breaking into a run.

'Stop! Iskra! Stop!'

It was the desperate tone in Bryden's voice, which made Iskra stop running just before she reached the cave entrance.

'Why. Bryden? Why do you want me to wait for you?' she asked in a perplexed voice.

Bryden hurried up to her, a bemused Chaz behind him. 'I'm sorry if I frightened you Iskra but I had a horrible premonition. Something is wrong here, very wrong.'

'Oh for Gods sake Uncle. Not more Mumbo Jumbo,' and with that Chaz stalked off towards the cave's exit.

Bryden, grabbing Iskra by the arm pulled her along as fast as he could, saying, 'Come on, we need to catch up with him.'

They needn't have bothered. Chaz was standing stock still in the middle of the path, his mouth wide open. He was pointing towards what should have been the admin block and ticket booth.

They were not there. They had disappeared, along with the car park and all the other trappings of the twenty first century.

5

They were looking out into a vista of scrub and trees with a rough track winding down the valley where it met a small river.

'Uncle! Uncle Bryden! What the hell has happened round here?'

Chaz held his injured hand to his chest and started to run along the track. It was covered with weeds and tufts of long grass. Stopping to catch his breath, he turned round and shouted hoarsely, 'There's no one here. Do you hear me? There's nobody here!'

Bryden and Iskra walked down the track, too stunned to say anything. Reaching Chaz, who was now trembling with shock at what he had just experienced, Bryden opened his arms and hugged both Chaz and Iskra to his chest and held them tight.

'Whatever has happened to us, I promise to do my upmost to put it right. Right now we must be strong and stick together. We need to find out where we are and the date. That to me seems the most important thing to know. What date is it?'

They stood apart looking at each other. Then Iskra took a deep breath and said. 'Well it's obvious where we are. This is the Magura Cave isn't it.'

Bryden sighed and said, 'Yes, you are absolutely right but I repeat. Where are we? What year is it?'

'Come on. What are you saying Uncle?' asked Chaz, somewhat recovered. You think that we've transported to another world. Get real.'

'Actually Chaz, you may not be far wrong with your assumption.'

'Before you two start falling out,' interrupted Iskra, 'Have you noticed how dark it's getting. Where are we going to spend the night?'

'Yeah, and when are we going to eat?' added Chaz,

looking round as though hoping to find a McDonald's hidden among the trees.

'You're both right,' said Bryden briskly, suddenly feeling a bit more in control of himself. 'Let's assume that some of the 'old' villages are still around here. So Iskra, where's the nearest place?'

'I'd say Rabisha. It's about, was about 1km over that ridge.' She pointed in a south-easterly direction.

'Right then, let's get going,' said Bryden. 'It will be dark soon and I don't fancy a night out in the open.'

Iskra, now the appointed guide, led the way down the track towards the river. When they reached it, the river current was flowing strongly. 'We need to cross it and then climb that ridge.'

'Is there a bridge?' asked Chaz, 'I can't see one. Can you Uncle?'

'Well I wouldn't actually call it a bridge,' Bryden said, pointing to a pine tree trunk about 5m long lying across the river.

'That thing!' cried Chaz in alarm, 'No way am I going across that!'

'Look Chaz,' said Bryden with as much patience as he could muster, 'Think about it. We have to get to that village before dark, right. That log is our only way across this river. We just haven't time to look for somewhere else to cross. OK.'

'Yeah but…'

'Chaz! There's no other way.'

'Well if you can do it I suppose I could.'

'OK. I'll go first, then you Iskra.'

She nodded in agreement.

Bryden looked more closely at the log. It was about 30cm wide with most of the bark still intact. *At least that will help to keep my feet from slipping.* Making sure his anorak was zipped up tight he slowly edged his way onto the log. Placing one foot at a time firmly in front of the other with arms outstretched, it only took a minute or so for him to reach the other side of the river.

Jumping off onto the riverbank, Bryden wiped the sweat from his face. Despite his outward appearance of calm he had to admit to himself he had been terrified of falling into the river. He couldn't swim a stroke.

'Come on Iskra. It's a piece of cake.'

'What has a piece of cake got to do with anything?'

Bryden just smiled and called back across the river. 'Never mind, I'll explain later. Now come on. Chaz wants to cross.'

Chaz looked across at his uncle. *You must be joking*, he thought.

Without any more ado, Iskra flipped her shoulder bag round her back and tightened the strap. Then she hitched up her long skirt and calmly walked across the log.

'Jeez!' Where did you learn to do that,' Chaz called out.

'We did a lot of gym work at school.'

Well I can't do that,' Chaz said as he bent down and slowly straddled the log, his legs dangling just above the fast flowing river. Then, leaning forward, he grasped the log with his hands. He had forgotten about his inflamed hand. It stung like hell. Trying to ignore the pain, he half-lifted himself off the log and pulled himself along at the same time. He moved forward about 10cm.

Bryden and Iskra could do nothing but watch, as he painfully pulled himself across.

The inevitable happened just over the half way mark. Chaz lost his grip and slipping sideways, saved himself a ducking by wrapping his arms and legs round the log. It was a precarious position made worse by the fact that he found he was hanging upside down under the log.

'Uncle Bryden! Uncle Bryden! Help! Help me!' The urgent cries rang out along the riverbank.

Bryden and Iskra stood transfixed.

Then Bryden broke the spell and shouted out, 'Hold on! Chaz. Hold On! I'm coming!'

Unfortunately Chaz couldn't hold on. His injured hand,

throbbing like mad, had lost its grip and he began to fall into the river.

To his amazement he stopped falling. Two pairs of what felt like small hands had suddenly gripped hold of him and were now carrying him to the riverbank where Bryden was standing by the end of the log and Iskra who looked flabbergasted.

The next moment Chaz was on the ground on his back, staring up at the evening sky.

'Are you alright?' Iskra was at his side looking down at him. 'That was completely incredible. I can't believe what I just saw. It's unbelievable.'

'Chaz! Chaz! My God you're safe. What the hell happened? I saw you fall into the river and the next minute you're up here.' Bryden was totally confused. He didn't know what to believe.

'Don't ask me,' said Chas sitting up. 'All I know is that two people picked me up before I fell into the river.'

'But there was nobody there,' spluttered Bryden, more confused than ever.

'There was actually,' said Iskra, who even in the darkening light, looked pale.

'What do you mean?'

'I believe Chaz was probably saved by legendary Water Sprites, friendly spirits that were believed to inhabit rivers, streams and lakes. I saw a shimmer of light appear around Chaz the moment that he began falling. It took him to where he is now.'

'Now look here Iskra.' Bryden looked at her and said in a condescending voice, 'I know lots of strange things have been happening recently but this is ridiculous.'

'Uncle Bryden!' Chaz's excited voice interrupted him. 'Look! Look at my hand. It's better. I've been cured. It doesn't hurt a bit.'

Bryden turned away from Iskra and looked down at Chaz. Feeling that the ground had just been taken from under his feet, he crouched down next to Chaz. 'OK,' he said with more vigor than he felt, 'Let's see the miracle hand.'

Chaz shoved it right into his uncle's face. 'See, there's nothing wrong with it.'

The little bugger's right, thought Bryden after a brief examination. *This puts another complexion on our situation.*

'Well! I hold up my hands to the fact that your hand is cured. I'm very pleased for you Chaz. However, I'm not too sure about how it happened.'

'I saw what I saw,' said a defiant Iskra.

'OK! OK!'

'If you're up for it Chaz, we'll get on,' said Bryden looking at Iskra for some support.

Nodding, she set off followed by Bryden and a moment or two later, Chaz, who started to moan that he felt stiff all over.

The climb up the small ridge took them about ten minutes to reach the top. Stopping for a breather, Iskra stared down the hill towards the village of Rabisha.

In a clearing near the banks of another small river, a group of primitive looking houses were set in two rows facing each other. They looked like earth-covered ridge tents. 'I can't believe I'm seeing this,' she exclaimed. 'Those are medieval houses. I'm absolutely positive they are.'

'I think you've answered one of my questions, Iskra,' said Bryden as he walked over to her. 'I agree, possibly the thirteenth century and furthermore it's a time when the extra-ordinary has become the ordinary.'

'Pull the other one Uncle!' said Chaz disparagingly, as usual the last to arrive. 'I know some funny things have been happening but the thirteenth century. Come on!'

'Bryden is right,' said Iskra, pointing to the village. 'This morning that village was full of brick houses with windows, paths, gardens and cars. What do you see now, Chaz? It's a medieval village.'

Chaz stood for a moment denying the logic of his eyes. Then with a shake of his head said, 'How in hell are we going to get back home?'

'Before I answer that, let's get down there and see if anyone will give us some food and shelter for the night,' Bryden said urgently. 'I can hardly see the damn place now. Come on!'

A narrow track wound between the trees on the upper slope of the ridge, making for a faster descent than they dared hoped. By the time they reached the first dwelling it was practically dark.

'Hallo! Is anyone there? Hi! We're lost, can you help us?'

Bryden stopped shouting and said quietly to the others, 'I'm going to knock on the door of the first house, OK.'

So he edged closer and could just about make out the shape of some sort of a doorway and knocked. No response. He banged again. No answer. He yelled as loud as he could, 'Hallo!'

'It's no use,' said Chaz. 'No one's in.'

Iskra suddenly whispered, 'Have you noticed that no one in the other houses has come out to see what the noise is about.'

Bryden looked around. 'It would appear that the village is deserted.'

'What the hell are we to do now?' Chaz chuntered.

'Well, I'm freezing,' said Iskra. 'I vote we go inside this place now. We can always apologize if the owner turns up and then offer to pay them something.'

'With what! Gold or silver coins,' said Bryden wryly. 'However, I'm with you Iskra,' and with that he tried to open the door. 'There's no handle,' he said in surprise.

'Allow me,' said Iskra pushing him to one side. Then fumbling by the right-hand side of the door she pulled a small piece of twisted hide. The door opened with a squeak of its leather hinges.

'How did you do that?' asked an impressed Chaz.

41

'Actually, it was quite simple. Here in Bulgaria, many country cottages have a similar type of door latch. You pull a string and the bolt on the other side of the door lifts up. QED.'

'Iskra, is your torch still working?' asked Bryden, 'We need to see what's in here.'

'OK, I'll have a look in my bag. It should still be there.' The sound of rustling could be heard in the darkness. 'Yes. I've got it.'

A blaze of light dazzled them for a second until their eyes adjusted to the glare.

They were standing on the threshold of a small, narrow room. A central wooden post supported the steep wooden roof. A sunken floor of bare earth was covered with straw and was about 1m below their feet. They had to climb down some steps to reach it. In the far corner was a stone oven and a long wooden bench was placed along the wall by the door. Some sort of bedding was lying on the straw across the room.

'Ugh! What a dump,' said Chaz holding his nose. The air was very ripe.

Then Bryden gave a loud gasp. 'What the hell is that!' he said pointing towards the oven.

A strange little figure had suddenly appeared and was calmly sitting there. It was like a tiny dwarf complete with big ears, long straggly hair and a huge beard down to its knees. It was holding a broomstick and making a funny noise, a kind of chuckling.

'God! What is it!' cried Chaz in alarm. 'Where the hell did it come from?'

'I think they used to be called *Schopanyn* in the old days,' said Iskra. They were supposed to be house guardians.'

'What do you mean by the old days,' cried Chaz, his eyes bulging. 'It's here now.'

'Yes,' said Bryden and looking at Iskra, asked her if it was ever dangerous?

'As far as I can remember the old stories said that they were more mischievous than bad,' she replied. 'Oh yes, they also mentioned something about keeping them happy. By giving them presents I think.'

'Jeez,' Chaz nearly irrupted, 'Give that little runt a present. You must be joking.'

Before anyone could say another word, a small three-legged stool standing in the corner by the oven, flew through air and crashed into Chaz's left knee.

'Ow! For f....s sake, what happened then?' he cried, hopping on one leg and clutching his other knee.

Bryden, catching on very quickly said, 'I should watch what you say Chaz. Those are very big ears. Good for hearing don't you think.'

Still bent over rubbing his knee, Chaz jerked upright. 'You don't think mini-granddad did that, do you? Don't make me laugh.'

Without a sound the stool flew up again and knocked his elbow, the funny bone to be exact.

'Aaaggh!' Chaz yelled out again. It hurt like hell and he tried to rub it better as the stool clattered to the floor.

Iskra decided that it was time for her to intercede on Chaz's behalf. 'Don't say another word Chaz. Don't say another word. I'm going to try something.'

Tugging her shoulder bag round she rooted about inside for a minute and pulled out a roll of mints and opened it. She palmed a couple and went over to the Schopanyn and offered it the two sweets.

The Schopanyn leant forward and sniffed them. It smiled. A long thin red tongue flicked out between two rows of blackened teeth and snatched the two sweets from Iskra's hand and then the Schopanyn disappeared.

'Thank God the little bastard's gone,' Chaz said with feeling. 'I was worried sick that the sod was going to whack me on the head with that frigging stool.'

'Calm down, Chaz! Calm down! He's gone. Is that right Iskra?' asked Bryden.

'From what I remember, if the present is well received the Schopanyn will treat everyone in the house as its friend.'

'Now that's settled we had better see if we can make a fire in that oven thing before your torch gives out. I don't know about you two but it seems to be getting colder in here,' Bryden said. 'Any ideas Chaz?'

'I went to a US summer camp last year and did some outdoor activities which included making camp fires. I actually enjoyed camping outside.'

'Good, said Bryden. 'See if you can get a fire going will you.'

'Right!' said Chaz, perking up now he had something to do. 'Iskra, would you come over to the oven corner with me and keep the torch steady while I see what's around for the fire.'

The oven was set right in the corner of the house. A mound of stones had been placed carefully around and on top of a set of flat stone slabs, which made a central cavity, in which a fire could be made. A bundle of small sticks and several small logs were laid out next to it.

'Anyone got any paper or something I can use to light these sticks with?'

'Just a minute Chaz,' said Iskra, 'I've got a few used tissues in my bag. They should be dry now,' she joked.

Two minutes later, Chaz had a fire blazing away in the oven. He thanked his lucky stars for remembering to bring his emergency survival kit, which included a ferro stick and striker. The spark maker did everything it said it would do on the tin. The extra light from the fire illuminated the small room enough for them to see several clay pots along the wall they had missed earlier. Two with skin lids on.

Bryden opened one and found it contained a couple of litres of drinkable water, the other one, three hunks of what looked like rye bread.

'Well aren't we the lucky ones,' he said.

Chaz and Iskra were sitting on the bench watching

Bryden when Chaz started to cough and then he blurted out, 'My eyes are stinging like mad. It's that bloody fire. It's because there's no chimney. I thought it would be alright because there wasn't much smoke.'

Then Iskra and Bryden joined in with a coughing fit. 'Open the door Chaz,' gasped Bryden, 'It's not just the smoke. This place has no ventilation. The air is getting stuffy, the carbon monoxide could be getting to a dangerous level in a small room like this.'

Chaz limped over to the door, his knee still sore from the knock that the stool had given him earlier and pulled it open. A sudden gust of fresh air rushed in and cleared the room in seconds.

'Wedge it open, Chaz. There must be something near it. These people must suffer from the smoke just like us.'

Scrabbling around, Chaz found a large chunky pebble. 'This must be it,' he said as he propped the door open.

'Once the fire dies down, it should be safe to close it,' Bryden said and added hopefully, 'There'll be little or no smoke then. In fact, I suspect it will get quite warm when the oven stones heat up.'

Sometime later they were able to close the door and it was warm enough for them to remove their anoraks and in Iskra's case, her woollen cape.

'Let's try this bread,' Bryden said, taking out one of the rye cobs from the storage pot. He broke it into three pieces and gave them one each.

'I could eat a horse,' said Chaz, taking a big bite. 'Jeez, I nearly broke a frigging tooth then.'

'I suggest that you eat small mouthfuls and at the same time have a swig of water.'

'I've still got a bit of water in my water-bottle,' Chaz replied. 'I'll use that first. You don't know what that stuff in that clay pot is like.'

'Since beggars can't be choosers, I'll go first.' Bryden looked at Iskra who nodded. He went over to the water pot and was surprised to see two wooden beakers next to it.

45

'Well, well,' he exclaimed, 'All mod cons.' Lifting off the skin lid, he rinsed both beakers and then, half filling them gave one to Iskra and took a small sip from his own. 'A bit stale,' he said, 'But definitely drinkable. Skol!' He toasted Iskra and sat down to eat his bread.

Chaz, meanwhile, was idly chewing like mad on a piece of crust. Taking another drink of water, he looked around the room and saw a small, strange object sticking out of the wooden wall opposite him. It looked like a thin, short stick poking out of a clay holder fixed to the timber.

'I say Uncle, what do think that's for?'

Before Bryden could speak, Iskra said, 'That's a rushlight. It's what the peasants used for lighting. They're much easier to make than candles. You just soak the dried rushes in tallow and dry them. Quite simple, eh.'

'How do you know all about this peasant stuff?' Chaz was impressed.

'Well! If you must know,' said Iskra, 'As part of my studies I covered the early history of my country. That's one of the reasons I'm wearing this peasant's costume. It's part of my course.'

'In that case,' said Bryden with a grin, 'Will you do the honours by lighting that rush for us.'

'With pleasure,' replied Iskra taking the rush out of its holder and going over to the fire. As she poked one end of the rush into the red-hot embers it lit immediately. Quickly pulling it out, Iskra went back and replaced it into the clay holder. It gave out a reasonable amount of light but the tallow smoked and gave off a peculiar smell.

'Jeez! What a stink.'

'Don't be ungrateful Chaz,' said his uncle. 'Be glad that you spotted it. It saves the torch batteries and if I'm not mistaken there must be other spare rushlights about here somewhere. They'll come in useful for us I'm sure.'

Then, Iskra stood up. 'Excuse me. I'm going outside for a moment. I won't be long.'

Chaz looked at her, puzzled, 'Going out now. Why?'

His uncle called out, 'For God's sake Chaz, sometimes you ask the dumbest of questions.'

'Oh, Yeah,' said Chaz, blushing a bright red.

To cover Chaz's embarrassment, Bryden asked him to help look for the spare rushlights.

They found them wrapped up in an animal skin by the oven, obviously to keep them dry. It was the warmest place in the room.

Once Iskra had returned, Chaz and his uncle took turns to go for their night walk.

Iskra chose to sleep on the bench so Bryden and his uncle, after a quick check through the so-called bedding for creepy crawlies, lay down on the floor, covering themselves with their anoraks.

'Jeez! I'll never get to sleep down here on these stinking rags.'

'Chaz! Can it. We're all in the same boat. OK. So count sheep or whatever and go to sleep.'

Surprisingly, he did and so did the other two. The strain of the day's strange events had finally caught up with them.

The next morning Bryden slipped out first, partly to have a look around and partly well…. He met nobody in or around the village so he went back, the noise of the door opening waking the other two.

'What time is it?' asked Chaz, stretching out his arms and legs and uttering a big yawn. Then he sat bolt upright when he realized where he was.

'Jeez! It's not a dream is it?'

'It's just after six am,' said his uncle, 'So up on your pegs Chaz. I don't want to hang around here all day.'

'Why, is it dangerous?' asked Iskra, sitting up.'

'Well,' said Bryden, 'I'm not too happy about the fact that there's no one here. Where are they? Why did they go? Did they flee from something? I think we should leave as soon as possible.'

After Iskra and Chaz had sorted themselves out and their 'sumptuous' breakfast was over, Bryden said that they had to take anything of value like the rushlights, beakers and a big surprise to them, the iron tipped spear that he had found on the far side of the doorway, together with the rest of the bread of course. 'There's not much left,' he added. 'God knows when we will eat again.'

Iskra listened with a thoughtful expression on her face and said, 'I've got to collect something and I don't want either of you two to laugh at me. OK.' With that, she went over to the now cold oven and picked up several tiny pieces of charred wood that had survived the fire.

'What on earth are you doing?' cried Chaz.

'I'm taking a part of the Schopanyn with us. He will help in a time of need.' Carefully wrapping the cold charred pieces of wood in a couple of tissues she placed them in her bag.

Without another word the trio left the house.

Outside Bryden broke the silence. 'Which way?' he asked Iskra.

'Follow the river, I think.'

So they went down towards the river and were fortunate enough to find a track of sorts next to it. They were travelling through an area of pine and oak trees on the upper slopes with patches of scrub dotted alongside the river. The place was devoid of any sign of life, human or animal. Then at a bend in the river they came upon a small beach of pebbles. A body lay sprawled on the edge of the water. It was obviously a dead man.

'Stay here,' ordered Bryden, giving Chaz the spear, 'While I go and see what's happened.'

Clambering down the riverbank, Bryden made his way across the pebbles to the body. It looked like a peasant. He was appalled at what he saw, an elderly man dressed in a simple hemp white shirt covered with an embroidered waistcoat and white cotton trousers with tied leggings held up with a wide belt. The feet were bare and a sheepskin hat lay by the head.

It was the bearded face, completely desiccated, eyes wide

open in terror, mouth gaping in a rictus grin, the tongue half bitten through that made Bryden blanche. Then he saw the wounds in the neck, four large punctures under the left side of his jaw.

'My God!' he exclaimed in horror. 'This poor devil's had his lifeblood drained from him by something like a giant vampire.'

***

The body was at least half an hour behind them. Bryden was still recovering from the horror that he had seen. He had scarcely uttered a word except to say that they needed to press on and find somewhere safe to rest, somewhere out of prying eyes he had emphasized. They passed many more bodies; all dried up and shrivelled, more victims of the 'vampire' as Bryden now thought of it.

Some time after mid-day Chaz called for a halt. Typically he wanted something to eat. The urge to get as far away from the dead bodies had steadily diminished the further they went downriver. Finally he rebelled, actually, he just stopped and sat down.

'Can't we find something to eat,' he called out in a plaintive voice. 'I'm bloody starving.'

His tone of voice seemed to get through to Bryden who for the first time in hours responded with some semblance of normality.

'I've already told you why we must save the bread for later. It's a last resort. But I agree with you Chaz, we do need to look for something else to eat.'

'Like what, grass?' asked Iskra in a tired voice. Since the *bodies*, she had not spoken and had lost all that sense of vitality and confidence which was so much of her personality.

Bryden pointed over to the river, which at that point was disappearing over a small waterfall. 'I bet you at the bottom of that, there is a pool full of fish.'

The thought of something other than a piece of rock-hard

bread jerked Chaz to his feet. 'I've got some hooks and line in my ESK (emergency survival kit) pouch,' he said eagerly. 'Let's try it.'

Half an hour later, he was the proud owner of a hazel rod his uncle had fashioned with the help of the multi-tool blade that was part of Chaz's ES kit. He sat on the far edge of the rocky pool, formed eons ago by the erosive force of the waterfall. He was far enough away from the turbulent backwash of the waterfall to see several darting shapes in the clear water. Mentally crossing his fingers, he cast his line and a hook baited with a red berry.

He couldn't believe it when in seconds he had a bite.

'Careful Chaz, easy now,' his uncle advised, 'Remember you don't have a reel.'

The hazel rod bent as the fish tugged at the line and by gently lifting and lowering the rod, Chaz played the fish until it tired and he was then able to ease it to the edge of the pool.

'You little devil,' chuckled his uncle. 'You've done this before,' and he bent down to pick up the still lively, wriggling fish, big enough to give each of them a fair sized meal.

'Well to be honest,' said Chaz, 'We did a fair amount of fishing when I went to that summer camp. An hour later, sitting by the small campfire they had made to cook the fish, they decided unanimously that was the best meal they had ever had.

Now fully rested and fed, Chaz's hip flask refilled with fresh water, Bryden set off in the lead to hopefully find somewhere safe to spend their second night in this strange in-between world.

The next stage of the journey proved more difficult. They kept encountering outcrops of rock that forced the track to move away from the river so that they were forever climbing up slopes and thrashing though thick under-growth, which blocked the little used track. Now in the late afternoon, they heard sounds of some kind of animal crashing through the nearby woods.'

'Jeez, I hope that isn't one of those wild boars,' said Chaz looking wildly around.

'I suggest that Iskra and I look for two stout sticks. I should have thought about it before. Chaz, light a small fire. If we can find them quickly, we can burn the ends into spear points. '

'I don't like the sound of that,' said Iskra. 'Are we in danger?'

'Just being prepared,' said Bryden calmly. 'We need to be able to defend ourselves. Just in case.' He looked at Chaz. 'And before you say it. I don't know from what.'

Leaving his 'borrowed' spear with Chaz, Bryden and Iskra went into the woods.

Carrying Chaz's multi-tool with the knife blade open, Bryden pushed his way through some more thick undergrowth. They had been searching for about ten minutes when Brydon turned to Iskra who was patiently following him.

'I'm looking for a clearing,' he explained. 'Open spaces usually mean smaller trees and shrubs,' he added. 'I can't very well chop down a seventy-five metre tree with this thing can I?' He flourished the multi-tool blade in Iskra's face.

She laughed.

Thank God for small mercies, he thought. *It looks like she's getting back to normal.*

'Bryden! Bryden! Stop!' Iskra suddenly called out. It broke his reverie. 'Look. Is that what you are looking for?'

Through a gap between two huge oaks, a small glade could just be seen.

'Well done, Iskra. I missed that. Sorry, my mind was elsewhere.'

'Come on then,' she said, squeezing between the two large oaks trees.

'Hang on, I can't get through there,' laughed Bryden. 'I'll have to go round these monsters.'

'You need to cut down on the fish portions,' she replied with a grin.

Once in the glade, Bryden did a quick survey with his eyes. *A couple of possibles*, he thought. 'Over here, Iskra if you don't mind.'

Walking over to him, Iskra watched Bryden pull down a thickish branch of a small tree. 'This is a mountain ash,' he said. 'A good hard wood is just what we want. This will suit Chaz perfectly. It's too thick for you Iskra, so we'll cut this one to size and then get one for you, OK.'

'Are you sure I need one?'

'Look Iskra, I don't like saying this but you have to realize that in this place we are in potential danger at all times possibly from things that we can't even comprehend. So we make spears, comprende.'

'I guess so.'

'Good,' said Bryden, trying to hide his relief that Iskra had understood his point. It then took him several minutes to trim the branch to his satisfaction. He ended up with a spear shaft of about 2m long. 'That should do it,' he said. 'Now for yours.'

This time he was much quicker. Once he had selected a branch thin enough for Iskra to hold comfortably, the job was done in half the time as the first one.

The journey back was uneventful; Bryden had blazed a trail as they had walked through the wood. Iskra had wondered why he had cut notches on trees as they went by. *What a clever idea,* she thought.

The smell of burning wood smoke told them that Chaz had done his job too.

'About time too,' he called out in greeting. 'Wow! Those spears look great.'

'They're not the finished article yet, Chaz,' his uncle replied, admiring the fire.

Chaz had made a ring of small rocks to contain the fire area and had even managed to collect a fair sized stock of brushwood. A good blaze welcomed Iskra and Bryden.

Even more welcome, were the piles of dried bracken that Chaz had placed as seats around the fire.

'Ah! That's better,' said Bryden, sitting on his pile of bracken. 'Could I have a drink from your water-bottle Chaz. Oh! Sorry, where are my manners. Chaz, pass it to Iskra first, if you don't mind. You must be gasping for a drink Iskra.'

She nodded and accepted the water-bottle from Chaz, had a drink and passed it to Bryden.

After a few minutes rest, Bryden stood and picked up the two spear shafts. He had already sharpened the tips, so carefully pushing the points into the glowing embers on the edge of the fire and taking care they would not ignite, he turned them several times and when they began to char he pulled them out and scraped off the burnt bits.

'There you are, two functioning spears,' he said passing them over to Iskra and Chaz, who was chuffed to bits with his.

Then looking wistfully round their campfire, Bryden said, 'I think we should crack on and look for a secure place for the night.'

So they dowsed the fire with handfuls of earth and worked their way back to the river. It was still the easiest way to travel down the valley.

They soon became tired of the up and down nature of the terrain. It seemed hours since they were relaxing round their campfire when in fact it was only some forty minutes as Bryden found when he checked his watch.

At last they reached a fairly level stretch of riverbank, the woods a fair way back up the slope. An area of grass and wild flowers made a wonderful change of scenery. Iskra was captivated and soon had a colourful halo of blooms peeking out from her headscarf.

It was a few minutes of fun that ended with a loud shriek from Chaz.

'Jeez! Would you just look at that.'

He was pointing to a large Brown bear crouching next to

a rock in the middle of the river.

As they watched, the bear in a sudden flurry, scooped up a large fish with its paws. Then, it nonchalantly bit the fish's head off. Still holding the fish in its big paws it began to eat its catch.

Bryden was suddenly worried stiff. 'Chaz! Chaz!' Keeping his voice as low as possible, Bryden put a finger to his lips and signalled to Chaz to do the same.

Chaz acknowledged he had understood with a thumbs-up sign.

Turning to Iskra, he indicated the woods and pointed to her. Then he pointed to the woods again, saying in a quiet voice. 'Go! Go!'

Nodding her head, she scooted up the slope, half crouching until she disappeared into the trees.

The bear must have been aware of the movement because it dropped the remains of the fish and on all fours splashed its way to the riverbank, growling loudly.

Bryden, fearing the worst, looked over towards Chaz and said, softly, 'Just listen and do exactly what I say. Turn round and walk and I really mean walk, up to the woods. Don't, for heavens sake, look back. Then take Iskra right inside the trees, well away from the edge. OK. Don't answer. Just do what I say. Go.'

For once, Chaz didn't argue. He could feel the urgency in his uncle's voice. So he began to walk slowly up the slope and he hoped, the safety of the trees.

Bryden gave a sigh of relief when he saw Chaz fade out of sight among the trees.

With a start, he realized the the bear was now lumbering up the riverbank, roaring and growling and it was only about one hundred metres away from where he was standing.

Shit! He thought. *He knew that a man could not outrun a bear, or even climb a tree for safety. Bears can climb better than man too. His only chance to survive was to kill it.*

Bryden quickly examined his 'borrowed' spear. It had a

hefty shaft, a good two metres long, with a strong, sharp iron tip.

A quick glance at his immediate surroundings brought a big sigh of relief. He was standing two or three paces away from a small outcrop of rocks. A quick shuffle and he was standing just in front of them.

A growl made him look up. The bear was coming at him on all fours at a tremendous speed, mouth wide open. Bryden flinched when he saw the huge canines. They could tear him apart in seconds.

The bear reared up on its hind legs, at least two metres tall. Two massive front paws, with unsheathed claws as sharp as razors opened out wide and it lunged at him with a fearsome roar that was deafening in its intensity.

Taking a deep breath, Bryden praying to all the gods he had ever heard of and to all of those that he might have missed, that he be saved, rammed the foot of the spear into a crack at the bottom of the rocky outcrop and aimed the iron tip at the lunging bear's chest. At that moment, he wished that he had become that train driver he always wanted to be as a kid.

The spear point buried itself right through the heart. The huge bear stood impaled, paws still outstretched, spittle dribbling from its gaping muzzle. Then its eyes glazed over and it toppled over sideways to the ground.

Bryden, frozen in shock by what had just happened stood still for a few moments before he slumped down to the ground weeping with relief.

6

In a glade in the wood above Bear River as Chaz now liked to call it, a hunk of bear meat was roasting on a spit, a branch fixed between two other Y- shaped branches placed on either side of the campfire Chaz had made about an hour or so earlier.

Iskra and Chaz had ignored the plea by Bryden to hide deep in the woods and had watched in horror as the bear attacked him. They couldn't believe their eyes when the bear fell first and cheered like mad. Then the sudden dread when Bryden slumped to the ground. They thought he had been killed too.

By the time they had rushed down from the wood, Bryden was up and about. He had pulled out the spear from the dead bear and was sitting on the rocky outcrop contemplating what to do next. Iskra and Chaz ran up and hugged him, over the moon that he was still alive.

Once the joyful reunion was over, practicalities took over. Using the multi-tool blade, Bryden cut off a haunch of meat from the bear, a task made more awkward by the fact that the blade was so small. He had asked Chaz before he'd started to find a suitable place for a campfire up in the wood, preferably not too far away. He had also enquired of Iskra if she had any experience of basket making.

'Yes,' she replied, 'I've made several as part of my traditional craft course.'

'Fantastic,' said Bryden, 'I was beginning to worry about how we were going to carry some of this bear meat.'

So that is how Iskra was drafted in as chief basket maker, with the proviso that they be simple, shallow basket shapes and quick to make. So, armed only with the scalpel from Bryden's emergency pack, Iskra went down to the river to gather some reeds.

***

Leaning against the trunk of a fallen tree, which lay to one side of the glade Chaz had chosen for his campfire, Iskra laid down the last of the three reed baskets. *More like trays with a hoop handle,* she thought. *Not bad though, taking into account the time constraints she had worked under.*

Bryden was more than pleased with them. 'It gives us a chance to carry the meat,' he said

The meal of roast bear meat had raised their spirits no end, especially as Bryden had found several wild mushrooms, which, when held on a thin stick and dipped into the hot fat dripping off the roasting meat and toasted for a minute or so, were delicious.

Chaz had put three more hunks of bear meat on the go, sizzling away on the home made spit and he stood guard whilst Bryden and Iskra went off to scout round for some more wild mushrooms and maybe fruit berries.

Around an hour later, they returned, each carrying an armful of mushrooms and berries wrapped in a bundle of large leaves.

'Hi Chaz,' called Bryden, across the campfire, 'Talk about luck. I had been puzzling on how to protect the cooked meat when we leave this place when, would you believe it, right next to these mushrooms was a patch of horseradish. Just look at the size of these leaves, I ask you?' Bryden held out a huge leaf from his bundle. 'Just look at that! Will it wrap up our meat or what? It's nearly as good as a piece of greaseproof paper wouldn't you say?'

Chaz grinned and said, 'Jeez! Uncle, what would we do without you.'

'Cut the crap,' replied Bryden with a chuckle. 'Give Iskra and me ten to recover from our walk and then we can split from here. You my lad, use these leaves to wrap the meat and put them in Iskra's fine baskets. OK.'

'Just a minute Bryden,' interrupted Iskra. 'What does 'split' mean?'

'Oh! Sorry, It's just slang for let's go.'

Before anyone else said anything, an eerie sound echoed through the wood, a wolf in full cry.

Grabbing his spear, Bryden jumped to his feet. 'That's all we need,' he said anxiously. 'They've picked up the scent of the dead bear. They'll be here soon.'

Needing no more incentive, they dowsed the fire and each carrying a spear and their basket of food, they left their little oasis of tranquility.

'We'll keep to the high ground,' Bryden said, 'At least for next half hour or so.'

Following the edge of the wood, they could see the river rippling along the valley with flashes of reflected sunlight glinting like dewdrops in the early morning sun.

The howling of the wolves came nearer. 'Faster,' urged Bryden. Then it stopped.

'We don't have to worry for a while now they've found the bear carcass,' said Bryden. 'Let's have a breather.'

Iskra and Chaz were too breathless to say anything. They just sank to the ground.

'That's what I like to see. Two fit young people enjoying themselves,' Bryden said with a laugh.

'God! At times Uncle Bryden, you're the pits,' gasped Chaz.

Iskra looked over to Chaz. 'Don't take him too seriously. He's only trying to take our minds off things. Aren't you, Bryden?'

'Very astute, Iskra. The way things are going in this Netherworld, it could drive people in our position mad.'

Bryden went on, 'Do you realize, we've only been in this 'world' and I use the term 'world' advisably, for two days. To survive we need to adapt and adapt damned quickly or we die. Bluntly, it's as simple as that.'

Chaz glanced at Iskra and held up a hand and said, 'I think I get your point Uncle. This thing we're in is unbelievable. I still find it hard to accept that mumbo jumbo stuff is real around here and that this place is hundreds of years in our past.

I mean that cave is only a few miles away, right?'

Bryden nodded in agreement.

'Yet to us it's hundreds of years in the future. Jeez, you're right. I am mad.'

'While you're thinking about that,' said Bryden, 'I suggest that we go back into the wood and make our way over the ridge. We need to put as much distance between us and that wolf pack as possible.'

'Why would they follow us?' asked Iskra. 'Surely they have enough food with the dead bear?'

'Maybe for now,' said Bryden thoughtfully but they are voracious animals. It won't be long before they're hungry again.'

'What I don't understand,' said Chaz, 'Is why they would want to hunt us.'

'Look around you. How many living animals can you see?' asked his Uncle. 'None! Not one bird, rabbit, anything. Those wolves were probably starving and once on the hunt again and they get our scent, what do think will happen Chaz? That they'll run away in fear of man. In this place and in this time, I don't think so.'

Bryden took a look round and said, 'Enough chatter, let's go,' and he turned and led them into the wood.

7

Half an hour later they came upon a clearing. A small stream bubbled and gurgled its way along one edge, passing by a wooden hut. At first glance it appeared to be a normal woodcutters type of place until it suddenly rose up in the air as they watched, on four giant bird-legs. The 'hut' walked about the clearing for a minute or so and then touched down, a normal looking hut again.

'Stay still,' whispered Iskra. 'That looks like the hut of Baba Jagka, the Old Hag of the forest. You would call her a witch.'

Chaz began to roll his eyes in disbelief when the door of the hut opened and a hideous figure stepped outside.

She, for it was woman, then turned and dragged out a large cauldron across the threshold and placed it by the doorway. Gasping and wheezing from the effort, she leaned against the doorway to catch her breath. The wide gaping mouth exposed two or three yellow-green teeth. A long, bulbous hooknose dribbled onto her upturned chin, which was covered in red-brown warts, several of which sprouted spiky grey hairs. The rest of her blotchy-mottled face was partly hidden by a set of straggly eyebrows, which screened a pair of mismatched squinting eyes. Lank, lifeless grey hair hung down to her waist, giving a sense of false modesty to the dangling pendulous breasts that her filthy looking shift and shawl couldn't.

Then, to the astonishment of the onlookers, she hitched up her skirt and straddling the cauldron, relieved herself. Adjusting her dress, the old hag, wheezing and coughing, slowly lifted the cauldron by the rim and emptied the contents over the ground. Still coughing, she then dragged the cauldron back inside the hut. Within seconds, the hut stood up on the four bird-legs and walked round the clearing before touching down again.

'What on earth are we to make of that,' asked a

bewildered Bryden.

Chaz just looked gob-smacked, speechless at what he had just witnessed. Iskra tried to be all efficiency to hide her embarrassment. 'Of course you know that people of all kinds can and do display idiosyncratic behaviour. However, this is not one of them. Bearing in mind what you said earlier Bryden, this is I believe an example of normal behaviour in the thirteenth century.'

'Jeez!' said Chaz with some feeling. 'How the hell are we to get out of here? Rub a magic oil lamp or something.'

'Well! Idiotic as it might sound, we go and ask that old lady.'

'What!' Exploded Chaz. 'Ask that cross-eyed lavatory attendant. No way.'

'Steady. Chaz. Steady,' said his uncle. 'Remember where we are. We need help. Special help. Alright, maybe from someone who knows a bit about Mumbo Jumbo as you have so eloquently put it. As someone once said, *Cometh the hour, Cometh the man.* Well in this case, woman.'

Bryden looked at them and said, 'Shall we go and introduce ourselves then.'

Crossing the clearing, Bryden led the way to the hut and stopped in front of the door. Before he could knock, it flew open and the old hag stood there, stooped over holding a broomstick in her gnarled hands.

Her bulbous nose dribbled and she gave a big sniff before wiping it with the ragged end of her shawl. She lifted her head and squinted at Chaz but spoke to Bryden in a shrill, squeaky voice. 'What do you want from Baba Jagka?' Then with a grimace which Bryden took for a smile, said in a wily tone, 'Have you brought Baba Jagka a present?'

Chaz gave a gasp of astonishment. 'I could understand what the old bat said. Every frigging word.'

Without warning, the broomstick jumped out of the old hag's hand and whacked Chaz across his head before returning to her.

61

'Ouch!'

Baba Jagka's mouth opened wide, showing her yellow-green teeth, just tiny gaping stumps and sniggered, 'Don't be cheeky to Baba Jagka young man or she might get angry.'

'Jeez! Er... I mean sorry. I didn't mean anything, honest.'

'If it pleases you Baba Jagka.' Iskra winked at Bryden and bowed and went on, 'We're travellers in need of help. Your fame and wisdom is known far and wide.'

'Well-said, young maiden. I see that you at least have some manners. You may come in.'

Baba Jagka then turned and shuffled back into her hut.

Somewhat hesitantly, they followed the old hag into the room. They got another surprise. The room must have been three times larger inside than outside.

They passed the cauldron set by the door on a stone slab big enough to build a fire on. The wall next to it had rows of wooden pegs, fixed to hold a variety of dried herbs, skins of different animals and a range of lucky charms. A three-legged stool that had a huge leather bound book perched on the seat, was next to an oven.

The central part of the room contained a long wooden bench along one side and rows of clay pots of different sizes were set against the other. The far end, blocked off by various animal skins hanging from the roof of the hut, was probably the sleeping area.

The old hag waved them to the bench and they sat down.

'Does this room remind you of anything, *Doctor*, Chaz said as he winked at his Uncle.

'Who . . .?' Bryden nearly laughed out loud at the remark.

Then he remembered where he was and just nodded.

'What are you two playing at?' whispered Iskra. 'Don't upset her again.'

Leaning on her broomstick, Baba Jagka stared at them for a while and then pointed to Iskra. 'Tell me,' she demanded forcefully.

Iskra thought it best to give an abridged version of their plight and at the end of her explanation Baba Jagka went to one of the jars and took out two eyeballs of some large animal. Popping one in her mouth she began to chew. With only three or four teeth this proved to take some time.

They all watched in fascination as first one cheek in her face bulged out and then the other as she tried to crunch the eyeball enough to swallow it. All the time her bulbous nose dripped constantly onto her chin. At last she managed it. Unfortunately they had to watch the whole process all over again.

Eventually satisfied with her afternoon snack, Baba Jagka said that it was possible to help them but they had to prove to her that they were worthy of her help.

Bryden, glad that their transition to the Netherworld had facilitated the ability to understand and speak the local language, asked the Baba Jagka what was necessary in order that she assist them.

A big sniff followed the ritual wipe with the end of her shawl. 'Show me some of your magic. If what you say is true you must be wise and know many things.'

Bryden was stumped. *How the hell could they show this old bat, to coin a Chaz phrase, something magical?*

A hand tugged his arm. It was Chaz. 'Uncle I've got an idea.'

'Well, I certainly haven't,' said Bryden. 'What is it?'

'My iPod!' he said excitedly. 'It's full of recordings and it should work. Iskra's torch did, didn't it?'

Baba Jagka watched suspiciously as Chaz brought out his iPod from his cargo pants pocket.

'It's one of the latest models. You can play it without headphones just like a radio but the music is downloaded into its own hard-drive.'

'OK Chaz, switch it on,' said Bryden. 'What have we to lose?'

A blast of rock music filled the hut and Baba Jagka's

63

mouth dropped open. It was not a pretty sight. Then her cross-eyes uncrossed for a moment and she let go of the broomstick and they both fell to the floor, she in a swoon.

Baba Jagka was out for the count for a few minutes before she began to stir. Mumbling something to herself, the broomstick moved along the floor and once in her hands lifted her upright.

'That's a good trick,' whispered Chaz to Iskra who hurriedly stood up to help her.

The old hag backed away from Iskra, giving them all a funny look. (*Well it looked funny to Chaz but with her cross-eyes who could tell,* he thought) and went to the cauldron at the far end of the room.

After picking a selection of herbs and a couple of dry, brittle animal skins, Baba Jagka took them to a clay mortar and pounded them with a pestle to a fine powder. Then she went to a clay pot and pulled out a handful of smelly, gooey black stuff, which she put with the already powdered ingredients and stirred with a stick. Satisfied with the results, the obnoxious brew was emptied into the cauldron.

A bout of coughing stopped the proceedings for a few minutes. Then wheezing painfully, Baba Jagka shuffled over to the row of clay pots again and got one that sloshed as she picked it up. Awkwardly, she shuffled back to the cauldron and poured in the contents of the pot before placing it on the floor. Then, stooping over the cauldron, she began to stir, using a long wooden spoon. The action of stirring caused her body to gyrate and as the spoon went round and round the cauldron, so her pendulous breasts, unencumbered by her shift, swung in unity and harmony.

***

They used the time Baba Jagka was busy to rest. Whatever she was doing they didn't have a clue. Chaz though, was rocking to some band or other. *Thankfully,* Bryden thought, *with his earbuds in.* So Bryden asked Iskra where they might go if as looked likely Baba Jagka was going to help them.

'The only place I can think of that may be of any use to us is Balogradchik. It's the biggest place round here.'

They were suddenly interrupted by a sneeze. Bryden recoiled from a shower of spittle over the back of his head and neck. Looking round he saw Baba Jagka wiping her nose with the end of her ubiquitous shawl.

Hoping his disgust wasn't apparent he gamely tried to smile.

'We go, where?' wheezed Baba Jagka, who was holding a clay pot in her gnarled hands. Without waiting for an answer she tipped the pot and a stream of fine sand poured onto the wooden floor. Putting down the pot she used a small stick to smooth out the sand. Then she made a cross on the edge of the sand and pointed to herself.

'Jeez,' said Chaz. 'She's making a map.'

Iskra quick on the uptake, used her finger and drew a line from the X to a half circle, (the cave) and pointed to herself, Bryden and Chaz.

Baba Jagka nodded. She understood.

Then Iskra drew a wiggly line away from the X and a series of inverted V's (^^^^^).

Again Baba Jagka nodded.

'This is the hard bit,' said Iskra. 'I'm assuming the rocks we know are the same as the ones she knows.'

It sounded like Double Dutch to Chaz, but Bryden began to squirm with ill-concealed excitement.

Iskra then drew the inverted v's again and put a stick figure of a man and a woman on top of them.

Baba Jagka studied the shapes for a moment and started to cackle and nod her head.

'She knows they're the Belogradchik Rocks,' Iskra said, clapping her hands.

Brydon pointed to the stick figures Iskra had drawn, then to Baba Jagka. 'We go.'

Baba Jagka nodded her head and scooping up as much of the sand as she could, she put it back into the clay pot.

Then, pointing to the bench, indicating that they should sit down, she pulled out a small bunch of feathers from inside her shawl and dipped them into the cauldron. With the tips of the feathers now covered with the nasty smelling concoction, Baba Jagka began to daub each wall in turn, leaving streaks of her brew trickling down to the floor.

With one last look to see if they were still seated on the bench, Baba Jagka sat down in the middle of the room holding the feathers and began an incantation. Her shrill voice began to chant a monotonous series of sounds. Then the hut began to move and rock.

The bench seat began to slide across the floor. Then the hut finally levelled out and the bench came to a halt.

'Jeez! We're frigging moving,' cried Chaz. A muffled thud, thud, came from the outside and the hut rolled slightly from side to side.

'I believe that this hut is, to coin a phrase, legging it,' said Bryden with a grin. 'Full marks to the lady of the house,' who happened to be still sitting on the floor in a kind of trance but could still wipe her dripping nose with the corner of her shawl. *It must be a reflex action,* mused Bryden.

About an hour later, the hut stopped moving and with a lean this way and a lean that way settled down with a gentle bump.

Baba Jagka, sprawled across the floor was out cold, her gnarled hands twitching and writhing, the bunch of feathers crushed.

'Come on. Lets get the hell away from here,' cried Bryden and they rushed out of the hut and found themselves amid a set of rocks, many of unbelievable shapes and colours.

'Welcome to the Belogradchik Rocks,' said Iskra with a beaming smile.

8

Both Chaz and his Uncle were impressed, very impressed by the towering sheer rock face of the nearest pinnacle. It soared straight up for more than one hundred metres and they seemed to be surrounded by them.

'They go on for kilometres in isolated groups, just popping up here and there all over the place,' added Iskra. 'From the look of this place I think we are quite near to the Fortress.'

A sort of moan made them all jerk round. Baba Jagka's hut was lurching upright on its huge, long legs and with a sudden sideways movement, began to stagger awkwardly away before picking up speed and disappearing out of sight around one of the towering rocks.

'Well, I can't say I'm not glad to see the back of her,' said Chaz. 'I wouldn't have trusted her with a frying pan let alone with a sodding cauldron.'

'Come on! Chaz, stop wittering and follow Iskra. We don't know what to expect so get a move on,' said Bryden irritably.

The lower slopes of the area were covered with trees and bushes so progress was slow. The fact that they were not used to carrying spears let alone home made baskets with wonky handles, didn't help either.

'Iskra!' Bryden called out to her and she stopped and turned round.

'Yes, Bryden.'

'A minute ago you said that we were near a fortress. What did you mean?'

'Well,' she said as Bryden walked up to her. 'These rocks have been used since Roman times as defensive positions. They were the first to build walls between the higher rocks. It was a quick and simple way to build a fort. Half of the walls (the tall rocks) were already there to be utilized by them. Later on Bulgarian Tzars made them bigger and stronger. I believe the walls are twelve metres high in places.'

'Hm,' said Chaz, rolling up last as usual. 'They should keep the draft out, shouldn't they. Heh. Heh.' He sniggered at his own feeble joke.

Iskra continued to lead the way for the next half hour or so, silently hoping it was the right way when Bryden stopped and called out, 'Hold on. I can smell smoke.'

They were in a small valley, following a stream that quietly meandered between trees. Up ahead, towering over everything, were the jagged peaks of another group of sheer faced rocks.

Then Iskra said in an anxious tone, 'I can hear people talking.'

'Away from the stream, quick,' whispered Bryden, pulling Chaz by the arm toward the shelter of some bushes. Her face white, Iskra ran at a crouch to join them.

Huddled behind the bushes, they saw a group of people approaching; three adults, (a man and two women) with two small children, the women dressed similarly to Iskra. The man's garments were similar to those of the dead man they had encountered. The two children wore simple smocks. They were all shoeless.

Carrying a spear similar to Bryden's, the man led the way alongside the stream. The women and children were carrying reed baskets.

They were of a much better quality than the ones Iskra had made of course. *Well, they would be*, she thought. *They've spent all their lives making them.*

The group began to chatter again to each other as they passed by. They were wondering if they should go back to their camp. There were no fruit berries around here a woman said and there was no game worth a rushlight the man moaned in a weary voice.

As previously, Bryden and the others understood every word but before he had made up his mind whether to say something to the man, one of the children screamed out in fear, pointing skywards.

'Mama! *Man-vamp! Man-vamp!*'

Bryden looked upwards and saw a vision of hell. A giant bat was swooping down, huge wings beating with a thrum thrum sound. Then Bryden saw the face and he recoiled in horror. The skull was completely hairless. It was a human-like face but what a face. The eyes were a pair of yellow orbs, a snub nose could barely be seen because of a large top-lip curled right back to expose a set of long thin canines. A long, red tongue protruded like the head of a small snake. Dark brown hair straggled down below the mouth in a sticky mess of drool and saliva. The naked body seemed hairless and had a yellow tinge.

Bryden then realized that the wings, giant leathery wings, were attached to the back of the body. The hands and feet were of human shape and proportions except for the claw like nails, transformed into long razor sharp talons.

He took all this in during the seconds it took for the monster to slash the child (a boy) across his back with one of its taloned hands. Blood spurted as the child fell and before he hit ground the man-vamp snatched the body and flew away.

The women screamed in terror. Another man-vamp was plummeting down, arms out-stretched and ready to grab one of them. The man with the spear rushed over, jabbing at the monster. It veered off for a second and then made a grab for the woman who was trying to protect the terrified child. It was a clever feint. As the man turned to protect the new victim, swinging his spear round, the man-vamp reversed his flight and using its feet, slashed the man on his shoulders causing him to drop his spear. Defenceless, the man sank to the ground, crying out in pain. The man-vamp, roaring in triumph, landed by the stricken man and knelt, wings flapping slowly above its head to suck the lifeblood from him.

With a howl of rage, Bryden stood up and running towards the monster, threw his spear. It hurtled through the air and pierced the man-vamp's left wing and then his lower back. A shriek of agony split the air as the creature tried to take flight. The spear shaft had pinned the left wing to the man-vamps body so it couldn't fly. It turned round, one wing flapping fruitlessly. Then, snarling and chittering, it tottered unsteadily on taloned feet towards him, unused to walking on them. Its canines clashed with desire to get hold of his throat as it drooled and slobbered on its mission to kill him.

Bryden knew he could move fast enough to get away but he thought of the others. This monster was still capable of killing any of them.

He was still weighing up his options when the man on the ground rolled over and grabbed his own spear.

Grimacing with pain, the man slowly stood, and without a sound and with all of his remaining strength, rammed it in the man-vamp's back. He used so much force the tip of the spear went right through the body. It uttered one screech and fell to the ground, dead.

Bryden and the man stared at each other, neither quite believing what had happened. A moment later, the man collapsed to the ground, bleeding profusely from his shoulder wound.

'Iskra! Over here now!' called Bryden urgently.

Running as fast as she could, Iskra came from behind the bushes up to Bryden and asked, 'How can I help?'

'We need to see to this man's wound as quickly as possible. I think he's bleeding to death. God! I need bandages and something to suture that gash with. Otherwise he's a goner.'

Standing up, Iskra threw her bag down and without any pretensions to modesty, lifted up her long skirt and pulled down her white cotton petticoat and began to tear it into strips.

Meanwhile, Chaz had walked slowly over in a daze. Two dead bodies plus the killing and carrying off of the little boy were proving too much for him to take in.

'Chaz!' Bryden snapped at him, no time for niceties. 'Take some of those cotton strips from Iskra and go and wet them in the stream. Quick as you can lad, this man's dying.'

Fortunately, the stream was only some twenty or so metres away and Chaz, jerked back to his senses by Bryden's tone, grabbed a handful of torn strips from Iskra and rushed over to the stream to wet them.

To save time, Bryden as gently as he could, removed the blood-soaked waistcoat and shirt from the man. As he did so he looked across to Iskra and said, 'Thanks for the bandages. Now, all I want is a needle and thread.'

Iskra stopped tearing her tattered petticoat and bent down and picked up her shoulder bag and rummaged around for a minute before producing a small zipped case.

'If that is what I think it is,' said Bryden with a smile, 'Would you mind threading it for me with the strongest thread you have. I'm trying to stop the bleeding by holding the wound closed.'

Nodding her head, Iskra complied and was ready to hand the needle and thread to Bryden when Chaz rushed up with the dripping cotton strips.

'Thanks Chaz,' said Bryden as he quickly wiped the wounds with one of them. 'Now stay here and press one of these wet strips I've wadded into a ball over that wound there.' He pointed to a place on the man's back. Then wiping his own hands clean of blood, he took the needle and thread from Iskra.

Chaz couldn't look while his uncle sutured the open wounds, only moving away when ask to remove the bloody cloth he was pressing on the most serious gash.

Iskra moved in to take Chaz's place using one of the wet cloths to clean the stitched wounds.

'Thank God that's over. He should be alright now. Just a bit of R and R needed,' said Bryden a few minutes later as he stood and stretched his aching arms. He hadn't done anything like that for years and he thought back to the time he was in the Territorial Army (TA). Then he realized that he was being watched.

The two women and the other child, a girl, who was crying and clinging to what looked liked her mother, stood staring at Bryden like he was a man from Mars.

Then he remembered he was dressed like no other man they had ever seen. *So that's what it feels like*, he thought.

One of the women found the courage to speak. 'Is Teodor dead?' she asked in a quivering voice.

'No,' replied Bryden with a smile. 'But he will need plenty of care for the next few days. We need to get him home as quickly as we can.' He was hoping that they might be accepted by these women and taken to their camp.

'How can we do that? We can't carry Teodor?'

'I've got an idea,' interrupted Chaz. 'Why not make a stretcher. There are enough of us to carry him if it's not too far of course.'

The two women understood all of what Chaz was saying but for the word stretcher.

'Good idea,' said Bryden and knowing that the two women needed an explanation, he asked Chaz to go to the head of the injured man whilst he went to his feet. 'Now Chaz, pretend to pick up a stretcher, OK.'

The puzzled expression left Chaz's face and he bent down with his uncle to mime the pick up. They had to do it twice before one of the women clapped her hands and nodded her head.

It was a makeshift effort but it worked. Finding two stout poles was no problem and using thin saplings bound with vines (*the women being very adept at tying them)* as cross pieces, the stretcher was soon ready.

Bryden supervised, making sure the injured man was placed face down. Then with Bryden and Chaz each holding a rear position, the two women in front and Iskra holding the little girl's hand and looking wistfully at the baskets of food they had to leave behind, they set off.

It proved to be a more of an ordeal than it seemed. They had to find out by trial and error how to keep in step without jiggling the injured man too much. Eventually after many rests, they rounded another huge rock and saw their destination.

It was the fortress.

9

Towering high above the valley was a ridge, peppered with rocky pinnacles that reared hundreds of metres up into the sky.

What surprised Bryden even more was the scene around the base of the ridge. There were hundreds of makeshift huts made of a few wooden poles lashed together with vines for a simple frame and then covered with small branches, grass, leaves, anything that would help keep the weather out. These, it would appear, were the homes of hundreds of people who were terrified of being taken or killed by the man-vamps. Small fires, all over the camp sent up plumes of smoke which drifted away in the direction Bryden and his party had just come from and the smell of roasting meat pervaded the air everywhere.

Well at least now I know where that smell of smoke came from, thought Bryden.

The slope leading up to the ridge, denuded now of trees, led to a huge gate set between stone fortified walls which filled the space between two vertical rock faces.

As the stretcher party approached the gate, a group of armed men ran up to them. The leader, a Bolyar carrying a sword, ordered them to stop.

They put the stretcher down and one of the women explained what had happened. The Bolyar bent down in concern to look at the injured man and after giving him a pat on the shoulder (which fortunately he didn't feel because he was unconscious), he then ordered four of his men to pick up the stretcher and take it inside the gate. Only then did he give his attention to Bryden, Chaz and Iskra to whom he raised his eyebrows and smiled.

'I would like you three strangers to come with me,' he said quietly but authoritatively.

Iskra let go of the little girl she had been looking after. The young girl ran happily over to her mother. Of the three spears Iskra had also been carrying, she returned those belonging to Bryden and Chaz.

The Bolyar didn't seem to notice or mind. With a wave of his hand he led them through the huge gateway into the interior of the fortress. In the shadow of the twin rocky pinnacles was a large open courtyard confined between two more fortified stonewalls which led to another large gateway also nestling under a huge rock face.

The courtyard had three rows of wooden huts facing one wall. Opposite them a wooden stockade enclosed about thirty large horses. A nearby open-sided barn contained bales of hay and other bits and pieces needed for them. In the centre of the courtyard was the well, protected by a low stonewall. A wooden winding apparatus straddled it, the pail floating in the already filled stone trough.

'Keep close,' the Bolyar said impatiently as Chaz stopped to gawp at the well.

The small group approached the second gateway; this was also huge, although there was only one giant rock face from which to build the fortified stonewall which confined the second courtyard. This was obviously the military centre.

The huts were larger and much longer. Judging by the number of armed men around, this was probably the barracks or whatever they called them in these times. They passed another stockade with a similar number of horses, and the fodder shed. As before a well occupied the centre. The smoke from what looked like a forge drifted over them, the clanging sound of a hammer beating on metal confirming it. Three large stone ovens further along the wall were radiating a tantalizing smell of baking bread.

To Bryden's surprise they came to another gateway, a pair of massive rock faces buttressed this time and he could see even more towering pinnacles on the far side of it.

The third courtyard was the smallest and the most protected, being surrounded by the tallest rock faces of all and with one entrance and exit. The Bolyar led them past several small wooden huts, probably for the guards and of course, a well, towards a large two-storey stone building, comprising a long, ground floor hall with several smaller rooms above.

Gesturing to the following guards to remain outside, the Bolyar led them up a steep wooden staircase and through a narrow doorway into the large hall.

Chaz shuffled in and nearly ran out again. 'Jeez, It stinks like shit in here.' He looked down the hall and saw a central open hearth surrounded by stones with a log fire burning brightly in the dark room. The tiny window openings high up on the walls allowed little light in.

The long narrow floor was covered with rushes and straw within which bones, bits of food, excrement, (hopefully only cat's or dog's) and wet patches, which smelled of beer, could be seen.

A few rushlights were dotted about, jutting out of the walls on clay holders, casting flickering eerie shadows amongst the smoke drifting up from the fire through a louver, a lantern-like structure in the roof with side openings.

At the far end of the hall, was a raised dais of stone slabs on which two massive wooden chairs were placed in front of a long, transverse wooden table.

The Bolyar walked past a pair of trestle tables and the smoking hearth, leading them to the high table.

Muttering under his breath and praying he didn't walk on something smelly, Chaz was followed by Bryden and Iskra who were whispering conspiratorially behind him.

Chaz almost bumped into the Bolyar as he stopped in front of the high table and knelt down on one knee.

'Down strangers,' the Bolyar ordered anxiously. 'Kneel to the Great Strator.'

As they complied with his order, Chaz whispered to Iskra, 'Who the hell is he on about?'

'If I remember right, historically the Strator was a sort of military governor,' she whispered back.

The Bolyar turned and looked daggers at them so they shut up.

A sudden noise made them all look up.

Behind the massive chairs was a large wall tapestry. A huge turbaned guard, carrying a nasty looking curved sword, was drawing a part of it aside to enable the Strator to enter the great hall.

The Great Strator was wearing a sheepskin hat (a kalpak). A pair of piercing blue eyes stared at them over a straggly, full-length beard. His black waistcoat, which was stitched with intricate gold embroidery, sparkled in the firelight, emphasizing the long sleeved white shirt. He sported a pair of blue leggings, tied with a wide leather belt from which a jewelled, silver-handled dagger protruded.

The Strator strutted into the room, his dark red cloak fastened around the neck by a silver pafka, (hook buckle) and bedizened with golden discs draping his shoulders. Surprisingly, he was wearing a pair of pigskin Tservuli (peasant sandals).

Sitting down in the massive chair, the Strator looked smaller than at first appearance. His voice though, was impressive. 'Who are they, Bolyar Chaydar?' he commanded in a sonorous tone.

'My Lord,' Bolyar Chaydar began, 'Please forgive your humble servant. We have not had time to interrogate them for they have just arrived carrying Teodor. He was badly injured by a man-vamp. The strangers saved him.'

'What! The man-vamps so near?' the Strator asked, a feeling of dread visibly flowing through his bones. He licked his lips and asked curtly, 'And who are these strangers?'

Before Bolyar Chaydar could speak, Iskra said, 'My Lord, these two strangers are from Epirus.'

'Ah! Epirus. I thought they were dressed strangely. Now tell me how you saved Teodor.'

Bryden begged leave to stand and when the Strator nodded, he rose to his feet and leaning on his spear shaft told of how they had come upon Teodor and his group and how the first man-vamp's sudden attack had killed the small boy and then snatched up the body, carrying it away.

He then explained how he ran to help the defenceless Teodor before he himself was saved by the last desperate thrust of Teodor with his spear.

Before the Strator could ask any questions, a commotion at the door of the hall made everyone turn.

The Strator stood, his face red with anger.

'Who dares disturb the Great Strator,' he roared. 'Answer quickly or your guts will be fed to the swine.'

A Malki (junior) Bolyar followed by a guard crept in. 'My Lord! I beg your indulgence and clemency.' The Bolyar then fell to the ground trembling in terror.

'Speak!' commanded the Strator.

'My Lord, I bring bad tidings. The man-vamps have attacked a group of woodcutters gathering fuel. At least four hands (twenty, whispered Iskra) were attacked and had their life's blood taken from them.'

The Strator staggered back and collapsed on to his chair. 'By all Saints, this is the Devil's work,' he muttered in strangulated tones.

Then, standing again, he called out loudly to the Bolyar, 'Bring in the bodies. They must be buried with all Holy Rites. Send for the Friar.'

The cowering Bolyar got to his feet, bowed and scurried out followed by the equally terrified guard.

The Strator looked down at Boyar Chaydar. 'Take these strangers to the guest hut. We will talk tomorrow.'

With a flick of the wrist, he dismissed them and stalked off through the opening behind the tapestry, escorted by his guard.

'Come,' Bolyar Chaydar said, leading the way out of the Strator's hall.

'We need to talk about the man-vamps.'

'Yes,' replied Bryden.

'Perhaps you can tell us a bit more about them first. We

have not come across them before today.'

Bolyar Chaydar's eyes widened. 'You have never heard of the man-vamps? Where the hell have you been?'

'It's a long story. Maybe another time, eh!'

With a shrug, the Bolyar led them out of the inner courtyard into a bustling outer one.

A group of mainly women and children were gathering at the gatehouse. An air of expectancy was very apparent with many whispering voices. A lot of women were white faced, some weeping. They had already been informed of the deaths of their husbands.

One hut was situated away from the others, being near a massive stonewall. 'Here we are. I hope this will be sufficient for your needs. I will send a platter of food for you shortly.'

Bolyar Chaydar looked closely at Bryden. 'Then we talk.'

10

The hut was similar to the one at Rabisha they noticed, as they descended the steps. It was now late afternoon and getting chilly so they were grateful that the oven fire was lit and radiating pleasant warmth across the room.

The bench across the wall had several small animal pelts on the seat. Iskra sank down. Chaz, who had been unnaturally quiet for most of the time, joined her and let out a big groan. 'What a frigging mess,' he said to no one in particular. 'What do we do now? Anyway, where's the blasted food? I'm starving.'

Suppressing a smile, Bryden was just about to ask Chaz to be patient when a scuffle at the door made him pause. He walked over to the door and pulled it open. Two young girls stood there, each holding a shallow wicker basket.

The two girls burst out laughing when they saw Bryden's hiking outfit, nearly dropping the baskets in the process. Smiling back at them he thought, *maybe he did look like a clown to them, just as medieval troubadours wore outlandish clothes.*

Calling Iskra to help, he took one basket containing three platters of cut meat, cheese, apple and hunks of dark bread and passed it over to her. Taking the other basket, which held three wooden beakers of beer, Bryden thanked the girls who ran off giggling loudly.

A few minutes later, a large belch from Chaz signified that he was feeling much better. He then asked Iskra why they had been given beer to drink.

'I'm sure you remember the reason. Every kid gets taught about the lack of clean drinking water in medieval times. Well, here we are and you are getting drunk on beer.'

'I'm not!' spluttered Chaz with another burp. 'Oh! Sorry,' and he began to get a fit of the giggles.

A sudden outburst of shouting and wailing caused

Bryden and Iskra to rush outside. A large wagon pulled by four horses was coming through the gateway. A crowd of wailing women ran to the wagon and tried to see who was being brought back.

As Bryden and Iskra watched, Bolyar Chaydar came up to them. 'I would like to see you,' he pointed to Bryden. 'Come with me. I'm sorry, I don't know your name.'

'It's Bryden.'

'Thank you, Bryyyden,' Bolyar Chaydar said. 'That is a new name to me.' Then he looked at Iskra and smiled. Blushing a little, Iskra gave her name.

'Would you mind if I take Bryyyden away from you for a while?'

'Of course not,' replied Iskra. 'Anyway I think Chaz might need a bit of supervision.' She laughed and mimicked drinking from a beaker.

'Another strange name, Chasss,' said Bolyar Chaydar. 'I suppose it is popular in Epirus.'

Bryden just nodded.

As Iskra turned to go back to Chaz, she watched Bryden and Bolyar Chaydar walk towards the central gateway.

***

'Where've you been?' asked a slightly truculent Chaz. 'I've been stuck in here for ages with that little bugger.' He pointed to the oven.

A small impish figure, dressed in black was watching them. He had a pointed hat on and was holding a beaker in his hand. A cheeky grin was plastered over his face which was half covered with a grey beard long enough to cover his chest.

'Is it one of those things we saw in the other hut?' asked Chaz, remarkably calm after his previous outbursts.

'Yes,' she replied looking closely at it. 'It looks like another Schopanyn ….. Chaz! You're all wet!'

'I know. The little sod threw water all over me.'

'Why?'

'Well, I sort of threw an apple core at it.'

'Serves you right then. It was only doing its job.'

'Doing its frigging job. I'm soaking wet.'

'Don't you remember they're house-guards?'

'Oh, for God's sake! I'm going!' Chaz made a dash for the door.

The small figure by the oven lifted his beaker and a shower of small black dots swept over Chaz and as they hit him they developed legs. 'Aaahh! Spiders! Millions of the buggers! Get them off me! Get them off me!' screamed Chaz. 'I'll kill the bastard if I get my hands on him,' he promised vehemently as he brushed himself trying to get rid of them.

'Just stay where you are and don't move,' Iskra said, as she fumbled in her bag.

'Don't move! You must be joking,' yelled Chaz, dancing about, arms waving everywhere.

Iskra began to sidle across the room towards the oven and the little impish figure, not sure what she was doing, turned to watch Chaz who was still jumping up and down yelling obscenities at the top of his voice.

Seizing her chance, Iskra opened her hand and tossed the small parcel she was holding into the oven. The hot embers on the bottom of the oven's fire-shelf ignited the tissue paper and the tiny piece of charred wood inside it.

Whoosh!

Sparks and black smoke erupted from the oven and then cleared in a few moments. As the smoke dissipated another form emerged into view.

'My God! Not another one of the little sods,' Chaz cried out in dismay, as he continued scratching his arms like mad. 'Wait a minute. It's that little bastard that did my knee in.'

'Careful what you say Chaz,' warned Iskra, as she pulled out another small object from her bag and crouched down to say hello to the Schopanyn from Rabisha.

Holding his little broomstick like a walking stick, the

82

house-guard smiled and held out a hand. Iskra obliged by giving him a mint. If anything, his smile got bigger when she pointed to the impish figure on the other side of the oven (which by the way was trying to look indifferent to the situation). It got even larger when the broomstick left his hand and began to float over to the other Schopanyn but before any fireworks could begin, it disappeared in a puff of smoke, along with all the tiny spiders that had driven Chaz crazy.

'Jeez! Never again,' said a mighty relieved Chaz. 'Where's the nearest sweet shop. I want some mints.'

'Sorry, you'll have to wait until you get home,' laughed Iskra.

They looked round to thank their new house-guard but he too had disappeared.

***

Meanwhile, Bolyar Chaydar had taken Bryden to see Strator in his Great Hall. This time they were allowed to sit on a stool.

'My friend from Epirus,' began the Strator, 'We need your help and knowledge to defeat the man-vamps. As you have seen, many of my people have died and the camp outside the gates is getting bigger daily. Soon there will be no one tending their farms in this region and we will all face starvation unless we can defeat these monsters. Have you any ideas?'

Bryden looked directly into the Strator's eyes and thought he saw a man of honour. 'My Lord, as you say, I am a stranger here and may need your help too in the not too distant future.'

'Say no more, stranger. If you rid us of our peril, I, as Strator give my word to help you. Go now with Bolyar Chaydar and plan to rid us of this pestilence.'

***

Bryden followed Bolyar Chaydar to the Guard hut. It was

empty although with room enough for about twenty men. They found a corner with a couple of benches covered in soft skins and took a moment to fill two beakers of beer.

Bryden had been giving plenty of thought as to how to tackle the problem of the man-vamps and he had developed a couple of theories. After about half an hour a plan had been thrashed out and he had persuaded Bolyar Chaydar that it might be feasible.

With about an hour left before sunset, Bolyar Chaydar had six trusty men collect their weapons and a large skin-wrapped bundle along with several long wooden staves. Stopping only to mount a horse each, the party of eight men left the fortress.

Travelling fast, the troop rode to the place of death, the site where the woodcutters had met their tragic end.

It was on the edge of a large clearing. Half trimmed trunks lay strewn about. A pile of cut logs ready for loading was left abandoned and a bloody waistcoat was hanging from a branch, swinging in the gentle evening breeze.

'Dismount,' ordered Bolyar Chaydar. 'Zltan, Borislav, unwrap the skins quickly. The rest of you stand guard and look out for man-vamps. Your lives depend on it.'

The unwrapped skins revealed a pile of fishing nets and ropes.

'Bring them over here,' Bryden called to the two men carrying the nets. He was standing in front of a range of trees, open ground behind him. 'Fetch the staves and fix two here.' He pointed to a large shrub. 'Tie the nets to them first.'

Bryden then walked across the open space to another convenient shrub. 'Fix the staves here and like before, tie the nets on first.'

Working as only desperate men can, they soon had a fishing net stretched between two shrubs, which served to hide the staves. Bryden and Bolyar Chaydar then walked away from the nets and had a look from the edge of the clearing. They were invisible.

'I have my doubts,' confessed Bolyar Chaydar. 'But we have to try something. You are a man of great wisdom.'

'Let's light the fire. It's getting dark.' *Let's hope it's not too dark,* Bryden thought, crossing his fingers.

A small fire sent up a trail of smoke drifting into the darkening sky. With the men in hiding by the two shrubs, Bryden lay down next to it, spear by his side, ready for a long wait.

It happened so suddenly. A swoosh and hiss of air was the first warning. Then came an almighty screech and the fishing net seemed to explode. A huge shape was entangled and desperately trying to escape. 'Get the ropes!' yelled Bryden. 'Get the frigging ropes round the bastard!'

His ploy of putting the fire behind the fishnets had worked.

The Bolyar's men rushed forward with their ropes and began the dangerous task of roping man-vamp alive. A scream rent the air as one of the men was ripped almost in two when a foot talon disemboweled him. The scream died into a howl of agony, then silence.

The man-vamp had a rope around its throat and was being slowly choked to death. 'Easy on that rope,' cried Bryden. As the weakening creature stopped struggling, they were able to add more ropes around it, pinning the wings and those lethal talons.

'Now,' said Bryden feeling a sense of relief, 'All we have to do is to get this critter back to the Fortress.'

11

The pit was 4m deep. Once an ancient grain pit cut into the solid rock, it made an excellent dungeon. At the bottom, standing in his own filth and securely chained against the wall, the man-vamp strained to get free. Iron shackles on his ankles, manacled wrists and his wings tied together, it was a hopeless endeavour.

Bryden stood on the edge of the pit, which was between the rear of the Strator's hall and the fortress wall.

Ever since the site became a fortress, hundreds of years ago, the pit had been a place of terror and torment. No one had ever escaped with no way out except up, by ladder or rope held by someone on top and no one ever left them there *in situ.*

Bryden tried again to explain to a sceptical Bolyar Chaydar the reasons why the man-vamp must be kept alive. 'As I have already said, the first time I saw one, I thought there was something odd about the skin colour. Well, I didn't think of that right away of course. It was a sub-conscious thing really.'

Bolyar Chaydar raised an eyebrow.

God! thought Bryden, getting a little exasperated. *I'm not getting anywhere with him.* 'Look at that man-vamp down there. The skin is yellow. You can see that, can't you?'

Bolyar Chaydar nodded.

Good. Now we're getting somewhere. 'Well I think he has a disease, I …..'

The look Bolyar Chaydar gave made Bryden stop.

'What is diissis?'

Jeez! How the hell am I going to tell a thirteenth century man about the red blood cells in his body? 'I …, I …. Oh shit. The man-vamp is sick, not well.' Bryden looked at the Bolyar and rubbing his stomach, made retching noise.

'Ah, I see. Diissis.' Bolyar Chaydar smiled.

Thank God. 'We watch for three days, then, if the man-vamp dies, we tell the Strator about my plan. No food, no water. Three days, right.'

Still not sure why he should trust Bryyyden the Bolyar nodded in agreement.

***

It was the third day. Woodcutters and hunters were still being killed daily by the man-vamps despite being protected by armed men. The camp was now so large, fuel and meat needed replenishing every day.

A strangled cry came up from the pit, followed by gasps and wheezing. Hoarse, heavy breathing and then a choking, rasping cough echoed in the damp evening air.

Bryden and Bolyar Chaydar shoved the guard away from the edge of the pit and looked down at the man-vamp.

He was dangling from his manacles fixed to the wall, his chest heaving from the exertions of trying to breath. Mouth wide-open, dribbling drool, yellow eyes staring at the sky, he writhed in his chains and with a huge effort, straitened his body and then with a loud gasp, collapsed in a dangling heap, dead.

Now comes the tricky part, thought Bryden. *Trying to persuade the Strator to accept his idea.*

'We must see the Strator right away.' Bryden looked at Bolyar Chaydar earnestly.

The Bolyar looked once more down into the pit at the dead man-vamp and nodded in agreement.

***

It took a while, the Strator was a busy man.

That was the impression he tried to give to his people anyway.

Bending on one knee before the Great Strator, Bryden muttered to himself, *if this is going to be a regular thing I'm going to bring a sodding kneeling pad.*

As before, the gracious Strator allowed them to sit on a rock-hard stool

87

'My Lord,' began Bolyar Chaydar, 'I bring glad tidings. The man-vamp is dead.'

'I know that! Imbecile,' raged the Strator, giving vent to his relief that the monster was dead. 'Why did it take so long? Three days. Why?'

'Allow me, My Lord.' Bryden stood and bowed. He was well aware that he needed all his wits about him if he was to convince the Strator of his strategy to rid the area of the man-vamps.

'May I remind the gracious Lord that I am from Epirus, a far away land that many wise and learned men have visited. I believe the Emperor himself has sent envoys there in order to acquire secrets that only Emperors can be allowed to have.' *In for a penny, in for a pound,* thought Bryden.

The Strator nodded knowingly.

'It was there I met several wise men who had travelled far and wide in search of knowledge. One, I remember had just returned from Adrianople. (The Strator raised his eyebrows. It appeared he liked what he was hearing). He was the one who informed me of the sickness of the yellow skin.'

The Strator leaned forward in his huge chair, avid for more.

'My Lord.' Bryden wanted to '*reel in*' the Strator but he knew he had to be careful. 'The scholar in Epirus told me their secret. I know that the man-vamps have the yellow skin sickness. I also know that to remain alive, they must drink human blood at least once in three days. If they don't, they will choke to death, just like the one in the pit.'

The Strator leaned back in his chair, dumbfounded by the news he had just heard. He was silent for a few moments and then said. 'My friend from Epirus, that may be so but how will that help us stop the man-vamps terrorizing and killing my people?'

Bryden smiled to himself. *Hook, line and sinker.* 'My Esteemed Lord, *pile it on Bryden pile it on.* You must forgive a humble servant like myself for being so presumptive as to give you advice on such serious matters.'

The Strator held up a hand and said firmly, 'I insist that you tell me if you have found a way of killing the man-vamps.'

'The only way, My Lord, is to remove their food.'

'Their food! What do you mean? You have just said that they only....'

The Strator stopped speaking. His face flushed a bright red, 'You expect me to lead my people from here, their homeland. How dare you propose such a thing!' He was nearly raging by now. Then he jumped up.

'I'll have you flayed alive,' he spluttered. 'Guards, Guards.'

Bryden blanched with fear. *God. I didn't frigging expect this.*

'My Lord! My Lord!' Bolyar Chaydar actually raised his voice to be heard. 'I beseech thee not to be too hasty. Stranger Bryyyden is not familiar with our ways. My Lord, please let him explain his plan. On my honour, he speaks truly.'

The Strator sat down again, still red faced, breathing heavily. Leaning over the arm of his chair, he picked up a golden goblet and after taking a large gulp, threw it across the room.

Slightly calmer, he looked down at Bryden and said in a sterner, more unfriendly tone, 'Lucky for you, Stranger, I value the council of Bolyar Chaydar. Speak.'

Bryden got to his feet and trying not to let his trembling hands betray how he felt, put them behind his back and bowed. He wasn't feeling so cocky now, in fact he felt shit scared.

'My Gracious Lord, I beg your forgiveness for offending you. I assure you on my honour that it was not my meaning. I spoke loosely and apologize most deeply. It was not my intent to imply that you lead your people away from their homeland.'

Bryden went on, hoping the Strator had enough patience

to let him finish. 'I truly believe that the only way to save your people is to bring them all and I mean all, into the safety of the fortress.' He held up a hand, 'My Lord, just for three days. The three days that will kill the man-vamps if they cannot feed on humans.'

The Strator said nothing. He just stared fixedly at Bryden, his blue eyes as cold as ice.

'My Lord,' said Bryden earnestly, 'On my journey here, we passed many bodies all drained of their life's blood. (The Strator shuddered at the thought). The reason that the man-vamps are attacking near the Fortress is because most of the humans in this area are now camped outside the gates or inside them. If everyone in the camp brought enough food for the three days, the man-vamps will die, just like the one in the pit.'

Bryden paused for a moment, then crossed his fingers behind his back. 'I also believe, that the man-vamps are not aware of their sickness. They will keep attacking your people because, forgive me for saying so, from their point of view they are easy pickings.'

Bending on one knee, *I hope this is the last frigging time I do this,* thought Bryden. 'I urge you to consider this plan, My Lord. It is the only way, I assure you.'

'Leave!' The Strator said grimly.

With a sinking heart, Bryden stood and turned to go. Bolyar Chaydar got off his stool and walked over to him.

'Wait!' commanded the Strator.

Bryden froze. *God, what now* and looked back at the Strator.

'Bolyar Chaydar, get all available Bolyars and go and inform the camp that no-one must leave the camp today and that they must be ready to enter the Fortress by the sound of the Angel Bell.'

***

Chaz lay on the bench listening to his iPod. Iskra had just put a small log on the oven fire when Bryden stormed in.

'You won't bloody believe it but I was just about to be carted off to be flayed alive by that balm-pot, idiotic Strator.'

'For goodness sake, sit down and tell us what happened.' Iskra indicated the other bench as she sat on the floor by the oven fire.

Taking a deep breath, Bryden related his morning with the Strator, 'And he threw a golden goblet at me,' he said, exaggerating the situation somewhat.

'Jeez!' said Chaz, 'Who were you going to play with. I didn't know you could play an instrument, Uncle?'

'God give me strength,' Bryden said, giving Chaz a look that would freeze water.

Coming to Chaz's rescue, Iskra ask Bryden what was going to happen now.

'Well,' Bryden thought for a moment. 'The man-vamps have definitely got a form of jaundice. I thought as much when I saw the yellow tinge to their skin and the yellow eyes. I had to test one in order to see if they had a mutation, one that could prove to be fatal. If they had, it meant that they would develop a sickle cell infection that would affect their ability to breath. If they did not get a regular supply of human blood within three days they would die. That one did.'

Bryden paused. 'Hell!' he shouted, suddenly jumping up, 'We've got to get three days of food in. Now! Right away. God! I hope were not too late?'

'What's all the fuss about?' said Chaz, suddenly realizing he should have turned his iPod down.

The whole bloody place will be crawling with people this evening. Didn't you hear a blasted word I said?'

Chaz was saved from any further diatribes by a polite knock on the door.

Bryden, breathing heavily, realized that that he was suffering from delayed shock. *Poor Chaz, he really got it in the neck. Never mind, he'll get over it.*

He opened the door to a young man-at-arms, minus his

arms. Bryden giggled, *minus his arms. Ha, Ha. God, I'm going mad,* he thought. Still grinning, he saw that that the guardsman had a sort of sledge piled high with baskets of food and skins of beer.

'Bolyar Chaydar ordered me to bring these to you with his compliments,' and he proceeded to unload everything by Bryden's feet.

'Oh! Before you go, please ask Bolyar Chaydar to come and see me. Say it's urgent.'

The guardsman nodded and left dragging his sledge behind him.

Bryden had to call Chaz twice before he came out to help bring in the supplies. They had just finished when Bolyar Chaydar knocked and came in.

'You wanted to see me Bryyyden.'

'Yes. Thanks for coming so quickly. Can we go outside so I can show you something.'

Bryden took the Bolyar round the back of the hut and pointed to the pit (toilet). 'Have you considered that there will be maybe several hundred people wanting to use these?'

Bolyar Chaydar looked blankly at Bryden.

'Oh! Yeah, numbers,' muttered Bryden to himself. He held up his hands and began to quickly, open and close them. 'People,' he said, pointing to the fortress walls and then to the pit.

'Ah, people. Many,' said the Bolyar, nodding.

Bryden pointed to the pit, opened and closed his hands several times again and then shook his head. Then he walked to the pit and opened his hands wide. 'They need to be much bigger,' he said, pointing to the fortress walls again. 'Many people for three days will want to use these. Not good.'

The Bolyar looked at Bryden and shrugged. *So what,* he seemed to say. *What can I do about it?*

Bryden pointed to the wall. 'Come,' he said to the Bolyar.

92

Then using a stick, Bryden drew two parallel lines for about ten metres and half a metre wide. He then mimed digging, pointing to the pit.

The penny dropped. Bolyar Chaydar grinned and nodded. He called over to another Bolyar and issued the order to find suitable places by the wall and dig the long pits as fast as they could, using as many guards as necessary. They had to be ready before the Angel Bell.

Suddenly feeling hungry, Bryden went back to the hut for something to eat.

12

A bell began to ring. Iskra had spent most of the afternoon sorting the various baskets of food into some semblance of order and filling as many receptacles that would hold water as possible since she was very aware that later on, the area round the well would be swarming with people, each one trying to get access to the one and only pail. Jerked awake by the clanging, she became aware that she was lying on a brown bearskin in front of the oven fire.

'Welcome back to the land of the living,' Chaz chided gently.

'What's with the bells?' Iskra asked, her head still fuzzy with sleep.

'It's the Angel Bell. It's rung each night just before sunset.' Bryden had stopped sharpening his spear point to answer her question. 'Have you forgotten, the Strator has allowed the camp people sanctuary inside the fortress for the next three days.'

'Ah! Now I remember.' Stifling a yawn, Iskra stretched like a cat in front of the fire.

Chaz, lying on his back on his bench, hands behind his head, admired the view.

The Angel Bell continued to ring but its sound was beginning to get drowned out by an incessant noise. The clamor of voices grew louder and louder as the crowd of camp people streamed into the fortress courtyard.

Iskra went to the door and looked out.

Family after family were spreading out, each looking for a small space to call their own for the next three days. Animal skins, woollen cloths, even bundles of straw were put down to stake a claim. Then, sitting or lying down, they laid out the few personal possessions they were allowed to bring; wooden platters and beakers, small clay pots or jugs, animal skins filled with beer, (clean water was a luxury in the camp. They would get a surprise when they heard about the well.) and parcels of food wrapped in leaves, cloth or animal skins.

Children of all ages wailed, played or squabbled. Anxious parents were calling to one another about this or that. And still they kept coming.

Chas deigned to have a look. 'Jeez! Just look at that. Is it a free happy hour or what?'

'Knock it off Chaz. This is serious,' Bryden called from the hut.

'Sorry.'

***

By the time the Angel Bell had stopped ringing, every square metre (except for the walkways between the gates, the well and the long pits (toilets), was taken up by family groups.

Once everyone was in and the gate locked, some sort order was established and people began to settle down for the night. The novelty of the situation had put everyone in a cooperative mood since many of the camp had lost a loved one to the man-vamps or knew of others who had. There was an air of compliance and there were few grumbles about the overcrowding.

***

High up on the fortress walls, which were scarcely visible in the twilight, two guardsmen were talking quietly, against orders if the truth be known. They should have been keeping a sharp lookout but things had been quiet all day until the buzz they got from bringing in the camp people to the fortress. It had been a welcome change from the boring regime of guarding a normally quiet outpost.

Their post was on the west side of the fortress wall and above the first courtyard. The last rays of the dying sun pierced the gloom and glinted off their helmets and spear points.

It was the sudden gust of wind that warned one of the guardsmen and looking up, he froze in terror as he saw a grotesque apparition falling through the air towards him. A gaping maw, full of fangs and emitting ear shattering shrieks. A man-vamp.

Then, with arms reaching out to grab the guardsman, the man-vamp crashed into a wall of netting, fishnets strung along the top of the fortress wall like giant flycatchers of later years. (Bolyar Chaydar had copied the idea from Bryden and had set them up).

Entangled in the net, momentum carried it over the wall and then it fell at speed to the ground, shrieking and roaring. The mass of writhing limbs and metres of fishnet swirling around and then falling on top of the slumbering forms of the camp people, caused pandemonium. (Most peasants sleep from sundown to sunrise). The man-vamp crashed down onto a woman nursing her baby, knocking her head with great force against a clay pot which shattered into lethal shards, one of which pierced her eye straight through to the brain.

The baby, trapped beneath her body, was suffocated within minutes. Her husband, frightened out of his wits, not knowing what was happening, tried to sit up. A taloned hand gripped his throat and pulled out his windpipe. Gasping for air, as blood spurted over the man-vamp's arm, the man tried to escape but he too, got caught in the fish net and as he slowly bled to death, the man-vamp now with one arm and leg free, dragged him over his dead wife and son.

The adjoining family of four scrambled to their feet in the gloomy shadow of the fortress wall. Terrified by the roaring, shrieking apparition, they didn't know which way to turn. A part of the fishing net trailed over their patch of ground and one of their two children was trapped in it. The desperate parents hindered by the darkness, tugged and pulled at the net.

Feeling the tugging, the man-vamp turned and lashed out with his free leg. The taloned foot ripped across both parents' backs, severing both their spines with one blow. Screaming in agony, they fell to the ground writhing with pain. The child trapped in the net whimpered and sobbed at the sight of his injured parents screaming. His elder sister rushed forward, heedless of the danger, wanting to help.

The man-vamp, twisting round, saw the girl and grabbed her by the hair and flung her over the heads of several approaching guardsmen, some carrying flaming torches, others spears at the ready. Seeing the armed guardsmen, it roared a challenge and tried to free its entangled wings.

The nearest guardsman threw his spear at the man-vamp, wounding it in the thigh. It gave shriek of pain and ripped at the net with its hand talons, the light of the torches actually helping it. Two more spears flew through the air and hit the body, one in the chest the other in the stomach. Trying to pull them out, the man-vamp slipped in its own blood and fell to the ground with a screeching howl. A Bolyar ran up and jabbed a spear down its throat. The man-vamp reared up and then slumped to the ground, dead.

By now the courtyard was full of screaming, frightened and panicking people. Some tried to run to the main gate but couldn't get through because too many of the others had the same idea. Others ran towards the second courtyard gate, now open to let out a stream of guardsmen.

In the darkness whole families were split up. Many people, lots of them children, were trampled underfoot. Most fallers suffered broken limbs, a few died, mainly from injuries sustained when the hysterical mob pushed them down onto broken pieces of pottery.

It took most of the night to clean up the courtyard as best they could by torchlight. The injured were taken to the second courtyard to be tended by the guardsmen. The bodies wrapped in white shrouds lay by the gatehouse.

The rest of the families huddled the best they could on their patch of yard, waiting grimly for daylight.

The man-vamp's body was dumped outside the main gate.

13

It was a sober morning. Grieving parents, children, other family members and friends clustered together in little groups, trying to console one another.

The Friar held an open-air service in the mid-morning, right after the clean up had finally been finished. The burials then took place immediately after the service had ended.

The Strator had ordered the guard's bakers to make enough bread for everyone as well as insisting that an ox be roasted and enough beer to quell any thoughts of the peasants' growing desire to plan a raid on the unknown lair of the man-vamps. They soon became too drunk for any kind of action.

During the afternoon, several teams of guards were sent back to the empty camp outside the fortress walls to collect anything of value, to replace the damaged goods caused by the previous *'Night of Terror'* as it had now become known. Items of value were distributed according to need. By now the whole fortress was in jittery mood.

Trying to calm down the people's fears, the Strator ordered the guards to be doubled along the walls of the fortress.

***

Chaz had been bored out of his mind. He couldn't very well wander the courtyard with all the cleaning going on and then there was the service. So Bryden had no trouble enlisting him into the water detail, arranged with Bolyar Chaydar to stop the squabbling, which had erupted several times around the well.

Bryden had suggested that water carriers be appointed and only they were to be allowed access to the well. So a group of teenage boys, now to be helped by Chaz, were drafted in to do the job.

Iskra had already made herself useful by helping tend the

injured, her knowledge of basic first aid proving most effective. The cleaning and dressing of wounds was transformed by her ideas of basic hygiene such as making sure all the 'nurses' had clean hands. A number of the patients would be ever grateful to her for saving an arm or leg from being deformed by the simple treatment of fixing splints, all be it, by using simple sticks, to their fractures. Of course there was resistance to her ideas but Bolyar Chaydar, much impressed with Bryden's thinking, gave her his full support and she was soon in demand as the new *healer.*

The Bolyar and Bryden had spent a good part of the day trying to plan for as many different scenarios as possible. The man-vamps, they both knew, would attack again and soon.

***

They were tested that evening just before sunset, when seven man-vamps hurtled down out of the twilight sky and were about to land in the middle of the first courtyard. The lookouts gave the alarm immediately. Cries of *Man-vamp! Man-vamp!* mingled with the blare of warning horns blown by other watch keepers.

At once, everyone standing fell to the ground as ordered to that afternoon. That is, except for the five groups of guardsmen of four spaced around the courtyard, each guard standing back-to-back, spears by their sides. They were each wearing a hooded full-sized cloak as a disguise.

The man-vamps were startled at first by the raucous blare of the warning horns. Then, deciding that the standing guards were the easier targets, they split up and attacked.

Every guard had two spears. As the man-vamps got within range, they each threw one. Four of the demon creatures were hit, three falling severely injured to the ground where the peasants, now armed with sickles, set upon them. Before the injured man-vamps knew what was happening, all three had been dismembered and beheaded.

The four remaining man-vamps flew towards the standing guards, separating as they did so. The leading creature, a spear dangling from its side, was shrieking with rage, its wings flapping just above ground level, making a swish swishing noise. Then in a graceful arc it twisted in the air so that the taloned feet were foremost, ready to strike the nearest guardsman.

Standing firm, the guardsman jabbed his spear between the legs, deep into the belly of the man-vamp.

The impact of the oncoming creature hitting the spear knocked the guardsman back into his comrades and all four sprawled onto the ground, the mortally wounded man-vamp on top of them, screeching, thrashing wings battering and taloned hands raking any flesh within reach.

Scrambling to his feet, the guardsman had only one chance to save his own life. Seizing the spear that was sticking from the beast's side, (The one thrown earlier) he rammed it straight through the heart.

The second man-vamp was more successful in that it evaded the first thrust of a spear-wielding guardsman and swiped at his head with a taloned hand. Jerking himself backwards to avoid the strike, he knocked into his fellow guardsman, pushing his spear sideways right into the path of the third man-vamp as it reached out to grab one of them. The point of the spear entered the left eye socket, penetrating the brain. One shrill shriek came from the gruesome, grimacing mouth as the vile creature fell, dead, to the ground.

Taking advantage of the death of one of its own, the man–vamp swerved away from the guardsmen and spying a child that had disobeyed the instruction to stay down and had just bobbed up curious to see what was making the noise, swooped lower still and seized the child by its smock.

Screaming in terror, the child wriggled and twisted so much, the homespun smock was ripped apart by the razor sharp talons. Like a pea in a pod that was suddenly popped open, the naked child dropped to the ground on top of a matronly woman who squealed in terror and pain before realizing what had fallen onto her ample bosom.

The remaining man-vamp suddenly veered in the air as it realized it was on its own. It hesitated for a moment, apparently disoriented, hovering too long.

Three spears flashed through the air, one after the other, into the body of the man-vamp. The first one entered the right thigh by the groin, the second one, through the right rib cage puncturing the lung, the third one lodged in its throat.

Spiralling down, the wings hardly fluttering, the man-vamp crashed into a hastily evacuated space in the courtyard, where the crazed peasants pulled it to pieces with their bare hands.

***

The rest of the night passed by in a fitful manner, most people too afraid to sleep. By morning, droopy eyed and yawning, Chaz poked his head out of the hut. The courtyard was filled as usual with recumbent forms in the most peculiar positions.

'Jeez!' exclaimed Chaz, 'I hope I don't look like that.'

He was looking at a prize specimen who was sprawled half naked across his bedding, a hairy butt exposed to the world, a face looking up to the sky, drool dribbling from his half-open slack mouth, showing a set of greeny-yellow teeth, several of which were missing. The sound of his snoring, mixed with the other scores of snuffling, wheezing individuals made a kind of macabre morning chorus.

By mid-morning the main courtyard was awash with the tension. There was an unspoken feeling that something 'big' was about to happen. Small groups gossiping would suddenly stop and as one, look up to the sky.

Chaz, on water duty, had been told to carry his spear at all times. 'Hells bells,' he complained, 'It's bad enough carrying a great big blasted pail of water half way round this damn courtyard without a bloody spear.' He took it all the same and was often seen furtively glancing up at the sky just like the others.

Iskra went to see her 'patients' straight after breakfast as usual, literally right after the crack of dawn. Her main task was supervising her helpers to make sure they were keeping to the 'new' hygiene standards.

The patients were now under cover, well partly so. Some off duty guardsmen had set up a wood and reeds lean-to shelter. It gave some sort of privacy that the injured and wounded appreciated. Iskra got the impression that normally the injured had to more or less grin and bear it and if you got better, you were lucky, if not, tough.

Bryden was having his usual talk with Bolyar Chaydar. They were both trying to second-guess what the man-vamps would do next. It was, according to his reckoning, the fatal day when his forecast of the demise of the man-vamps would happen.

He was worried, very worried. It was a worry he could do without. If the truth be known, he was terrified that his forecast would prove to be wrong. That bastard, the Strator, would have his guts for garters, he was sure.

This recurring thought was nearly paralyzing him. When the Bolyar asked a question he had to mentally shake himself in order to give a coherent answer.

He now knew that the Strator had a force of one hundred guardsmen (twenty hands) and twenty Bolyars, (Four hands) with Bolyar Chaydar as his Majordom. He was the go-between or buffer with the Strator and the peasants. His word was law in this Sanjak (District), answerable only to the Emperor, the Strator and the *Veliki* (Great) Bolyars.

The best that Bryden could come up with was to encourage the Bolyar to prime his guardsmen to act in a disciplined way to any order given to them.

Keep it simple, he advised.

They formalized a list of rules, like the, *Drop to the floor if you hear a warning horn* or, *All guardsmen were to go around in groups of four with spears ready.* Bryden also suggested that each guardsman be given a water-filled skin and a hunk of bread so they became a more independent, self-contained force, each with a warning horn too.

As evening approached, Bryden's fears intensified. His future was going to be decided one way or another and soon.

***

As on the previous two nights, the setting sun was the catalyst to the events that followed.

The first courtyard had been cleared of the women and children who had been sent to the inner courtyards, protected by twenty guardsmen. Every peasant, each armed with his sickle or borrowed spear supplied by the guardsmen, was ordered to lie prone on the ground.

Ten groups of guardsmen, dressed in long hooded cloaks, were in place around the courtyard. Twenty guardsmen were patrolling the fortress walls, which had been freshly topped with strengthened fishnets.

The Bolyars were being held back as a reserve force, ten by the main gate, ten on the far side of the courtyard, by the inner gate.

Bolyar Chaydar and Bryden were with the Bolyars at the main gate, each armed with a spear.

The Strator, as were Iskra and Chaz, was reasonably safe indoors.

The blare of a warning horn broke the spell. It came from the far wall, midway between the main gate and the inner one. This was the darker side of the fortress, in the deep shadow of the nearside wall, cast by the fading sunlight. It was difficult to see why the alarm had been sounded. One effect though, was the immediate lighting of scores of torches previously arranged for this very purpose. The extra illumination brought a gasp of horror from the prone peasants, many of whom had to twist round to look. Gyrating above the fortress wall was a swarm of man-vamps waiting to attack.

The guardsmen on the wall threw their spears and missed. The canny man-vamps were flying too high to be hit. Then a group of six man-vamps zoomed down shrieking like banshees. Two, missing the net by a whisker, snatched a guardsman each but the weight was too much for them and they were pulled down towards the courtyard. As they fell below the height of the wall, a flurry of spears were thrown at them, several hitting their mark.

With squeals of pain as the spears hit them, the man-vamps tried vainly to gain height, stubbornly refusing to release their prey. Another volley of spears hit them and mortally wounded, they crashed down onto the courtyard on top of several prone peasants. The area around them erupted as those not flattened by the falling man-vamps and the two guardsmen, rose to their feet as one, screaming obscenities as they began to stab and slash the man-vamps to pieces. The two guardsmen were lucky to escape alive such was the pent-up bloodlust among the peasants. They staggered away half naked, covered with cuts and bruises.

The other four man-vamps, roaring and shrieking, landed near two guard groups who were at the ready with spears pointing, but instead of being back to back they had made a line. Trampling over and slashing those too slow to get out of their way, the man-vamps flapped and hopped towards the line of guardsmen, who being much nimbler on the ground quickly encircled them.

The spears jabbed, prodded and thrust their sharp points deep into the snarling raging man-vamps. Chest, belly, thighs and throat. Wings were full of holes, flapping uselessly. Out-reached by the spears, the man-vamps stood no chance and soon the last of the four crumpled to the ground, blood spurting from a multiplicity of wounds, dying as it fell.

Across the courtyard, cries of alarm rose as tens of man-vamps descended from the sky and began to harry the peasants, who panicking, broke ranks and tried to flee from the horrors of their nightmares come true. Their run for safety, anywhere but here, was in their minds but impeded the guardsmen as well. Too often, trying to defend themselves, let alone fight a man-vamp, they had to force the peasants back from where they had come from, in order to establish some sort of buffer zone between the man-vamps.

Then even in all of the yelling and screaming of the fighting, a loud voice got through.

'Look, Look at that!'

Swooping down into the courtyard, past a burning torch, was a female-vamp carrying against her breast, her young offspring. Her mouth was wide open, screaming. A taloned hand, outstretched, was tying to grasp a running peasant, who sensing her presence, turned and cried out in horror as the talons ripped his face wide open, an eyeball dangling on his bloody cheek.

Concentrating on what she was doing, the female-vamp did not see a burly peasant heft his spear and throw it so forcibly at her, that it pierced the child at her breast and through her heart too. Tumbling to the ground her body smashed into the spear thrower, spear shaft first, puncturing his stomach before it was dragged sideways, flipping a trail of intestines out of the wound in front of his horrified eyes.

Three peasants bore the full force of the falling body, squealing in terror, thinking they were about to be slashed to ribbons as they heaved the body off them. One screamed even louder when a broken bone in his arm suddenly protruded through his flesh as he pushed the body away.

Their neighbours wasted no time either. Sickles slashed and cut before they realized that the creature was dead. A roar of triumph erupted from their throats and the offspring was dragged off to a clear space of ground and trampled to a bloody pulp.

The piercing blare of the warning horns forced everyone to stare upwards.

More man-vamps had appeared and were descending

swiftly. They landed in one large group not too far from the main gate. Bryden urged Bolyar Chaydar to marshal his Bolyars, held in reserve, to use the one major advantage they had on the ground, agility.

Bryden had noticed that the extra reach a spear gave to anyone using it, coupled with the ability of changing direction quickly, meant they had a tremendous advantage over the man-vamps on the ground.

'Bolyar Chaydar,' yelled Bryden, trying to get his attention above the clamour.

'Yes, Bryyyden?'

'Get your men to copy those guardsmen who formed a line. Remember?'

Pausing for a moment, the Bolyar nodded. Turning to one side, he called to one of his men, Bolyar Zltan, and explained what he wanted the guardsmen to do.

Within moments, the guardsmen were in a line abreast, spears pointing forward. Waving his sword, Bolyar Chaydar gave the order to advance towards the man-vamps, now attacking a group of peasants desperately trying to defend themselves.

In a wide arc, the Bolyar spearmen quickly closed in on the man-vamps from behind. The surprise was total. Before they realized they themselves were being attacked, seven man-vamps were speared to death. The other six turned to face their new enemy, forgetting that two of the peasants had spears as well. Though not as well versed in their use as the guardsmen, they proved to be enough of a nuisance value to allow the fast learning Bolyars to dispatch the remaining man-vamps with efficient spear thrusts to the belly and then the throat.

There was one very worried person amongst all of the mayhem, Bryden. He had been anxiously waiting for signs of weakness among the man-vamps. There had been none so far.

Then a warning horn blew and a cry from the top of the fortress wall. 'There's more and more coming! We can't count them,' yelled an unknown, panicky voice.

'Form your groups! Form your groups! With your spears out,' shouted Bolyar Chaydar, with a quiver of fear in his voice.

All eyes in the courtyard were raised to the heavens and many a silent prayer was said.

***

The blare of the warning horn had jolted both Chaz and Iskra from the sense of security they had enjoyed since they had entered the hut. The noise of the fighting, shrieks from the wounded, the uncertainty, were becoming too intolerable to bear for Chaz and so he began pacing up and down the room, spear in hand. Finally, Iskra couldn't stand it any more.

'For God's sake sit down Chaz. You're driving me crazy.'

'Sorry, my nerves are shot. I've never been in anything like this before.'

'And you think I have?' yelled Iskra, immediately regretting her outburst. *She was the eldest*, she thought.

'Let's have a drink of beer. It might settle us down.'

'OK. Last one to finish is a cissy,' Chaz said with mock bravado.

They supped the beer in silence, unable to shut out the chaos outside the hut. The flickering flames of half a dozen rushlights cast jerky shadows along the walls.

***

A bump on the roof jerked Iskra awake. 'I can't believe I dropped off,' she mumbled to herself and then noticed that Chaz was slumped over on his bench, mouth half open, eyes closed.

'Chaz! Chaz! Wake up!' she whispered, 'Chaz!'

'What! Did you call me?'

'Quiet! There's someone on the roof.'

Crash!

The door burst open and a man–vamp tried to enter the hut. A pair of yellow eyes scanned the room as dribble frothing from its hideous mouth fell to the floor. It uttered a cry of rage when it saw them. Stooping, it tried again to enter the hut but its wings were too wide.

Stifling a scream, Iskra got to the floor from the bench she was using and crawled over to the far end of the room and crouched down next to the oven.

Chaz was completely awake now. *This wasn't a dream. It was a sodding nightmare.* He realized that his spear was on the far side of the door, past that walking horror show. Discretion being one of his better traits, he too crawled over to the oven side of the room.

'What do we do now?' he whispered, flinching, as the creature put one arm and part of a wing inside the doorway.

'I can only think of one thing.' Dragging her shoulder bag towards her, thanking the Gods she had left it there, she pulled out a small wrapped tissue and threw it onto the embers of the fire, which fortunately had stayed in. The tissue caught fire and a big flash of light dazzled them for a moment and a puff of black smoke choked and blinded them. When their vision returned, there stood a small hairy figure holding a broomstick. It was the *Schopanyn,* their house-guard.

Smiling, the *Schopanyn* held out a hand.

'God! I nearly forgot,' whispered Iskra, delving back into her bag. 'It wants a bloody mint.' Grabbing the tube, she took one and gave it to the house-guard.

A look of bliss came over his face, as he tasted the sweet.

'What about him?' Chaz said in a low voice, pointing at the door.

The man-vamp had succeeded in pushing his head and shoulders into the room, with his wings still stuck outside. It began to tear at the wooden wall with its razor sharp talons and soon strips of wood were being ripped away from it. A snarling growling roar, resounded throughout the hut as the frustrated creature redoubled its efforts to get inside the hut.

'Do something and do it quick,' pleaded Chaz.

Iskra just nodded and looked at the house-guard, who was looking at the man-vamp with a quizzical expression.

Clapping her hands to gain the house-guard's attention, Iskra pointed to the man-vamp and shook her head and then mimed a 'shoo away' gesture.

The little house-guard stood up and nodded vigorously, his long beard flapping in sympathy. Taking hold of his tiny broomstick, he waved it twice round his head and let go. Flying through the air towards the man-vamp, the broomstick flipped over and the broom bristles stiffened into sharp pointed tips.

The scream of pain as the now sharp tipped bristles stabbed into the face and eyes of the man-vamp, nearly deafened Iskra and Chaz. The creature staggered, blind, back from the hut doorway and flew unsteadily away, shrieking loudly.

'Jeez! Thank God it's gone,' Chaz said, white faced, as he stood up and after a moments thought, rushed over for his spear. 'This stays with me for flaming ever.'

Iskra got up, shaking with relief and feeling a bit stiff, stretched out her arms and looked for the little house-guard.

He was gone as quickly as he had arrived.

Chaz closed the door. The wall wasn't as damaged as he had first thought. Just deep grooves gouged out of the wood. He shuddered at the thought of those talons ripping into his own flesh.

Feeling a lot better at having survived the traumatic experience, Chaz stood guard while Iskra poured a beer out for him and herself. This time she didn't complain as Chaz began to pace up and down the room.

***

There must be over one hundred of them, Bryden thought. *If they get among the peasants it will be a massacre. There are not enough guardsmen to protect them and if the man-vamps can snatch enough bodies, they will be able to survive long enough on that blood to become a permanent threat since the fortress cannot protect the peasants any longer than today. (There just isn't enough food). They will have to disperse and fend for themselves, easy meat for the man-vamps (no pun intended).*

The swarm of man-vamps began to swoop down into the courtyard. Strangely, several of them went straight into the fishnets fixed on top of the fortress wall. Latterly, they had started to avoid them. As the nets collapsed with the impact and the entangled creatures fell to the ground struggling weakly to get free, a guardsman shouted out.

'Hey! These are only kid–vamps and a lot of them don't seem to be able to breathe properly. They can hardly move.'

'Stop yacking and kill them,' yelled a Bolyar.

Obeying orders, the nearest guardsmen began to spear the young helpless kid-vamps to death.

In the courtyard the mass of man-vamps dropped out of the sky and snarling ferociously, they began to lash out at the nearest peasant or guardsman with their fearsome talons.

'Form ranks! Form ranks!' The loud command from Bolyar Chaydar had an immediate response. Every guardsman moved to form a line of four, each with his spear pointing straight to the front. Turning to face the nearest man-vamp, each line then marched forward. Contact came quickly, there were so many man-vamp (and female-vamps) landing in the courtyard, it became a one sided slaughter. The spears kept the man-vamps' vicious talons out of reach whilst the guardsmen could now jab and aim in relative safety.

It soon became apparent that something was wrong with the man-vamps. Once on the ground, they were unable to fly away. Many were seen to be trying to flap their wings, faces contorted with the effort, mouths wide-open gasping for air. Others suddenly crouched down, arms holding themselves up from the ground, chests heaving, not even able to snarl at their executioners, for that was what the guardsmen now became.

It was over well before dawn. Every man-vamp or female-vamp was either killed or dead from the '*yellow skin curse*.' The bodies were dragged out of the main gate of the fortress to a flat piece of ground, where, as the sun rose to mark a new day, a huge fire consumed every last one of them.

The peasants slowly went back to the courtyard to collect anything of value and then, drained to the core by the last few days events, plodded out again back to their camp and a good rest prior to returning to their homesteads.

Bryden had already surmised that any man-vamps left in their lair would be dead by now,

Tired but elated Bolyar Chaydar sat with Bryden, Iskra and Chaz in the hut, each supping beer.

'Bryyyden!' the Bolyar said, 'You and your friends have saved us from a calamity. How can we possibly repay you?'

'It's strange you should ask that,' Bryden replied, 'I've got a sort of proposition I'd like to put to you.'

14

The mid-morning session with the Great Strator was very amiable, at least from Bryden's point of view. Now that he was not under threat of being flayed alive you could say that he was extremely happy at the summons from on high insisting that he be present forthwith for an audience with his Excellency.

Sitting in front of the Strator, yes by God, sitting in a woven wicker chair with a buckskin cushion, would you believe, instead of those arse-numbing stools they had had to endure before.

Bryden was basking in the glory of being right about the '*yellow skin curse*' and he was about to collect his reward. By his side Bolyar Chaydar was also sitting pretty smug too. Hardly a guardsman had been lost in last night's battle with the man-vamps and his standing as Majordom knew no bounds. Behind them sat Iskra and Chaz, who was squirming like a dog with worms, trying to get comfortable on his stool.

The Strator droned on and on about how grateful his people were and how he wished that the Savior from Epirus could stay a while longer. However, he did not want to stand in the way of the urgent expedition that the omens of the last few days had indicated that the Epirusians had to follow. He agreed that their special sagacity had to be shared with others in his province. Therefore, with great reluctance, he would give his agreement for them to leave with an escort of Bolyar Chaydar and two other Bolyars for the next ten days.

***

'How the hell do you expect me to ride that thing?' Chaz pointed to a rather big horse. At least to him it looked huge. The horse in question stood indifferently as Chaz was finally persuaded to mount it, using a handy rock as a step. Once in the saddle Chaz was slightly mollified. It wasn't too bad, in fact it seemed quite comfortable compared to that damned stool. *God, he still felt stiff from that bloody thing*. Feet in stirrups, *Hey, this isn't bad*, he thought, as Bolyar Chaydar passed the reins to him.

'Be gentle, Chasss and you will be alright.'

Everyone else was ready. They had been patiently waiting for Chaz to pluck up courage and mount his horse.

Bolyar Chaydar and Bryden took the lead, followed by Iskra and Chaz, then the two Bolyars, Zltan and Borislav who were in charge of the two packhorses carrying supplies. Each one, including Iskra carried a spear.

The slow gait continued down the slope toward the valley below, passing the still smoking embers of the fire that had incinerated the man-vamps.

'Jeez! What a stink,' Chaz said, as he held his nose and looked over to the small mound of charred bones and skulls which had survived the intense heat of the fire.

Iskra had a piece of cotton cloth she had saved pressed to her face and averted her eyes as she rode past the grim reminder of the last few days.

They descended the valley by following a rough track by the river. The further down they went, the more the trees closed in. Without the frequent steep rocky outcrops that dotted the route it would probably be impassible.

The valley eventually flattened out and they made better progress until around mid-day, Bolyar Chaydar called a halt where the riverbank was low enough to ease the horses down to the water. After seeing to their mounts and hobbling them to stop them wandering, the party of travellers sat down for something to eat. That is, all except Chaz, who was a little saddle-sore.

Zltan fetched a linen bag of bread and fruit as well as an animal skin of beer from one of the packhorses and shared food and drink out.

Whilst they were eating, Bolyar Chaydar picked up a

stick and using a convenient patch of sand, drew a simple map of where they were going.

'Bryyyden. You want to get to the Great Lake. Yes?'

'Yes, that's right. That area at least.'

'Strange things have been happening around here lately, the man-vamps obviously the worst of them, so I thought it safer to go by the longer route.' He jabbed with his stick.

'We go along this side of the mountain ridge, climb up and go through this pass and drop down to ……'

'Bolyar Chaydar! Bolyar Chaydar!' Borislav shouted from where the pack horses were feeding and came running up to them.

'We're being spied upon from the high ground. There!' He pointed to a nearby ridge. 'I'm sure I saw someone up there.'

Dropping his stick, Bolyar Chaydar turned and shaded his eyes with a hand, 'I can't see anything.'

Iskra jumped up, 'I can and it's a child, a small child.'

'What did you say?' Zltan suddenly went pale. 'A small child up there.' He crossed himself and took out a small object from his waistcoat; a bear's tooth. He rubbed it three times and put it back

'What's going on?' Chaz asked walking slowly towards them with a slight crouch, legs apart and leaning on his spear shaft.

Bolyar Chaydar looked at Bryden and said gravely, 'I think we're in trouble.'

'From kids? I can't believe that.' Chaz looked up at the ridge. 'Anyway, there's no one up there now is there?'

Bryden frowned at Chaz. 'Be careful with what you say. There are things going on round here that we don't have a clue about. We only arrived here a few days ago and I would advise you to watch and listen a bit more before offering your opinion. OK.'

Chaz felt his face go red and he shuffled his feet in embarrassment at his ticking off.

'I'm sure he meant well,' said Iskra, trying to help.

'All right, let's forget it. Bolyar Chaydar, what do you make of the *child*?' Bryden asked, trying to be diplomatic.

'It can mean only one thing out here in the wilds. The Gblyn. Though small, they have the strength of two men and they also have the ability to control animals for short periods of time. The main problem with them is their gold mine.'

'Gold mine!' Chaz said, interrupting. 'They own a frigging gold mine?'

'Yes. As I was saying, the problem is not the mine itself. It's the miners. They are all slaves. That Gblyn up there was probably a scout.'

'Am I right in thinking that we might be in danger of capture by these Gblyn's, Bolyar Chaydar?'

The silence said it all.

Everyone glanced up at the ridge and Zltan started to collect any uneaten food and stuffed it into the linen cloth as Borislav casually walked over to the horses and began to un-hobble them.

As soon as they were mounted, Bolyar Chaydar looked at them and said, 'I think we should go through this valley as far as Shifik, then take the high path along Slither Ridge.' He paused a moment, 'It can be dangerous but it should give us a head start on the Gblyns. They won't expect us to go this way.'

The afternoon was well and truly gone when they began to climb up to the ridge. At first the grassy pastures were a relief from the tiresome, twisting route they had been following along the valley. The river had seemed to sense that they were in a hurry, so it deliberately became obtuse, by turning first one way and then the other, even at times turning back on its self. Time seemed to drag as they went two steps forward and one step backwards, eventually making them more irritable and snappy with each other at the lack of progress.

The grassy slope began to become rockier and steeper the higher they went, until Bolyar Chaydar called halt.

'We shall have to lead the horses on foot from now on,' he said, 'It's too dangerous to ride.'

'About bloody time.' Relief flooded through Chaz as he half fell off his mount. 'God! Who'd have thought riding a frigging horse would be so painful.'

He soon changed his mind, stumbling on the loose rocks, which composed the supposed path for the umpteenth time. (It wasn't named Slither Ridge for nothing.) He banged his knee again and swore that he had broken his wrist as well.

As the path rose higher and higher it became even more uneven. To make matters worse, it narrowed to a ledge just wide enough for the horses to traverse. The ledge zigzagged up the side of the ridge, often with only a horse's hoof-width from a sheer drop of several hundred metres.

As twilight approached, they reached the top of the path. 'Look!' Bolyar Chaydar pointed ahead, 'Do you see it? A cave.'

The path had levelled out somewhat and under the overhanging rock face was the cave, quite big enough for them all, including the horses.

Just to stand on the flat ground felt like heaven. Then, breathing deeply to ease the tightness in their chests, and sitting down on a convenient rock to relieve the tense, quivering leg muscles, they took stock of their surroundings.

Just inside the cave mouth was a small enclosure made up from loose rocks, obviously for the horses. (Previous occupants having left their droppings as evidence) so Borislav, walking stiffly, led them in and unloaded the packhorses.

Zltan, grabbing the food bag, took it inside the cave where he found a large recess filled with dry straw and some animal fodder. Further inside was a small stone oven with a fair amount of wood beside it. 'At least we won't freeze tonight,' he said, his voice echoing round the cave.

Whilst Borislav finished hobbling the horses, just to make sure they didn't get any ideas and try to get out of the enclosure, he noticed with pleasure that a convenient pool would provide his charges with water. *One job less for me to do.*

Zltan used some of the straw to make a more comfortable spot on the rocky floor for each of them to sit or lie on.

Before they all settled down for a well-earned rest, Bolyar Chaydar came in and gave each one a woollen, full-length hooded cloak.

Only then did Zltan open the food bag and dole out some food, hunks of bread and cheese, followed by swigs of beer from the beer filled skin.

Though it was meagre, the now very weary party appreciated the meal and soon they were all trying to settle down as best they could. *At least,* thought Bryden, *They were under cover and though smoky, the oven was at last warming their part of the cave. It could have been so much worse.*

The howl of a wolf jerked them awake. 'I hope,' whispered Bryden to Bolyar Chaydar, 'That hasn't anything to do with our *friends* the Gblyns.'

'I'm afraid it could well be. The Gblyn are known to be able to control the wolf, at least for short periods. In fact, they have been seen riding them. So, Bryyyden, I feel that we are not out of the woods as the saying goes.'

At the back of the cave, Chaz listened to his uncle and the Bolyar leader with trepidation. He wasn't in a fit state to take part in any funny business. In fact he was feeling pretty rotten. His upper thighs, actually the inner parts in particular, were killing him. He had discovered that they had been rubbed nearly raw by that sodding saddle and he had nearly told his uncle that he wouldn't be able to continue.

Then Iskra interrupted his thoughts, 'Chaz, Chaz. Are you awake?'

What a stupid question, of course he was bloody awake, with that damn wolf howling like mad, making enough noise to wake the devil. Who wouldn't be?

'Er. Yeah. I am.'

'I couldn't help noticing how you walked into the cave. When I first went horse riding I suffered for days with sore legs so I know how you might be feeling. OK. Now don't take this the wrong way. Would you like some of my hand cream? It's better than nothing. I hope you don't mind me mentioning it.'

For all his many faults, Chaz wasn't stupid. He often acted like he was and genuinely regretted the times when he inadvertently upset people.

So, he thought, *Why not. Better still, would she put it on for him?* He fantasized for a few more moments before replying, 'Beggars can't be choosers can they. Pass it over, please.'

A few minutes later, Chaz couldn't believe how much better he felt. The burning sensation had gone and his will to continue returned.

'Thanks a million Iskra. That feels much better. What a relief!'

'Glad to be able to help. Keep the tube, you may need it later. Night! Night! Chaz. Sweet dreams.'

You bet your pretty…. I will.

15

The next morning, after the usual ablutions and a hurried breakfast, Bolyar Chaydar led the way with his horse along the still perilous path, which by now was just below the actual ridge. They were soon skirting the edge of a huge quarry-like depression in the mountainside.

It was awesome, a sheer drop of three or four hundred metres and the pace slowed in consequence. Of course it was sods law that it happened just there.

Over the top of the ridge came a pack of wolves, snarling ferociously. On the leader's back sat a grinning Gblyn.

'Get your spears ready and close up to me,' shouted Bolyar Chaydar.

Borislav and Zltan responded immediately and were by his side in seconds. Bryden and Iskra were not too far behind but Chaz, who was not able to walk fast let alone run, was left exposed. It was the not unexpected bolt of one of the packhorses that saved him. With a neigh of terror, it turned and ran back down the path.

The leading wolf turned and rushed after it despite the obvious urgings of restraint by the Gblyn, with the rest of the wolf pack naturally following their leader.

Scrabbling down the ridge slope, the wolf reached the path and launched itself at the packhorse, landing on its shoulders. The impact knocked it sideways and with a shrill shriek of horror from the Gblyn, horse, wolf and Gblyn fell.

Slowly at first and then with gathering speed, they plunged to the bottom of the cliff with sickening thuds and squeals of anguish both from the animals and Gblyn, as they bounced and splattered off the rocks, littering the ground with smashed legs, heads and bloodied bodies. This was followed moments later by three more wolves, howling in terror and abruptly silenced by three faint, squelchy thuds.

The rest of the wolf pack milled around, whining and

whimpering while one or two looked over the edge of the cliff, sniffing the air. Then as one, they turned and ran back to the top of the ridge and disappeared.

Because everything had happened so quickly, the rest of the horses had had no time to react. Once the wolves had disappeared back over the ridge, Bolyar Chaydar insisted on moving on straight away.

'Let's put some distance between us,' he said urgently. 'It will be a while before the Gblyn realize that their plan, whatever it was, has failed.'

Reluctantly the rest of them agreed. Though shocked by the recent event, they realized that they had to get off this vulnerable path as soon as possible, since the Gblyn had somehow found out where they were.

As Bolyar Chaydar began to lead his horse again and the small party shuffled along behind him, Bryden was wondering about this. Then he thought he might have an answer. Calling out to Bolyar Chaydar, he asked, 'Am I right in thinking that you said that the Gblyn have some influence over animals?'

'Yes I did,' replied the Bolyar. 'It is said so according to the stories I have heard but only to some degree. It's not a total thing so I've been told. They can communicate a little with them, simple commands and suchlike.'

'That's maybe it,' said Bryden excitedly. 'They may have used a bird, possibly a hawk, to spy on us.'

In a way they felt relieved that they maybe now had some idea of how they might have been discovered. The problem was how could they avoid 'a spy in the sky.'

Bolyar Chaydar, who had stopped for the moment pulled his mount by the reins. 'Come on, lazy bones, he said, coaxing it into a walk, 'Once over the next rise we should be able to ride again. If my memory serves me right, the path becomes much wider and easier.'

The news that they were to ride again shortly came as a blow to Chaz. He had worked out a strategy of walking with his legs slightly bowed. This meant that his thighs, well his pants, didn't rub as much and he felt he was coping very well under the circumstances. The thought of riding, *God, it didn't bear thinking about.*

About half an hour later they topped the rise and saw a valley far below. Mounting his horse, Bolyar Chaydar called out to everyone. 'I want to get down to the valley as fast as possible. If we are being spied on, the bird could return anytime.'

Bryden nodded and after mounting his own horse, moved closer to the Bolyar. 'We need to plan a way of outwitting that bird if there is one as we suspect. I can only think of one thing that might work.'

***

It took at least three hours to descend this side of Slither Ridge and it was not only Chaz who gave a sigh of relief when Bolyar Chaydar called a halt by a fast flowing stream that ran down the valley bottom.

'We need to rest the horses. I think they have done us proud,' he said patting his mount on the side of its neck. He was rewarded with a snicker and a snort, as well as a shake of the head.

'Borislav, will you attend to the watering whilst Zltan rustles up something for us to eat.'

Borislav nodded and collecting the reins of the rest of the horses, said with a grin as he walked off towards the stream, 'I can't wait for a hunk of cheese and bread.'

The rest of them sat down on the grassy bank of the stream and as one, pulled off their shoes, stiffly walked over to a nearby pool and sitting on convenient rocks, gently lowered their feet into the cool water. A collective sigh of relief came from them and Chaz, after a few moments of bliss, said, 'I'm going in for a dip. This water is just right.'

'Hang on Chaz. Just think for a moment,' Bryden called out just as Chaz was about to drop his pants. 'This isn't a holiday jaunt you know and we might have to leave here pretty quickly if that bird comes nosing around.'

'Sorry! Just for a moment I forgot where I was.'

'Easy done old sport,' replied his uncle.

'Now if our personal cook can get his feet out of this delightful stream, we might have something to eat.'

'Zltan,' he said, giving him a friendly pat on the back. 'How about it?'

'If I must, I must,' said Zltan with an impish grin on his face as, with a flick of his wrist, he splashed a handful of water at Bryden.

***

After an hour's rest, the sparse meal being eaten in record time, Bryden noticed the furtive look that Bolyar Chaydar gave him as he looked at his watch but with the confidence of an '*Epirusian*' traveller, ignored it. He had more important things to worry about. *What if they were wrong about the spy-hawk? What then? Hell, you could go round in circles with thoughts like that. Be positive Bryden. Be positive.*

Bryden looked around. The three Bolyars were chatting quietly among themselves. Further away, Chaz and Iskra were also involved in a quiet tête-à-tête.

'You must tell him,' Iskra insisted quietly, suddenly noticing Bryden looking in their direction. 'If you won't, I will.'

'Look, I can manage, right. I got this far didn't I?'

'Well, we don't know how far we're going do we?'

'I can't let my Uncle down. For God's sake, Iskra, don't you see that.'

'I suppose so.'

'Good. Let's see how I manage this afternoon. I promise to tell him if things get worse.'

'Bryyyden! Bryyyden!'

The call interrupted his thoughts. 'Yes. What is it?' he asked and walked over and sat down with the Bolyars.

'We've been wondering if you have thought any more

about hiding from the Gblyn.'

'Well, it's a long shot.' The three Bolyars looked at him quizzically.

'I mean it might not work. What I mean is, if one of us went over one of these mountain ridges and made a camp and a fire, then made some dummies. (another long look) I mean get some small branches and twigs, you know, whatever, and wrapped them in our cloaks, from high up it could be us. Don't forget, because of the man-vamps, not many people are travelling around at the moment. What do you think?'

Bolyar Chaydar slowly stroked his long moustache. 'I have never heard of such a thing before but you were able to deceive that man-vamp into crashing into a fishnet. It was a clever trick. I trust your judgment Bryyyden. We will do it. Bolyar Borislav, you will be the, the. . .'

'We say decoy in Epirus,' offered Bryden.

'Ah! I see, another strange word. Yes. Borislav, you will be the deecoy. Your skills with the ironstone and flint are just what we need and of course your skill with the horse is well known.'

Borislav nodded, then said, 'It will be done, Bolyar Chaydar.'

16

The loss of one of their packhorses had depleted their supplies by quite a bit. However, the most important items for solving their immediate predicament were the hooded cloaks. Because the recent daytime temperatures had been fairly hot, the cloaks had been loaded onto one of them. Bryden had given a big sigh of relief when he found out they had not all been lost.

Bolyar Borislav slung the bag containing the cloaks and a linen wrap with his bread and cheese behind his saddle and set off with a casual wave of his hand, not forgetting to pat his waist pouch for one last check to ensure he had not left his ironstone and flint behind.

Fording the river at a convenient shallow point, he began the long climb up the side of the mountain ridge. As he did so, he pondered on his instructions. The idea of using reeds and rushes was great and should work like the Epirusian said. *Funny people though*, the Epirusians. *How can they wear such ridiculous clothes?*

The descent into the next valley went smoothly for Borislav and he was soon easing his horse along a faint animal trail leading down to a river. A wooded hill overlooking it proved ideal. On the far downslope side, a rocky overhang contained a cave-like recess big enough to hide his horse.

After watering his mount, Borislav left it hobbled in the cave and went to gather some fodder. Satisfied that his horse was settled, he went down to the rivers edge and collected armfuls of reeds and rushes. Pleased with his efforts so far, he stopped for a quick meal of bread and cheese, slaking his thirst in the river.

Then back to work, he weaved the rushes into head shapes and the reeds into torso shapes, using long stems of twisted grass as thin ties where necessary.

Borislav used a decent level piece of ground in front of

the cave for his fire. Scouting around, he found enough small rocks to contain the burning area and the nearby wood provided plenty of dead timber so he soon had a pile stored to one side.

With layers of dry grass set ready in the centre of the rocky circle, he struck his flint on the firestone. After several goes, the grass caught and began to smoulder. Blowing gently, a flame suddenly flickered, and spread to the rest of the grass. He placed several small twigs into the flames and then some thicker ones. Watching with satisfaction as they too began to burn, Borislav could relax.

Once stoked up, Borislav threw some wet grass onto the fire. Immediately billows of smoke rose high into the sky. He then placed the deecoy figures. *Not too near,* he laughed to himself, *or they will go up in smoke too.*

Now he had time to spare. *Well at least,* he thought, *for something to eat.*

After a brief rest, Borislav went and collected several loads of wood. *Better be on the safe side*, he thought. It was as he brought the last load of wood back, that he saw the bird. It was hovering on the far side of the river. A kestrel.

'It's time for the play to begin,' he muttered to himself as he dropped the bundle of wood next to one of his deecoy figures. He crouched down as though he was talking. Then he went into the cave and took off his (kalpak) hat and waistcoat. Strolling across to another deecoy, he sat and waved his arms about as though making a point to someone.

After a while he decided it was time for a change of character so off he went to his changing room (the cave) where he took off his shirt and came back out half naked. This time he sat by another deecoy, which seemed to have the huff on because he hadn't talked to it yet.

The kestrel kept hovering and watched everything.

As nightfall approached, Borislav was worn out with all the to and froing and in particular all the talking he had to do to keep up the impression that there were several people in the camp. Gagging for a drink he went down to the river and saw that the kestrel had gone. After quenching his thirst, he ambled slowly back but with a deep feeling that he was being watched.

With a nonchalance he didn't feel, he went straight back to the cave and picked up his spear, then pausing long enough to un-hobble his horse, *just in case,* he thought, went back outside.

A flicker of movement caught his eye. On the far side of the campfire was a Gblyn, riding a wolf. The wolf saw Borislav and muzzle agape, with fangs exposed in a wicked snarl, it leapt forward.

Borislav reacted more by instinct and hurled his spear with all of his strength at that very moment.

It caught the wolf right in the throat causing it to stagger and roll sideways into the fire. The Gblyn's leg was trapped underneath the wolf's body and it screamed in agony as first the beard, hair and then the clothes burst into flames.

The eyeballs popped with the heat as the Gblyn head shrivelled up and then erupted into a fireball. The wolf's fur singed and then caught fire. A jerk of its legs and the blackened stump of a small twitching, child-like hand was the last thing that Borislav saw before a huge flame and a plume of smoke engulfed the two bodies.

The stink of burning flesh was nauseating and Borislav rushed to the windward side of the fire to escape it. He breathed heavily, trying to clear his throat and lungs when he heard the howl of a wolf. *My God,* he thought, *There's more of them.*

He turned to go back for his horse when a grey beast jumped into the light of the campfire. Borislav raised a hand to protect his face and screamed in agony as the powerful jaws of a wolf snapped tight on his upper arm. He fell to the ground, the wolf tugging at him. Half kneeling to keep his balance, Borislav snatched his knife clear from his belt and stabbed the wolf between its fiery red eyes. The wolf suddenly stiffened, eyes wide open and then fell to the ground, dead.

'Aaagh!' moaned Borislav, as waves of pain flashed through his arm. He staggered to his feet, praying that there were no more wolves. He knew he wouldn't stand a chance with a wounded arm.

He picked up a burning branch and staggered to the front of the campfire. He couldn't see much but he knew the burning flame would keep them away.

On unsteady feet, Borislav made his way down to the river and stuck the burning branch into the soft earth. The wound needed cleaning as soon as possible. A wolf bite was not good news.

Kneeling by the river, he managed to remove his shirt and using his knife, cut a long strip from it. After cleaning the wound as best as he could, Borislav scrabbled in the bottom of the river and then brought up a handful of mud. He packed his injured arm, making sure that all the puncture wounds were sealed with mud. That stopped the bleeding so he wrapped the strip of torn shirt round the wound.

Feeling slightly giddy, Borislav made his way back to the cave and led out his horse. *The others need to know what's happened.* Taking time just to collect the cloaks and the remaining food, he painfully mounted his horse and began the perilous journey over the mountain, aided by the ghostly light of a full moon.

17

As Borislav disappeared over the mountain ridge, Bolyar Chaydar led the remaining group down the valley, more or less in the opposite direction.

A nervous tension gripped them. Chaz was frequently seen glancing up at the sky, bird watching.

The afternoon wore on and the valley began to narrow and the track steepen, as did the stream, now a racing torrent tumbling over rocks in clouds of spray on its tumultuous passage to the sea.

'We shall have to dismount soon,' Bolyar Chaydar called out.

'Great!' Chaz said sarcastically, 'Just what I need, a frigging hike up a blasted mountain.'

He looked around, hoping no one had noticed him standing in his stirrups. His thighs were killing him again.

Iskra glanced over, catching his eye and nodding in sympathy.

Bryden eased his horse forward until he was riding next to the Bolyar. 'We need to rest and think about what to do about these Gblyn's,' he said quietly.

'Well, if it is still standing, there is an old shepherds hut at the top of this pass.'

'Good. I'll tell the others.' Bryden reined in his horse in order to let Iskra and Chaz catch up. Zltan, taking on Borislav's role, brought up the rear, leading the packhorse.

It was nearly dark when they reached the hut built next to the stream. Chaz limped manfully up to the door, leaning on his spear as usual and standing to one side as Bolyar Chaydar pushed the rickety door open.

A flutter of whirring wings swept past him as several bats, chittering at the disturbance flew out, making Iskra jump in surprise as they disappeared into the twilight. Zltan had the honour of taking their horses round the back and tending to their needs.

Going down the steps, it seemed large enough for them all. In the semi darkness they could just make out six benches along three walls of the one room. The ubiquitous stone oven was next to the door.

Bryden, going down the steps, looked at the oven and suddenly had a strange thought. *So far, in this Netherworld, the days had been pleasantly warm and the nights quite chilly but not one drop of rain. Was this normal for this time period or not? Time would no doubt tell.*

Since Zltan was busy taking care of the horses, Bolyar Chaydar went over to the oven and took out his ironstone and flint. A small heap of dried grass and twigs had been left ready, next to a pile of wood.

A few clicks of stone on stone later produced a small fire flickering brightly in the oven and everyone began to relax. At first the smoke was a nuisance but as the fire took hold it became more bearable.

Iskra and Chaz took two of the corner benches and sat whispering together.

The door suddenly banged open causing them all to jump nervously and Zltan stomped in. He nodded to them and went to the oven and reaching up, took a couple of rushlights from a skin-pouch hanging from a wooden peg stuck in the wall. Bending down, he lit them from the oven fire and fixed them into the two clay holders on the wall, now visible in the extra light.

The room seemed to become more homely, at least to the Bolyars. The others felt it impolite to sit holding their noses. The smell was terrible. The departed bats had obviously contributed their offerings of guano which when added to the other various odours in the hut, made for a nasty niff in the air.

Zltan, going back to his original role, picked up the linen bag he had dropped by the door when he first came in. 'This is the last of the food,' he said as he produced two hunks of bread and half a cheese wheel. 'As the saying goes, *a hungry man will eat anything*, so this meal could have been much worse.'

After they had eaten and everyone had settled down on a bench as best they could, it became very quiet as each one either dozed off or silently contemplated the future in the semi-darkness. The rushlights were making more smoke than light.

Chaz seized the opportunity to stand up and wriggle out of his pants and carefully apply a thin smear of Iskra's hand cream to his inner-thighs. He realized that he had to use it sparingly. After all he only had the one tube. He breathed a sigh of relief as it still worked its magic, the pain abating enough so that he could lie down again on the bench in some kind of comfort.

As the night moved on, the hut resonated with the various sounds of sleeping people, nasal breathing, a snort or two, intermittent snoring, the tossing and turning of someone in the throes of a dream.

Then the rustle of clothing as a person stood up. In the dim radiance of the oven's embers, Iskra crept to the door, fingers crossed that it wouldn't creak. She lost the bet. The dry, old leather hinges creaked and groaned as she opened it but no one stirred.

Outside, the moonlight of a full moon cast silvery shadows between the trees. As she made her way through them, she noticed a large boulder. Thinking it would be a good spot for what she had to do, Iskra went behind it, musing, *It was at times like this that she missed modern conveniences.*

Without any warning, two pairs of hands grabbed her and pulled her to the ground. Before she could scream for help a small hand covered her mouth. Terrified, she looked up and in the light of the moon saw two ugly hairy faces gazing down at her. *Gblyns.*

Rolling her over, they roughly tied her hands together and with a linen cloth gagged her mouth. (Strangely they didn't bother about her shoulder bag, which for some unknown reason she had slung over her head before leaving the hut). Then with extraordinary ease, they lifted her up by the shoulders and feet and without a sound, carried her though the woods.

They only stopped when they reached a clearing in which a small hut could be seen. The two Gblyns carried Iskra into the hut and dropped her to the floor.

For some reason she thought she had been in it before. A long room with a cauldron by the door and a row of clay pots of differing sizes along one wall, all seemed so familiar especially the figure sitting on the bench opposite the stone oven. *Stone oven!* Iskra gave a muffled gasp; *It couldn't be, could it?* Not *Baba ... What's her name?*

It wasn't. Similar yes, but it wasn't. This one was even uglier. One piercing green eye gleamed malevolently, the other, a cloudy white orb wept tears down her cheek, a bulbous nose with a yellowish, hairy wart sticking out of her left nostril. The mouth was turned down at one side, leering at her, the single tooth reaching up to bite the wart but not quite able to reach it.

Iskra, scared witless by the turn of events, could only stare in horror, unable to speak because of the gag.

Waving to the Gblyns to sit on the bench, the Baba pulled a small bunch of black feathers from her shawl and hobbled over to one of the clay pots and dipped the feathers into it. Taking the now dripping, blood red feathers, she went round and daubed each wall in turn. Then sitting down in the middle of the room, holding the feathers to her breast she began an incantation. Her shrill, squeaky voice began to chant an incoherent series of sounds. Then the hut began to rattle and shake and to Iskra's horror, to move.

It must be a Bird-Leg hut similar to the one they had travelled in only a few days ago, she realized. *Where is she taking me?*

18

Daybreak. Consternation. No one had heard Iskra leave the hut but a search of the local area had found signs of a scuffle near the big boulder and tracks leading away deeper into the wood. Bryden stopped pacing the hut. 'I would say that it is pretty certain that Iskra has been abducted and by the odd footprint we found, by the Gblyn.'

'Why the hell kidnap Iskra?' Chaz began. A sign from Bryden checked him.

'What I meant to say was. Why would the Gblyn want to take Iskra in the first place?'

'I think it was a chance pick up. One of us out alone. It was too good an opportunity to miss I would say,' said Bryden. 'It could have been any one of us.' He looked over at Bolyar Chaydar, 'Where do you think they have taken her?' he asked.

'There is only one place. The gold mine.'

'Jeez,' How far is that?' Chaz was clearly upset.

'If we ride hard, one full day,' replied the Bolyar solemnly.

'Well, since we have nothing to pack, I think we had better start right now.' Bryden looked at each of them and they nodded in agreement.

'What about Borislav?' Zltan asked. We can't just leave him.'

Bolyar Chaydar looked at Zltan. 'There are times my good friend, when hard choices have to be made. I ...'

'Hey! I can hear a horse coming,' Chaz interrupted. 'Who the hell can that be?'

'Spears! Now!' The voice of command spoke. Following his own advice, Bolyar Chaydar grabbed his spear and leapt to the doorway. He stood ear to the door and waved to Zltan to join him. 'On my command we rush out.'

Zltan nodded.

'Bolyar Chaydar,' a weak voice cried.

'By the Gods! It's Borislav,' Zltan shouted and pulling the door open, ran outside, the others following as fast as they could.

Borislav was slumped over the horse's neck, one hand wrapped in its mane, his other hand dangling, blood dripping from the wound in his upper arm.

Zltan rushed to his friend and gently lowered him to the ground.

Bryden, with his military experience took over. 'Chaz, tear a piece off your shirt and go and wet it in that stream. Fast as you can please.' While Chaz limped to the stream, Bryden examined the wound. He nodded knowingly when he saw the remains of the mudpack Borislav had made.

'Here you are, Uncle.' Chaz, out of breath, passed the dripping wet strip of his shirt over.

'Thanks. Now if you could all give me a bit of room I'll attend to Borislav.'

***

Borislav sat on one of the benches wearing a sling made from parts of Bryden's shirt. He had objected at first, not knowing what a sling was for. Now he was feeling the best he had felt for over a day. Whatever the Eripusian had done to him was working well. Pity there was nothing for him to eat.

Bolyar Chaydar was full of praise for Borislav after hearing the full story and commended him for his courage and bravery in his fight with the Gblyn and the wolves. He was also pleased to know that the fact that Gblyn could control animals was true.

'Now we know what to expect we can plan accordingly. Is that not so Bryyyden.'

'Yes, from what we now know, I think we can make one or two observations. The fact that we have seen two Gblyn riding wolves tells me that they have to be either near or on them to keep control. Small creatures such as birds they seem to have a stronger influence over. What we do with that information is a different matter.'

The hut door banged open and Zltan came in smiling broadly. 'We have dinner,' he said proudly throwing down three rabbits.

***

'I think that we should give a round of applause to the chef for a succulent meal,' said Bryden, sucking a greasy finger.

Then, realizing his mistake as the Bolyars stared at him, added, 'We Epirusians like to thank the makers of a good meal. Thank you Zltan.' He gave a clap in which Chaz joined with a puzzled expression.

Bolyar Chaydar got to his feet. 'If Bolyar Borislav can ride, we have a young mistress to rescue. Are you ready, Bolyar Borislav?

Standing awkwardly, Borislav said intensely, 'Give me my spear.'

19

The Bird-Leg hut shuddered to a halt, the Baba sprawled on the floor, exhausted from the mental effort of directing it. The green eye was closed and the milky white orb of the other continued to shed tears down her cheek. The half-open mouth exposed the one tooth, which jutted out like a tiny tombstone in a misty churchyard through the frothy drool, which dribbled down her chin from her twisted lips.

The Gblyns, who had abducted Iskra, pulled her to her feet, still bound and gagged and dragged her outside. The bright moonlit scene made her blink. The Baba hut had settled down next to a wood and Iskra could just make out the shape of a large steep hill looming over what seemed to be a village.

Rows of what in the semi-darkness looked like hovels, rickety huts that seemed about ready to fall down, were set along one side of it. Trying to make out what was going on, Iskra shrank back in alarm. Two Gblyns riding wolves, were patrolling between the huts.

Before Iskra could see any more, she was pulled roughly towards the wood. As she got nearer, she was astonished to see in the moonlight, the shadowy outline of tiny huts set high up in almost every tree she could see. *Well, tiny to her but not to the Gblyn*, she thought. *This is where they live* and she was not surprised to see a small figure shin down a ladder from a nearby tree.

Iskra was dragged deeper into the wood until she reached what looked like an enormous oak tree that held the biggest hut so far. *No doubt the chief or leader's place.*

Untying her hands and removing her gag, her captors gestured to the nearest ladder and pointed upwards. Not having any choice, Iskra climbed slowly up until she reached a platform large enough to stand on.

In front of her was an open door to the relatively large hut. Stooping a little she was able to enter a long, sizable room with only a throne-like chair at the far end. Gblyns armed with spears stood along each side of the room. Clusters of rushlights in clay holders fixed to the walls, gave enough if smoky, flickering light.

An ancient Gblyn, long-haired and bearded sat on the throne. Two large orange tinged eyes peered unblinking at her through a set of eyebrows which fell nearly to his bearded chin.

He must have opened his mouth to speak. Iskra couldn't tell but it took all of her self-control to stop herself from laughing out loud. A high-pitched child-like voice asked her to tell him why she had come to the land of the Gblyn.

'Don't even dare to lie to Zrysatav the Bold,' he squeaked. 'Our hawks have been tracking you. The Bolyar are our enemies. Why are you, (he pointed a tiny finger at her) a stranger, helping them?'

Iskra didn't know how to answer. So, she thought, *in for a stotinka, in for a lev.*

'May I, your most humble maidservant explain.' The Gblyn sneered but Iskra took it to mean a smile of encouragement. 'My two friends and I are from Epirus and we happened to be passing through the territory of the Great Strator while the man-vamps were attacking his people.' At the sound of the words man-vamps Zrysatav cringed back into his throne. 'My friend Bryden discovered the man-vamps had a curse and helped the Great Strator destroy them.'

'What!' Zrysatav shrilled loudly. 'The man-vamps are destroyed? What kind of maajik did he use?'

'Oh! I've no idea. After all, I am only a maidservant and do not have the powers of the Great Bryden.'

'Ah! So you can do maajik too?'

'Me!' Iskra tried to laugh. 'I can only talk to the spirits through the bones.'

Zrysatav's eyes widened, 'You can talk to the spirits?'

'Only when the spirits agree to talk to me,' replied Iskra. 'Many times I try but they do not listen.'

He nodded his head as though he had tried and failed to talk with them too.

Then he stared at Iskra with a look that made her feel afraid. 'I had mind to put you in the mines but I think that you will be more useful to me if you use your maajik to help me. You can tell what is going to happen, can't you? That's what the spirits do, don't they? Tell the future.'

Iskra swallowed hard. *God, what have I got myself into,* she wondered. *But what did he mean about the mines. God, this must be the Gblyn's gold mine. If they put me in them, I'd never get out alive.*

Zrysatav interrupted her thinking by squeaking at her demandingly (Not so funny now). 'Tell me are the Bolyar going to attack the Gblyn?'

Her face suddenly began to sweat. Iskra now knew that her very future, her life, was in the balance. *What the hell could she do to put the little bastard off?*

Then she had a wild, desperate idea. Last year she had taken part in a couple of geomancy sessions. Could she remember the basics? *God! I need more time.* Then she remembered the bone dice she had in her bag. *My bag!* She had completely forgotten about it. *Thank God for small mercies.*

Careful not to rush and alarm the spear holding Gblyns, she slid her bag round her waist and surreptitiously unzipped a side pocket. *Yes! They were there.* Taking them out, she palmed them in her hand.

Holding out her hand palm uppermost, Iskra called across to Zrysatav, 'My bones,' and held her hand even higher.

He leaned forward in his throne eagerly, and then looked a little disappointed at the small dice. 'They bring the spirits?' he asked dubiously.

'I have to do several maajik things first,' stalled Iskra, looking wildly round the room for something to help her. Then she noticed the floor was covered in a layer of fine white sand. *Thank the Gods,* she said to herself, the relief nearly making her wet herself. *Oh No! I really do need to go.*

Iskra bowed to Zrystav. 'To start my maajik I must relieve myself of all my body fluids. Have you a suitable room?'

Zrysatav looked at her speculatively but the desire of hearing a message from the spirits overcame his reluctance to let her out of his sight. Motioning to the nearest Gblyn guard, he waved a hand indicating that she go with him.

Iskra followed the Gblyn to a side room, trying not to rush. It wasn't that difficult with her knees pressed together, it really was that urgent.

The room was tiny for her and when she saw the hole in the floor, she gasped. Then gave a shrug. When in Rome, came into her mind.

Zrysatav was waiting impatiently for her return and sat up eagerly, so as to watch the proceedings.

Iskra walked to the front of the throne and bowed. Then kneeling on the floor she used her finger to draw a square and divided it into sixteen sections. Moving over slightly, she smoothed over a patch of sand. Taking out the dice from a small pocket in her dress, she began an incantation. *I hope the little devil falls for this or I'm dead.*

Taking a deep breath, she began to hum and roll her eyes. Mentally picking letters from the alphabet, she emphasized the sound by a factor of six or seven in as deep a voice as she could. This droning sound seemed to her to be quite effective. She began to sway her body from side to side and occasionally arch her back, arms outstretched and uttering loud shrieks.

After putting on the show for a few minutes, Iskra began to wave the hand holding the dice across the patch of sand she had earlier made smooth, creating an intricate pattern. Then with a moan and fluttering of eyelids she dropped the dice.

The white dice had fallen showing a three and a one. With a loud gasp, Iskra opened her eyes and looked down at the dice and moaned. Then using the forefinger of her right hand, she slowly drew two crosses in the first square.

Zrysatav, agog with anticipation nearly fell off his throne, he was leaning forward so far.

Suddenly the door to the throne room burst open and a Gblyn rushed in and fell to the floor wringing his hands. 'Oh! Zrysatav the Bold,' he cried, 'The slaves are trying to escape.'

'What!' He shrilled, jumping up from his throne. 'Send for the Master! Now, fool! Go!'

Iskra cringed on the floor not knowing what to do when the door crashed open again as another Gblyn walked quickly in. Taller than the average Gblyn, he had an enormous bald head. Eyes that were huge in proportion, peered hawk-like across a hooked nose. A tiny mouth opened to speak above a wispy, white beard. 'Zrysatav,' he said in a surprisingly deep voice.

'Master. You came promptly,' Zrysatav said in a relieved voice. 'What is your advice?'

The Master bowed 'My Seeye will guide us to the missing slaves and they will soon be caught, Zrysatav the Bold,' he said, holding an orb that flashed, strobe like with many colours. He then placed the orb onto a small pedestal, which was to one side of the throne.

Zrsyatav suddenly realized that Iskra was listening to them and stamped his foot in annoyance. 'Put this stranger in the tower,' he squeaked, 'And make sure you guard the door.'

Two of the spear carrying Gblyn left their wall positions and one, with a gesture with his spear-point pointed to the side door.

Quietly standing, she followed the leader and leaving the throne room they went past the small room she had used earlier. *Thank God I went then,* she thought as they went along a passage, which seemed to end at a blank wall. Then she noticed the ladder going up to the next floor.

The butt of a spear prodded her towards the ladder, so

she went up and climbed through a trapdoor opening into a small room just big enough for her to stand up in. A small opening in one wall acted as a window, letting in the pale moonlight. A pile of straw in one corner was obviously the bed and a shallow clay pot was the other convenience by the smell coming from it.

The Gblyn, who had followed her up, muttered something Iskra didn't quite catch and left, pulling the trapdoor down as he did so. *No doubt to stand guard as well*, she thought.

20

Though it couldn't have been avoided, Bolyar Chaydar was annoyed at the delay and he pressed hard to make up for the lost time. The descent down the ridge was swift, and for once the track along the river was rock free. A brief stop at mid-day, more for the horses was the only concession he made until they reached a small lake.

Bryden called for a halt and said forcibly to Bolyar Chaydar, 'If we don't eat something soon we will be fit for nothing when we get to the Gblyn mines.'

'What do you suggest that we eat. Grass?' the Bolyar said sarcastically. Then he quickly apologized by holding up his hand to Bryden.

'I'm tired and hungry too.'

'The only food round here I can see is in that lake,' Bryden said hopefully.

'How are we to catch fish? With our bare hands?' Zltan asked scornfully.

Chaz, dismounting, limped over to them and after rummaging in his waist pouch said, 'With this.'

He held up a shiny fishhook.

Borislav stared fascinated at the gleaming hook.

Oh! Oh! Thought Bryden, *Better watch out what we say about this.*

'Ah. Yes. My friend here has brought his maajik hook, made especially for him in Epirus for his coming of age ritual.

Now Zltan. If you don't mind getting a suitable rod from those bushes, we might get something to eat. OK.'

The lake proved to be as bountiful as Bryden had hoped. Chaz pulled out a good 'four hands' worth of trout like fish, far too many to eat at once. So after Borislav had insisted in making a fire despite his injured arm, which made holding the ironstone awkward, they cooked the gutted fish, head stuck on a stick holding them over the flames. Zltan made a rough and ready shallow reed basket to carry the uneaten catch.

Refreshed and replete they set off again. The horses being well rested were frisky at first but the fast pace began to take its toll.

By dusk the horses were dead on their feet, their riders saddle sore. Surprisingly, Chaz made it through the day quite well considering his lack of riding skills. His sheer tenacity and determination pulled him through. Bryden was quietly proud of him.

When a cloud of smoke could be seen over a series of hills in the distance, Bolyar Chaydar called a halt.

'That is the mine, he said pointing. 'The Gblyn have several forges for smelting the gold. They use a lot of charcoal so they need lots of trees. The production of it makes plenty of smoke. When we get closer, you will see how bare the hills are.'

They did not get much nearer that evening because they heard the howling of wolves.

'The Gblyn must have patrols out. I suggest that we rest up around here. We can't do much. The moon can be both a help and a hindrance.' Bryden looked at Bolyar Chaydar who, just visible in the twilight, nodded back in agreement.

A dip in the hillside gave them some protection from the wind and happily wrapped in their hooded cloaks, (Thanks to Borislav's foresight in bringing them back) they dropped off to sleep quickly and woke at dawn, stiff but refreshed.

Bolyar Chaydar spat out a fish bone. Over breakfast he was talking about the next step. 'I think we must proceed with caution. The Gblyn will be on the alert if Iskra's captors have brought her here, as we think. They will suspect that we will attempt a rescue, I'm sure.'

21

The trapdoor was slung opened and a Gblyn, holding a wicker basket containing a small amount of bread, cheese and a beaker of beer, pushed it next to the opening and then noisily pulled the trapdoor down.

Iskra was jerked awake with the racket, having slept all night despite her previous day's ordeal and the fact that her bedding might have contained a host of mini-livestock, i.e. fleas.

Feeling quite hungry, Iskra soon ate the meagre breakfast, then trying to make the best of it, brushed her hair and with a dab of toothpaste on her finger, *God what would she have done without her bag,* rubbed her teeth. Now she felt ready to face the day.

The tiny opening in the wall, which acted as a window, overlooked the village and the big hill. The tower she was in enabled her to see over most of the trees. After a look, she wished she hadn't. In the centre of the village, an open space was filled with scores of peasants being corralled by Gblyns riding wolves.

Then, along a side alley, she saw three peasants pulled down by a pack of wolves guided by a Gblyn wolf rider. They must have been hiding in a wood-pile, for logs of wood were strewn about the alley.

Two of the peasants were screaming in agony as their flesh was ripped from their bodies. The third peasant staggered to his feet howling with pain, desperately trying to hold in his intestines as they were being pulled out of his stomach by a snarling wolf.

On the far side of the village she saw that peasants had barricaded several mine entrances with rocks and timber and the Gblyn wolf riders were making futile attacks against their well defended positions.

No gold will be coming out of there for while, thought

Iskra, as sickened by what she had seen, she came away from the 'window.'

22

Bolyar Chadar led the small group through a deserted village. The Gblyn had obviously attacked it. The evidence was there to see. Several decomposing bodies of peasants, most badly mauled by wolves and the carcass of one wolf with an axe buried in its head, were lying in front of the huts. Strangely the huts themselves remained untouched.

Pressing on past the grizzly scene, they came upon a wasteland of denuded hillsides. Every sizable tree had been cut down to make charcoal. *The food of the forge!* Eventually they came to the foothills just before the Gblyn's valley of goldmines.

On the highest point of a hilltop, (The trees had been left untouched in this area of the Gblyn's own backyard) overlooking the Gblyn's village, their view was partially obscured by the smoking charcoal kilns but they could still make out the brutal savagery as they saw more and more peasants being herded back to the village from the surrounding woods. Any peasant that tried to escape was set upon by a pair of wolves under the control of the Gblyn riding the lead wolf and promptly torn to pieces in front of their family and friends.

'There must have been a breakout,' said Bryden. 'Not very successful by the look of it,' he said sadly. 'Maybe we might be able to help.' He had been appalled at what he had seen and had a germ of an idea.

He turned to Bolyar Chaydar. 'We can't rescue Iskra on our own, not after seeing that lot in action,' he said pointing down at the Gblyn wolf riders.

'It's impossible,' said the Bolyar. 'You just said we are too few.'

'What if we released the peasants and protected them from the wolves. What then?'

'Still impossible,' insisted the Bolyar.

'What if I used a little maajik,' suggested Bryden with a

145

grin. 'Will you trust me Bolyar Chaydar?'

There was silence as the Bolyar thought. He considered the way the man-vamps had been destroyed. *That must have been in part through Bryyyden's maajik.*

He nodded his head.

Bryden gave a sigh of relief and said, 'Right, some of the things I'm going to ask you to do will sound strange, even to you Chaz.' He looked at each of them in turn. 'We don't have time to waste. Iskra could be in imminent danger right now so please, no arguments. Just trust me.'

'Now Borislav, do you know of any hot springs around here?'

Borislav looked surprised at the question but nodded. 'There is one, not too far away from here. Why do you ask?'

'I want you and Chaz to collect some shiny yellow stuff coating …' He saw the look on Borislav's face. 'It's around the edges of the hot spring. Scrape off as much as you can. A sharp stone would do. Fetch it back to me any way you can, reed basket, your hat if you have to.'

Still looking puzzled, Borislav led a speechless Chaz to their horses and they rode quickly away.

'Now Zltan, that village we passed. Is there likely to be another one like it but nearer to us?'

Pausing for a moment to think, Zltan smiled and said that he could remember one.

'But why?' he asked, perplexed by the question, just as Borislav had been.

'What I want is for you to collect six, I mean a hand and one finger, mortar and pestles and shallow clay pots about this big. Bryden opened his hands. 'Then, as many small clay pots as you can carry, this big again.' Bryden opened his hands. 'Take the packhorse and wrap the stuff in the cloaks if there is nothing else,'

Zltan looked at Bryden as though he had just gone mad.

'Trust me, Zltan. Trust me!'

Scratching his head, Zltan went to get the horses.

Bolyar Chaydar smiled at Bryden. 'This is going to be good maajik. I can feel it in my bones. Where do we go, Maajik man?'

'Do you like dark caves? I need to find some bats. Oh and I'd like you to make some reed baskets for me on the way there.'

**

Borislav led Chaz through a series of valleys away from the Gblyn stronghold towards a mountain range of dark coloured rock, quite different to the area they had just left. As they got nearer, Chaz gave a cry of disgust. 'God, it smells of rotten eggs.' It got stronger and stronger until Chaz felt he was going to be sick.

A small stream came into view and the water was tinged yellow.

'This must be it,' exclaimed Chaz excitedly.'

Not far upstream, they came to a rock pool with wisps of steam rising from it.

'Hey! We've found it,' Chaz grinned happily. Even the taciturn Borislav smiled.

A closer inspection of the pool proved what his Uncle had said. Layers of yellow stuff (crystals) were exposed where the water had evaporated or leaked away.

Grabbing a sharp stone each, they began to chip away at the 'yellow stuff,' until they had quite a pile of it. Fortunately there were some reed beds further downstream and Borislav made two narrow baskets in record time. Tired, but pleased with their work, Borislav and Chaz made their way back to Bryden.

**

Zltan had backtracked down the valley and then turned to follow an overgrown trail, (more evidence of the Gblyn being there) up and over a ridge into the next one. A group of huts, *Maybe two hands,* he thought, were nestled in a curve of a small river. He could see one body, half decomposed, throat obviously ripped out and belly slashed with claw marks and the carcass of a cow, lying on its back with a bloated stomach and legs pointing stiffly to the sky.

Trying to ignore the rotten stink, Zltan led the packhorse to the nearest hut. As in the other village, nothing seemed out of place. The attack must have been swift.

Leaving the horses, he went in to see what he could find. *Small pots, that's what he wanted. Lots of them, though only the spirits knew why,* he thought. The single room had a collection of clay pots by the stone oven. Spotting a woollen cloak left on a bench, Zltan used it to carry the smallest ones, having got rid of their contents onto the floor. *Pity*, he thought, as the smell of stale beer wafted through the hut. Then he saw the mortar and pestle by the door, half full of grain. Adding them to his spoils, Zltan hefted the cloak and went outside to the packhorse.

Once the transfer of his haul had been completed, he went to the next hut and found a similar quantity of pots and another mortar and pestle. *Why so many of these?* he wondered. *Surely one would be enough?*

Zltan worked his way through the village and was pleasantly surprised when he couldn't fix any more items onto the packhorse. Whether he had enough or not, he had no room for more anyway. So, hoping for the best. Zltan began the journey back to camp.

***

Bolyar Chadar led Bryden back down the valley past the turn that Zltan had taken, urging his horse to climb a steep ridge and rode along the top of it for a while.

Bryden, unused to riding at the best of times, had to literally hold onto his horse's mane to stop himself from falling off. Then, wishing he could get off for a while, he had to urge his mount on in order to catch up with the Bolyar who had at last stopped.

'I thought you were in a hurry, Bryyyden?'

'I was,' gasped Bryden, 'But this is ridiculous. Anyway, where is this blasted cave?'

The Bolyar got down from his horse and walking to the edge of the ridge, pointed down and smiled.

Bryden eased a leg over the back of his horse and dropped to the ground. Walking stiffly over, he looked down and blanched.

'You've got to be joking!' The rock face dropped more or less sheer for at least thirty metres. Midway down was the entrance to a cave.

'Do you not climb rocks in Epirus, Bryyyden? This is a good place to teach children, would you not say.'

Bryden swallowed. They needed the bat guano so he said a quick prayer and said, 'I have managed a few small climbs but it was some time ago so I'm out of practice. Would you mind leading the way?'

Once the horses were securely hitched to a convenient bush and Bryden had made sure they had the bundle of linen sacks to carry the guano in, they set off.

Bolyar Chaydar slowly climbed down the rock face, feet searching for footholds while the fingers held on to tiny cracks. Bryden leant over the edge, watching the Bolyar carefully picking up the route as best he could. Then he followed. By the time he was five metres down, his toes were aching from the pressure of standing on them and his arms were trembling with the strain of holding on by his finger tips.

It came as a complete shock when a hand grasped his foot and Bolyar Chaydar said, 'Easy now, Bryyyden. There is a ledge just to your right. Give me your hand and I'll pull you in.'

'Jeez! I never want to do that again as long as I live.' Bryden slumped forward on his hands and knees, breathing heavily.

Then as his heart rate slowed down, he lifted up his head and looked into the cave. Straight ahead, a passage dripping water from the walls and roof went deep into the rock. The floor was slick and slippery with the white guano droppings mixing with the water.

149

'We need to find a pool. I hope to God there's one near here. We need to be able to see what we are doing.'

'What about here Bryyyden?' The Bolyar had moved forward and was bending down.

Bryden shuffled forward and keeping to one side, managed to see the pool. It was just about big enough, he thought. Over the years bat guano had fallen into it and had made a sort of sediment. That was what he wanted.

'Well done Bolyar Chaydar. You deserve an Oscar.'

'What?'

'Never mind, just an Epirus saying. Let's scrape up this stuff on the bottom of the pool.'

Using his knife, Bolyar Chaydar scraped up enough guano to fill the linen sacks they had brought. Then a tough twine made from a vine was used to tie the sacks two apiece so as to to hang around their necks, thus freeing their hands for the return climb. Bryden was so over the moon at finding the guano, he was on the top of the ridge before he realized it.

Bolyar Chaydar took the dripping bags of guano and placed them in the two reed baskets he had made earlier. He then tied them to the back of their respective saddles.

Bryden hardly noticed. He was so busy working out what he had to do next. The journey back to their base was almost over before he knew it.

23

Bryden was pleased to see that everyone was back, the mound of clay pots that Zltan was standing by and the smell of sulphur from the baskets Borislav had placed some distance away from the group, telling him they had been successful.

Dismounting from his horse, he untied the basket of guano and put it with the one that Bolyar Chaydar had laid down next to the pile of pots and mortar bowls.

'Well done everyone but first things first. We need to eat.'

Zltan, waving a hand at Bryden, went to his horse and produced a whole wheel of cheese he had found in the village.

'That's fantastic Zltan.'

Zltan beamed at the compliment.

'Now, if we had some meat?'

Borislav raised his good arm. 'I'll see if I can catch some rabbits.' He pointed to a glade not too far away. 'There are some burrows over there.'

'Great! As fast as you can. Good hunting.'

'Now Zltan, while I explain what I want doing, for God's sake pass some of that cheese round. I'm bloody starving.'

Taking a large bite of cheese, Bryden went over to the pile of clay pots and picked up a mortar bowl and its pestle. 'We're going to,' he mumbled, 'grind down the yellow stuff.' He pointed to the sulphur crystals. 'To a fine powder and I really mean fine.' Snatching another bite of cheese, he went on, 'Zltan, I hope you don't mind doing another job for me.'

Zltan raised an eyebrow and shrugged his shoulders.

'We need a load of charcoal, small bits if you can get them.' Bryden sniffed the air.

'If that smell doesn't lie, I think we are not too far away

from a charcoal kiln, right.'

Zltan nodded.

'Sorry to push you off before Borislav gets back with the rabbits but ...'

'I know,' Zltan said smiling, 'We're in a hurry, right.'

Bryden nodded as Zltan, carrying a hunk of cheese in one hand, stopped to pick up two of the cloaks he would use to wrap the charcoal in. A few moments later he was riding towards the smoking kilns in the next valley.

'I say! Won't he be seen by the Gblyn and er, captured.' *Or worse,* thought Chaz.

'Not very likely,' Bolyar Chaydar said. 'The kilns are left for days and are looked after by the peasants anyway. The wolf guard Gblyns will only come down when the kilns are ready to be opened. As you can see they are still smoking. They are not ready to be emptied yet. Zltan will be quite safe and there should be plenty of discarded charcoal around the old kilns for him to collect.'

Having finished his cheese, Bryden took the mortar bowl over to the baskets of sulphur crystals and half filled it with them before returning to the others. He then sat cross-legged, the bowl between his knees. 'We have to crush this to a powder,' he said, picking up the pestle, a piece of hard wood shaped like a dumpy drumstick, thicker at one end.

Bryden began pounding the crystals with the pestle, then after a while started twisting the pestle in a grinding fashion. He then repeated the process again and again until he had a mortar full of a fine yellow powder.

'There,' he said emptying the powder into one of the large shallow clay pots that Zltan had also collected. 'That's what I want.'

Chaz and Bolyar Chaydar both nodded, and picking a mortar bowl and pestle each, went over to the baskets of sulphur crystals, filling them as Bryden had done. Then sitting down at a convenient spot began the laborious job of crushing and grinding.

A shout made them look up. Borislav had returned with

several rabbits. He looked at the busy scene of mortars being used and indicated that he would make a fire to roast them.

Using the driest wood he could find, (it made little or no smoke) Borislav soon had a small fire going. Quickly skinning and cleaning out the rabbits, his injured arm being much better, he then made a spit of two forked branches placed on ether side of the fire and a long thin sapling fixed across them. Once the rabbits had been strung along the sapling over the fire, it was just a matter of waiting for them to be cooked.

The clatter of hooves broke through the concentrated sound of pestles pounding and grinding. Zltan was back with two tied cloaks full of charcoal.

'I wasn't sure how much to bring, Bryyyden. I hope there is enough here. I wouldn't want to go back. The Gblyn wolf guards have started to patrol the area. It looked like they were searching for escaped peasants.'

'Well done, Zltan. You are just in time. Borislav's rabbits are about ready,' said Bryden.

The rabbits were and all enjoyed them.

***

'Sorry to crack the whip.' Blank looks from the Bolyars.

'I mean we have to get back to work. Chaz, would you and Zltan start on the charcoal, the same idea as this yellow-stuff. You can show him the ropes can't you?'

Chaz nodded as he and Zltan, now armed with his mortar and pestle, (now he knew why so many were needed) went over to where the two cloaks of charcoal had been dropped. A quick lesson from Chaz and he was on his pounding, grinding way.

By mid-afternoon, Bryden called a halt. He had estimated that enough raw materials had been made. Now came the tricky, potentially dangerous bit. He had to mix all three ingredients in the right amounts in order to make black powder, now known as gunpowder.

Bryden had already graded three of the clay pots into size order. The smallest would represent 10%, the next 15% and the largest 75%.

He asked Chas to fill the small one with the yellow powder, Zltan to fill the next with charcoal and Bolyar Chaydar the largest with the guano (saltpetre).

While they all looked on, Bryden then very carefully began to add small amounts from each pot into the largest shallow pot they had and mixed them with a pestle, adding drops of water to keep the resulting paste moist.

He did this until he had used up all the ingredients. Pausing for a moment, he looked tiredly at Bolyar Chaydar. 'Will you take over and keep grinding this paste. When you have had enough, let Zltan have a go.'

Waving his aching arm in the air for a few moments, he looked at Borislav and said.

'I would have preferred honey but are there any trees around here that have a sticky sap?'

The blank faces said it all. So going to the nearest tree, Bryden touched the trunk then put his fingers together and mimed trying to open them.

Borislav gave a grin and said *glu* and pointed to the woods.

Silently thanking the Gods, Bryden went to the pile of clay pots and picking up a smallish one, gave it to Borislav and pointed to the woods. 'Can you fill that for me?'

Borislav nodded and grabbing the pot, ran off into the woods.

'Now!' Bryden said, 'I want to spread the paste in this bowl.' He pointed to the ground. 'Onto the open cloaks we haven't yet used. I want it to dry as fast as possible. Chaz would you get them for me please.'

Once the cloaks were spread out, Bryden, using Bolyar Chaydar's knife, smeared the paste thinly all over the cloth. After the second cloak had been covered, he slowly stood up.

'Agh! My aching back! That's it for a while. Let's go

and sit down.'

***

Everyone was sprawled out under the nearest trees, some dozing when Borislav returned with a pot of pine resin. He looked down at them lying there. 'All right for some,' he said a little sarcastically and sat down himself.

Bryden stirred and stood up. After a good stretch, he went over to the cloaks and saw that the paste had dried. 'Chaz! Chaz! Over here please,' Bryden shouted.

Grumbling at being disturbed, Chaz wandered over to his Uncle. 'Yeah,' he drawled, 'What do you want?'

'Grab hold of one side of this cloak, I want to carry it to that large pot.'

Careful not to spill any of the black powder, they stood by the pot and held up the cloak close together, making a runnel with the material, thus allowing the black powder to fall straight into the large pot. They repeated the process with the other cloak. The large pot was now brimful and Bryden was satisfied that they had enough powder for his purposes.

'Listen up everyone. I want each of you to get a mortar and grind, just one more time, a bowlful of the black powder. Then fill each of those small pots over there.' He pointed to the original pile of clay pots. 'Right to the brim, alright.'

A mutter of agreement if not of understanding reached Bryden's ears.

'Borislav, do you mind?'

He came over. 'Yes Bryyyden?'

'Look, I'm sorry. I seem to be asking you to do extra things all the time. It sort of happens. I don't mean to.' Bryden said apologetically.

Borislav nodded and said politely, 'What do you want me to do?'

'I need a handful of really dry rushes. Do you think you can find some for me?'

155

Borislav looked down the valley towards the small river meandering through it. 'No problem, Bryyyden,' he said as he went down towards the river.

The number of filled clay pots grew until they ran out of the black powder and so Bryden called the group together.

'I wish to thank you, especially the Bolyar,' he began. 'I know that you have been puzzled by what I have asked you to do and until we made these special pots, I couldn't be sure if my idea would work. Now I am.'

The sound of heavy breathing made him turn. Borislav came running up to them, a large handful of dry rushes in his hand.

'Ah! Just in time, Borislav. Just in time. May I have one of your rushes, if you don't mind? Oh and Chaz. Could you pass me that pot of glu, please.'

The others were now completely intrigued by what Bryden was about to do.

They watched fascinated as he used a small stick to smear some *glu* all over a strip of rush and then sprinkle some grains of black powder along it. Then he applied some of the bat guano, (saltpetre) he had set aside for this very purpose in a clay pot marked with a charcoal cross. Wiping his hands on a piece of torn cloak, he used two flat sticks as tweezers to hold the sticky guano rush and carefully pushed it deep into one of the black powder filled pots.

'Damn!'

Bryden was furious with himself. 'I forgot the wet clay. Can anyone see a bit of mud around here?'

Zltan was the first to speak. 'There's a small spring over there,' pointing towards a group of trees.

'Chaz! Will you pop over and grab a handful of mud. Not too wet mind.'

Knowing everyone was watching, Chaz raced over to the spot Zltan had pointed out. Sure enough, the spring was there and quickly kneeling down, he scooped up a handful of mud from the edge of it. Not too wet as ordered.

Bryden accepted the mud and packed most of it over the top of the pot, compressing the black powder tightly as he did so and making sure there were no gaps. The top of the rush stuck out by about 5cm.

Now the moment of truth. 'Borislav, would you go over to the fire. The embers should still be hot enough to light one of the rushes. I know it won't burn for long but bring it to me. I'll be over there.' He pointed to a large boulder about 50m away. 'Everyone else stay here, including you Borislav, when you give me the lit rush. Is that clear?'

Once Borislav had run back to the others, Bryden touched the end of the rush sticking out of the pot with the still burning one in his hand. A fizzing, hissing noise told him the fuse he had made was working. Running like a bat out of hell, Bryden had just reached the others when an almighty bang blasted his ears. Shards of broken pottery whizzed by and he fell to the ground hands over his head.

The Bolyars were transfixed, faces a mixture of terror and wonder. Chaz started to dance about, 'Right On, Uncle. Right On,' at the top of his voice.

Bryden didn't hear a word. He was temporally deaf but he now knew he could make gunpowder.

24

Bryden lay on the ground. His head seemed to be full of little men banging tin lids. Then he remembered they had done it; actually made gunpowder. He sat up and looked around. The Bolyars had gone over to the boulder where he had placed the primed pot. A blackened patch of earth was all that remained of the explosion. Of course he had known what to expect. The Bolyars on the other hand, had not.

'Bryyyden, you make very good maajik.' Bolyar Chaydar spoke for all of them. They were still in shock at what they had just witnessed.

Walking round the site of the explosion with an ecstatic Chaz in toe, Bryden discovered the range of destruction that his homemade grenade had made. Branches knocked down from nearby trees gave him a good estimate of the force of the blast and he was well pleased.

When everyone, including himself, had calmed down, Bryden said he needed to fit a rush to all of the pots filled with the black powder, as quickly as possible. So he split the group, Bolyar Chaydar and Zltan to collect the mud from round the spring and Chaz to pack and seal the pot once the rush had been put in. Bryden had the job of preparing the rush fuse with the still injured Borislav as a spare pair of hands, ready to help where needed.

The team worked wonders and the stock of grenades were finished in good time. In fact Bryden said that he wanted to have a closer look at the Gblyn village before it got too dark.

Then, realizing that they had not eaten for ages, he suggested to Bolyar Chaydar that they split up, Zltan to try the river with Chaz's fish hook and Borislav his rabbiting skills. It seemed a sensible idea and once Chaz had found his fishhook, they went their separate ways.

Bolyar Chaydar led the way, taking a side valley, which

he said would take them to the back of the hill that contained the mines. We shall have to hide the horses and continue on foot he explained, much to the disgust of Chaz, who now preferred to ride rather than walk.

An hour later they were scrambling up the steep slopes of the hill.

'God, can't we stop for a bit Uncle. I'm knackered.'

Bolyar Chaydar looked at him and Bryden jumped in quickly. 'It's an old Epirusian saying. We say it when we are very tired.'

'Well! What about it, Uncle? Just for a short while. It won't hurt, will it?'

Bryden gave the Bolyar a look as if to say, *What can you do with them!* 'Alright, just for bit then.'

When they reached the top of the hill, Bryden gave a whistle of surprise. It was quite a set up. The Gblyn huts were in the treetops over the far side of the valley.

He then noticed the lines of huts on the ground. Most of them had a wolf-riding Gblyn guard outside them. The central square was full of peasants surrounded by more wolf-riding Gblyn guards.

As he watched, a single wolf prowling along the perimeter of the crowd suddenly pounced on one poor unsuspecting peasant and dragged him to the ground. Anyone near shrank back in terror as the screams of the man suddenly ceased. The wolf nonchalantly went back to prowling the perimeter.

'My God! It's barbaric! Come on let's get closer. I want to see where we can do the most damage.'

Fortunately there was plenty of cover. Trees, shrubs, even some large boulders, shielded them from prying eyes.

Bolyar Chaydar stopped and held up a hand. Chaz and Bryden obeyed the agreed signal and stood still. A hand waved, palm down. Getting down on all fours, Chaz and Bryden crawled towards the Bolyar.

'We're at the top of the cliff. The mine entrances are below us,' he whispered.

159

Bryden estimated that they were about a 100m above the valley floor. *How the hell could he get within range to use his grenades?*

Before he could answer that, he needed to locate the targets. 'Bolyar Chaydar, he whispered, 'Can you tell me what else is down there?'

Shielding his eyes to the setting sun, the Bolyar quietly described what the Gblyn would miss the most. The forges, over to their left, the wolf pen way over to their right, and of course the tree village of the Gblyn itself.

'If we can neutralize those damn wolves …, sorry I meant to say if we can put the wolves out of action, we can free the peasants. Then we might stand a chance …' Bryden trailed off. *But how can we get near to the little bastards?*

A tug on his arm made him turn towards an excited Chaz. 'Uncle,' he whispered. 'What about the crusades? He looked across to the Bolyar who appeared not to be listening. 'I mean, you know, attacking castles with siege weapons.'

Bryden slapped his forehead with a hand. 'Chaz, you're a frigging genius. Why didn't I think of that?' He then sat back and began to think.

A bemused Bolyar looked at him for a moment and then looked away. *Epirusians,* he thought, *Mad.*

'Got it!' A stifled cry came from Bryden. 'A catapult could do it. A bloody catapult.'

'Er, sorry to put a damper on it, Uncle,' whispered Chaz, 'But where are you going to get one from? Amazon?'

'Look about you Chaz, look about you. Can't you see what's all around us.'

'What? There's nothing but treessssss …., Uncle, you're the genius.'

'Yeah, but how do we make it?'

Bryden started to examine the smaller trees and shrubs around them, going so far as to swing on one or two of them.

Definitely mad, Bolyar Chaydar thought.

There was just enough light for Bryden to select a couple of possible saplings. Anything thicker would be impossible with his limited resources and technical knowhow.

They managed to make it back to their camp and to their delight, a meal of fish and rabbit was waiting for them and nearly as good was the fact that Zltan had saved a couple of clay pots to be used as water jugs, thus avoiding frequent trips to the spring.

Sitting next to the small, yet homely campfire, Bryden explained what they had seen and what he wanted to do very early the next morning at sunrise.

25

Iskra was left alone in the smelly, poky tower room all day. Screams and cries of pain coming from the village below were the only sounds she heard. Closing the wooden shutters of the 'window' opening set in the wall to cut out the noise, proved impossible.

The stench from the 'convenience' pot became too overwhelming.

It was nearly dark when a Gblyn guard lifted the trapdoor just enough for him to push a hunk of bread and a beaker of tepid beer through and then disappear, the trapdoor dropping down with a solid thud.

Forcing herself to eat and drink and nearly in tears with a feeling of hopelessness, she lay down on the straw bed, praying that Bryden and Chaz would somehow find her and take her away from this filthy rat hole.

Somewhat to her surprise, Iskra woke to find that the sun had been up for some time. *How the hell did she go to sleep? God only knows.* The rattle of the trapdoor being lifted made her quickly alert.

Two guards. *Were they the same two that brought her here? She couldn't tell. Gblyns all looked the same to her.* They took her down to the floor below.

Zrysatav stared at her as she entered the throne room. He seemed distracted as he played with his bottom lip.

Then Iskra saw The Master, standing on the far side of the throne, bending over the small pedestal on which the Orb was flashing different colours. He too seemed out of sorts. Sweat was running down his bald head and face as he looked closely at the Orb, which suddenly began to pulse a bright red.

'What is it Master?' Zrysatav squeaked nervously, 'Have you found all the missing slaves and what about those Bolyar? Where are they?'

The Master didn't answer at first. Grabbing hold of the

Orb, he lifted it up and his face became a ruddy glow in the reflected flashing light and his eyes widened in fear. 'We're doomed! All doomed!' he cried.

'What's wrong? Master, What's . . ..'

A large boom from outside stopped Zrysatav in mid-sentence and the door to his throne room shuddered from the impact of what seemed to Iskra, hundreds of stones being thrown with terrible force.

It's Bryden and Chaz. It's Bryden and Chaz, Iskra thought joyously. *They've come to get me.*

26

A swirl of mist wafted through the rough and ready lean-to shelters of the camp as the sun rose over the hill and with the now usual groans, farts and mutterings about whose turn it was to get some fresh water, they woke to the new and maybe unforgettable day.

A breakfast of cold fish and rabbit didn't take long and Zltan and Borislav went into the wood, scouting for long creeping vines.

Chaz and Bolyar Chaydar loaded the packhorse with the primed grenades so when the vines, coils and coils of them, (How they managed to carry them was a mystery to Chaz) were brought into the camp, they were free to help make twisted ropes out of them.

Frustrated by the delay, Bryden was mighty relieved when the ropes were finished. It did however allow Borislav time off to catch some fish.

It took some coaxing to get the packhorse up the steep slope of the hill that overlooked the Gblyn village. Once there, it was hobbled and allowed to graze contentedly, having had its heavy load of grenades removed from its back.

Bryden was busy instructing Zltan to hack off all the side branches of his selected sapling, except for those that made a fork near the top of the trunk. Zltan's short sword proved ideal for the task.

Once the sapling was ready, Bolyar Chaydar, standing on his horse, tied one end of the vine rope they had made about three quarters of the way up the trunk. The other end of the vine rope was passed round a tree 10m behind it. A low branch, cut back somewhat, provided a handy notch for the rope to go under.

Bryden had actually done a good job in picking this site. It was a small copse, with his sapling on the forward edge. The other trees behind, he had realized, would have to be used to bend the sapling to a different angle if he wanted to aim at different targets.

With three of them on the vine rope, the sapling's top was dragged down low enough for one of their baskets to be fixed to the forked branch. To save their energy, Bryden advised Borislav to take the surplus end of the rope, and tie it round a nearby tree, thus taking the strain and allowing the other three to have a rest.

'About sodding time,' chuntered Chaz, looking at his sore hands. 'I'm going to wrap some cloth on these,' he added, waving them in the air.

'And another thing, Uncle. This isn't a proper catapult is it?'

'I wondered when you might spot that, Chaz. But think about it. Lack of time, proper tools and to be truthful I'm not sure if I could have built one anyway. Still, let's not waste any more time arguing semantics eh.'

The Bolyars looked on. The mad Epirusian's were at it again.

'Now,' said Bryden urgently, 'I need some small rocks about as heavy as our pots. I need to test our little machine.'

It didn't take long for Bryden to sift through several different sized rocks brought to him by the others to make the first choice. 'Let's do it.'

'Borislav. Get ready to untie your end. Everyone else take the strain. Pull on the rope, I mean. One last thing, stand clear of the rope. It will whip by like lightening.'

Bryden placed the rock in the basket and stood well back.

'Now! Borislav.'

Slipping the knot, Borislav leapt to the side. The other three, already having taken the strain, let go as one and the sapling straightened up with a swoosh, the rope lashing skywards.

Bryden, fingers crossed, watched the rock sail through the air and land as far as he could see on the edge of the Gblyn tree huts.

'Frigging hell! It worked. It frigging worked!' And smiling like an idiot, he went over and slapped everyone on the back saying, 'Well done, well done.'

Now for the tricky part, thought Bryden, *Plus a bit of Epirusian maajik.*

He secretly unzipped his body pouch and took out a gas lighter. There was no way he was going to use a slow fuse to light the grenades. His homemade fuses were not accurate enough to be trusted. He knew that trying to light four or five grenades at once with a slow fuse would be tantamount to committing suicide.

A brief discussion with Bolyar Chaydar had led to an agreed plan of attack.

So, as Bryden arranged the grenades into a more accessible position, Chaz, hands wrapped in strips of cloth, Zltan and Bolyar Chaydar began to pull down the sapling. Then Borislav tied down the rope as before.

The basket held five of the grenades and once in place, Bryden lit their fuses with his lighter as fast as he could flick the wheel.

'Now! Borislav.'

Working in unison, the rope was unleashed; the five grenades had been aimed at the wolf pen, which at this time of the day was more or less full with maybe one hundred or so of them. (They were lucky because this was feeding time. To ensure the full obedience of the wolves, the Gblyn had them penned and fed them daily with the meat of the peasants' cattle which were kept in a large cavern next to the goldmines).

Four grenades reached the target before exploding a few metres above the pen. The sound was deafening and scores of wolves were either killed outright or lacerated by the flying fragments of the pots to such a degree that they died within minutes of their horrific wounds. Those which had suffered minor injuries or had escaped unscathed, fled the pen in panic, howling in terror into the surrounding woods. This was one valley they would never ever return to.

The terrified animals carrying the two Gblyn wolf guards, who were supervising the slaughter of five oxen next to the wolf pen, unseated them when the first grenade exploded and they lay dazed on the ground as their wolves panicked and mingled with the others in the woods.

The peasants butchering the oxen cried out, terrified that the spirit gods were angry and had sent a demon to kill them. They crouched down praying for mercy. Then, realizing that they were unhurt and their tormentors, the Gblyn, were sprawled helpless on the ground, they grabbed their butcher's knives and pounced on them. Knowing that the Gblyn had phenomenal strength for their size, the peasants chopped and hacked the arms off them and then gouged their eyes out, before running off to leave the screaming pair to suffer a hideous fate.

The errant grenade arched through the air towards the Gblyn village and as it dropped closer to the biggest tree hut, it exploded, peppering the walls and door with fragments of pottery.

'Quick as you can Borislav. Bring the end of the rope to this tree,' Bryden shouted. He pointed at the same time as he rushed over to the stock of grenades.

Borislav ran to grab the rope which had been whipped up when the sapling had been let loose and had come down some distance away. The chosen tree had been selected and trimmed earlier by Bryden so it was just a matter of the team of rope pullers repositioning themselves.

'Heave!' cried Bryden and as the sapling was pulled down and secured, he loaded the basket with another lot of grenades. Hiding his lighter as best he could, he quickly lit the fuses.

'Now! Borislav,' the command rang out. Borislav and the other three repeated their earlier actions and the sapling sprang upright, releasing its lethal cargo.

This time all five grenades arched through the air and dropped into the middle of the Gblyn tree hut village. Two exploded on the roof of a hut, shredding the thatch. One burst on the ground amongst a group of twenty or so anxious Gblyns who were about to go to the wolf pen to see what had caused the big bangs.

The carnage was quite horrific. Limbs and heads were blown off by the blast, bodies torn open by the razor sharp shards of pottery. The Gblyns on the edge of the group seemed to have escaped injury but had suffered burst eardrums and deafness.

Only one grenade failed to explode, the fuse dislodged by the force of the launch.

The last grenade, in one of those events that can only happen once in a million, passed through the open doorway of one of the tree huts and burst in the centre of the oven fire. Pieces of burning wood were blown out of the hut by the grenade's explosion and were scattered by the wind onto neighbouring thatched roofs, which immediately caught fire.

Up on the hillside, Bryden had already switched targets. The forges needed to be put out of action. His team, now familiar with the technique swung into action again, using another tree to change the angle of attack.

The cluster of grenades straddled the three forges and blasted two of the work huts to bits. They were merely lean-to structures and caught fire very quickly. The third forge seemed untouched but Chaz said he could see several bodies lying on the ground.

Now the risky bit, thought Bryden as he called Chaz over. 'I want you to do a pretty dangerous thing for me Chaz. If you refuse I won't be offended.'

'What's that Uncle?'

'I know you play cricket and you are, so I've heard a good bowler. So I would say that you can throw well too.'

'Er. I suppose I'm not too bad. Who told you - Dad?'

'It doesn't matter who told me. Do you think you can throw some of our grenades over the cliff?'

'Jeez, you don't hold back do you. Throw a frigging grenade. You are joking aren't you?'

'Sorry Chaz but I'm not. We need to help the peasants trapped in the mines below us. A couple of grenades falling from heaven should get rid of the Gblyn wolf guards and give the peasants a chance to get out.'

'Well, if you really think I could do it. I'll give it a go.'

'Good. I knew I could depend on you. Come on. No time to waste.'

Telling Bolyar Chaydar, Zltan and Borislav to stay back, Bryden, carrying two of the grenades, led Chaz to the edge of the cliff overlooking the mines.

A quick glance down showed a large group of Gblyn wolf guards milling about.

'They seem a bit agitated,' Bryden said. 'No wonder, if the mind control thing they have has sensed the little presents we sent over a few minutes ago.'

He gave Chaz one grenade and he held the other. 'Now, as soon as I light the fuse, throw it outwards as far as you can. Then I'll give you this one. Same thing OK.'

Chaz nodded, beads of sweat forming on his brow as he did so.

'Ready.' Bryden lit the fuse.

Chaz threw the grenade.

'Next one, here.'

Fuse lit, Chaz threw.

They both leaned over the edge and saw the first explosion. Wolves and Gblyn alike were suddenly jerking like puppets, arms and legs in all sorts of unnatural positions, blood spurting from open wounds. The sounds of screams of pain mingling with the whimpering and howls of the injured wolves were interrupted by another explosion.

The second grenade had detonated.

Within a minute the Gblyn wolf guards had been destroyed.

Only the dead and severely wounded remained. The rest had fled in terror.

Standing up, Bryden noticed the plume of smoke rising

from the Gblyn tree-hut village. 'Oh, Oh, that doesn't look good.'

27

Iskra suddenly felt frightened by the words of the Master. What did he mean? She looked over to him. He was still standing by the throne holding that flashing thing. It was beginning to give her a headache the way it pulsed on and off, on and off. Then explosions, *Not too far away by the sound of them,* she thought, *But definitely in the tree village.*

Zrysatav was fidgeting on his throne, pulling at his beard and moving from side to side. He glanced sideways at the Master, maybe hoping for some enlightenment from him. The Master had replaced the Orb back onto the pedestal where it pulsated rhythmically with a red glow.

Making a decision, Zrysatav sent a guard to find out what was happening. When he opened the throne room door to leave, a waft of smoke came in followed by the crackling sound of wood burning.

'What's happening! What's happening!' Zrysatav's shrill voice, quivering with fear, echoed round the room.

The guards suddenly raced for the door, some of them throwing down their spears in the rush to get out.

'Stop! Come back you cowards. I'll feed you to the wolves!'

Zrysatav stopped shouting. The guards had gone. They had deserted him, he Zrysatav the Bold. *Just wait,* he thought, *The mines will be too good for those mutinous curs.* Standing up his on his spindly legs, he ignored the Master and Iskra and left the throne room by the side door.

Iskra felt anxious. The Master seemed unstable to her and she couldn't help remembering how he was only a few minutes ago. He had sounded as though he had lost his rag.

The Master seemed unaware of Iskra's presence and was looking closely at the Orb which had started to flash in different colours again. He was sweating profusely, his bald head was glistening, drops of sweat were falling into his eyes and he brushed them away irritatingly with his hands. Two distant explosions made him jump. Then the Orb began to pulse a deep red colour. 'No!' he screamed in a hoarse croaky voice and made a grab for it. As he lifted it off the pedestal, it slipped out of his sweaty hands and fell onto the sandy floor.

The Orb began to roll towards Iskra, who had been standing transfixed, unable to move, not wanting to draw the Master's attention. Now the spell was broken. The thud of the falling Orb had penetrated her consciousness. Without thinking, she picked it up and running across the throne room threw it into the oven fire.

'What have you done!' A wail of anguish burst from the Master and he scuttled across the room as the orb began to throb and vibrate. A continuous wave of colours swept across the room from the oven's aperture. Babbling incoherently, the Master reached the oven and bending down, grabbed the Orb. He found that he couldn't lift it out and when he tried to let go of it, he couldn't do that either.

His screams of agony as his hands began to burn, tore through Iskra but she couldn't move. The Orb began to make a shrill, wailing sound and the light suddenly became incandescent, blindingly brilliant. Then it went out as the flesh on the Master's body began to melt away, leaving a bony skeleton holding a blackened lifeless Orb.

Stifling a cry of relief as well as horror, Iskra turned round to find a wall of flames blocking her way out of the throne room.

28

It took some time for them to reach the bottom of the hill and the horses became skittish when they caught the odour of wolves. Suddenly, a blinding flash of light shone out of the tallest Gblyn hut. *What the hell was that,* thought Bryden.

The goldmines came into view. Scores of peasants were scrambling over their makeshift barricades that had blocked off the entrances to the tunnels and kept the Gblyn out.

Carrying anything that could be used as a weapon, the peasants surrounded the fallen Gblyn who had been trying to recapture them. Whether dead or alive, the baying mob hacked, stabbed, bashed with rocks or poked with sharpened sticks. The few Gblyn and wolves still alive from the grenade attack added their screams and howls to those of the frenzied peasants lusting for revenge after their years of slavery and suffering.

Bypassing the bloodthirsty mob, Bryden rode in the lead towards the peasants' huts, those that had been guarded by the Gblyn wolf guards. He was amazed to see several Gblyn bodies sprawled on the ground, each one torn to pieces, their throats ripped out. They stopped to look at them.

'The wolves must have turned on them,' Chaz shouted. 'Why would they do that?'

'Because they must have lost the ability to control them,' said Bolyar Chaydar.

'Look. They're still bleeding,' Chaz said in a worried voice. 'It must have just happened. Where are the wolves now?' He looked around anxiously.

'I wonder if it had anything to do with that flash of light we saw a few minutes ago? If it is, I reckon that Iskra must be in or near that big tree-hut the light came from.'

'If that's so,' Bolyar Chaydar said worriedly, 'I suggest that we hurry. The smoke from there is getting thicker. The fire must be spreading quite quickly.'

As they urged their horses forward, the doors of the huts burst open and untold numbers of half starved peasants stumbled out, looking bewildered at the dead Gblyns.

Bolyar Chaydar stood up in his stirrups. 'Good people,' he shouted, 'For now, the Gblyn are not in control of the wolves. Take your chance and leave. For the moment, I believe you are safe. Go! Go back home! Now!'

The crowd looked at him in silence. Then the full meaning of what he had said struck home. Cheering broke out and groups of friends and families began to form.

The peasants from the barricaded mines arrived, calm now that the bloodlust had been excised from their systems, wondering what was going on. Then on hearing the news, there were smiles, hugs and then a scurrying of people rushing back into huts to collect the few items of value they owned. Several didn't even wait. They had already started to leave the Gblyn slave village. They couldn't get away fast enough.

'Come on,' cried Chaz, who had been waiting restlessly for the Bolyar to finish.

'We need to find Iskra. Now! Before it's too late.'

29

Iskra watched in horror as the flames flickered around the doorway and felt the gusts of hot air being blown into the room along with myriads of sparks, some of which she had to hurriedly brush out of her hair.

What can I do? What can I do? Thinking furiously for an answer, Iskra backed further down the throne room. Her foot touched something hard. Turning round, she gave a loud scream. She had bumped into the Master's skeletal body, (a foot to be precise) which lay projecting from the oven and to her surprise the fire was still smouldering.

Smouldering

Of course, she thought. *The fire.* Pulling her shoulder bag round to the front of her body, she frantically began to search it. *Thank God it was still there.* Iskra pulled out a wrapped tissue and tossed it into the embers of the oven fire.

A flash of light caused her eyes to water and when she opened them she saw the little house-guard standing there, broom in one hand, with his beaming smile and his other hand outstretched. *God! I forgot the mints.* Diving back into her bag she slipped one out of the roll and passed it over.

Popping it into his mouth, his eyes crossing over with pleasure, the Schopanyn sniffed the air and stopped smiling as he looked at the flames now creeping through the doorway.

Iskra coughed loudly, pointed to the flames and then to herself and then after flapping her arms up and down a few times, indicated to the little house-guard that she wanted to leave the room. *God, it's getting hot.* She coughed again, this time because of the smoke.

The Schopanyn suddenly held out his broomstick towards her and nodded, so Iskra ran over and grabbed the end of it.

A cool breeze wafted her sweating face and with an air

of anticipation she opened her eyes. 'He did it! He did it!' she squealed and jumped around the ground with delight before stopping and looking about to see where she was.

An enormous oak tree soared up in front of her; the throne room was high above her head illuminated by the flames, which already were hungrily consuming the roof. Smoke was drifting between the trees, getting thicker all the time. *The whole tree village of the Gblyn must be burning,*

Before she could move to a safer position, a terrible high-pitched scream made Iskra jump. It came from above and as Iskra looked up, a fiery object came hurtling down from the top of the tree.

The shrill cries sounded familiar and with a horrible, crunching thud, Zrysalav the Bold, with hair, beard and clothing all on fire, fell not two metres from her. The body seemed to explode.. Limbs and the torso enclosed in burning clothing and emitting an odious smell were spread far and wide.

A lump of burning flesh brushed Iskra's foot making her recoil in horror. The action jolted her to her senses and she began to retreat backwards but unable to take her eyes off the gruesome spectacle.

'Are you trying to keep warm or what?' a voice came from behind her.

Whirling round in alarm, Iskra's eyes opened wide in surprise. 'Bryden!' she cried out in astonishment and ran over to where Bryden and the others were sitting on their horses, which were becoming skittish with the smoke drifting all around them.

30

The burning Gblyn tree village was now far behind them. They had passed several mauled Gblyn bodies. *Most likely ex wolf guards,* said a Bolyar. *When the signal from the Orb Iskra described was extinguished, they must have turned on them.* Of the wolves there was no sign. No one complained.

Iskra, who had been given the packhorse to ride, was talking quietly to Chaz about her recent experiences. He listened in amazement to her story before he filled her in with his rather, he thought, humdrum story.

Bryden was riding in front with Bolyar Chaydar, discussing how long it might take to get to the large lake. The Bolyar was of the opinion that it would take the rest of that day.

'How about some food then?' asked Bryden. 'I'm sure everyone is as hungry as me.'

Bolyar Chaydar stood up in his stirrups and looked around. 'I would say we are outside the influence of the Gblyn now, not that it matters anymore.' He examined the track running alongside a small river they had been following for some time.

'I can see fresh hoof marks so I would say that some sort of habitat is not too far away.'

'Is that smoke?' called Zltan, 'Or a low cloud?'

It was smoke and it was coming from a small hamlet of five huts. The inhabitants were apprehensive, being so near to the Gblyn area of control.

A few words from Bolyar Chaydar persuaded them to venture out and soon a happy group of peasants were celebrating the news of the destruction of the Gblyn.

A skin of beer was brought out along with enough wooden beakers to go round and soon a rowdy group was making merry. The lack of food had the effect of making Bryden, Chaz and Iskra in particular, very jovial. They joined in the dancing with gusto. The celebration went on until the skin of beer was finished and while the men and a couple of boys sat down on the ground breathing heavily but still talking and laughing nine to the dozen, the women and girls went into one of the huts and brought out a large pot of cabbage soup, bread and some kind of pie. Wooden bowls were passed around and then chunks of bread.

Chaz suddenly realized that there was no cutlery, especially spoons. He looked down at the bowl of soup he was holding. 'What do I do?' he whispered to Iskra who had reappeared with the women and had sat down next to him.

'Use your bread to dunk in it,' she replied with a laugh. 'When in Rome, remember.'

'Oh, Yeah.'

***

It was a very happy and satisfied band of travellers that left the little hamlet. The food and a much needed sleep had worked wonders and for a while no one spoke, each busy with their own thoughts.

Towards mid-day they decided to rest for a while and partake of some of the rabbit pie they had been given by the friendly peasants. The track was as usual in these parts, following the river and a handy spot with suitable grazing for the horses, along with several shady trees by the river itself, had come along just at the right moment.

As the party sorted themselves out and sat or lay down and Zltan hobbled the horses, Chaz said he'd just go downstream for you know what.

Pushing through the bushes that lined the bank, he was quite surprised to see a sort of canoe half out of the river. When he was closer he saw that it was more of a dugout, a carved out tree trunk. Strangely, it was covered in slimy weeds and bits of mud. As he was examining it, a squelching, gurgling sound came from behind him and before he could react in any way, a pair of slimy, webbed-like hands grabbed him round the neck and pulled him into the river. He just had time to get one glance of his attacker and wished he hadn't.

A greenish face was half covered by slimy, algae encrusted hair, with two slits where the nose should be and a pair of sunken, fiery red eyes glared at him. The scaly skin, of the semi-naked body and arms was reminiscent of fish.

Then, pulling Chaz up close to its hideous face, lips pulled back into a snarl showing a set of bony fangs, the creature exhaled a puff of noxious breath into his face and Chaz fell unconscious.

Without any apparent effort, the creature heaved the inert form of Chaz into the dugout canoe, not bothering that the right arm dangled in the water. A jerk pulled the watercraft free of the riverbank. It clumsily climbed in and using only its webbed hands as paddles, splashed its way awkwardly across the river.'

Unbeknown to the creature, an unseen observer had witnessed what he had done, a *Water Sprite*.

With a shimmer of light, the sprite wafted across the river until it reached the dugout canoe still being paddled in an erratic manner. Silently, without a ripple, the spectral entity sank beneath the surface and touched the dangling hand of Chaz before it flickered momentarily, surfaced and morphing into a dragonfly, flew away.

Twitching as though a small electrical current had passed through it, the skin pores on the back of his hand opened and a slow trickle of minute erithrocite fluid began to stain the river.

31

'Where's Chaz?' Iskra stood up and looked along the riverbank in the direction he had taken. 'Don't you think he's been gone a long time.'

Bryden looked at Bolyar Chaydar and said, 'With all that's been going on round here during the last few days I think we ought to investigate. Don't you?'

'Yes,' replied the Bolyar. 'I also think we should stay close together.'

'Yes. Good idea. Did every one get that? Zltan, would you get the horses ready please. Any one wanting to make a quick call of nature now is the time to do it.'

After the episode of Iskra's disappearance, no one was taking any chances with Chaz, so they made tracks pretty quick.

'He can't have got far,' said Borislav hopefully. He had developed a soft spot for Chaz ever since their little expedition together to collect the yellow stuff.

Zltan was leading the way on foot, the track being too narrow to ride on horseback and they had not travelled far when Bolyar Chaydar called out, 'Stop!'

He had seen signs of some sort of disturbance to the vegetation on the riverbank.

Borislav rushed over to the rivers edge. 'Look! The grass has been trodden down and that's fresh mud.' He pointed to a spot a few metres away. 'Some sort of boat was pushed up the bank, right here.'

After a brief discussion between themselves, the Bolyars convinced Bryden and Iskra that the best course of action was to carry on downriver, the obvious point being that they had been resting up river and Chaz had not come that way.

It was only a couple of bends in the river later, having picked up a bit of speed by being able to ride their horses again, that Iskra, lagging somewhat behind the others was idly watching the river when she noticed the coloured stain in the water.

'Bryden! Bryden!'

The others stopped and turning their horses round trotted back to her.

'What's up, Iskra?' Bryden asked.

She pointed to the river.

'By the Saints,' cried Borislav, 'That looks like blood.'

'Oh no!' Iskra cried out anxiously, 'It's not Chaz's is it?'

32

Chaz couldn't breathe. His mouth was wide open but he still wasn't breathing. His heart began to race and he felt dizzy. Jeez! *He was dying. He must be. I'm not breathing. I must be dead, well nearly,* he thought. He coughed and spat out a lump of foul tasting . . .. *What the hell was it. A hairy ball of something? No! Not hairy. It's a ball of tiny black fibrous fronds now floating in a pool.*

Where the hell am I? Then he remembered. *That thing came to mind, the monster from hell but nothing else.* His face was centimetres from the surface of the pool and feeling as weak as a kitten, he rolled over onto his back, one hand still in the water.

God, he felt cold. Then he sensed that he was lying on a slippery slab of rock, soaking wet. *No wonder I'm bloody cold.* And he gave a start. He was lying inside an enormous cavern dimly lit by what seemed to be clumps of plants growing from crevices in the rocky walls.

Sitting up, he pulled his hand out of the pool. Feeling a trickle of what he thought was water running down the back of his hand, he flicked his wrist to shake it off. Even in the dim light of the cavern he saw that it wasn't water. *It was too dark. Maybe red,* he thought.

'Red! My God! It's blood! I'm bleeding to death,' he shouted and held his 'injured' hand to his chest. As he did so it tingled and began to itch. As Chaz held it up to have a closer look, a shimmering light suddenly appeared, hovering just above his wrist before darting down and disappearing into the pool. The itching had stopped, as had the 'bleeding.'

'What the hell's happening to me?' A plaintive voice cried, echoing around the cavern. Chaz stood up slowly, careful not to slip on the wet slab. He could now see that the pool went to the far edge of the cavern and a dark stain of what he thought was his blood, was being carried by an unseen current in the water to what must be an outlet for the pool. *It must be part of an underground river,* he thought.

A surge in the pool made him jump and he turned round to see what it was. His nightmare was back. The hideous green face with glaring red eyes was emerging from the water and a pair of webbed hands grabbed the slab on which he was standing.

Chaz twisted round ready to run and froze in shock as three small goblin-like figures appeared from a passage he hadn't noticed. They each had bald, domed-shaped heads, large ears and a bulbous nose above a tiny mouth from which a long fang-like tooth, jutting out from the upper jaw, hung like a piece of dried nasal mucus.

They stopped when they saw Chaz, fixing him with a stare full of all the intensity of those with only a large single eye in the middle of their foreheads can.

The creature stood on the slab, dripping wet. His slimy, algae encrusted hair had lost none of its endearing features. A short ragged tunic did little more than give a modicum of modesty and the stunted legs with feet more like flippers were another surprise to Chaz.

A hiss from the creature jerked Chaz back to reality as the three goblins began to chant in a warbling intonation. The single eye of each of the three goblins changed from violet to orange. Not only did their eyes change colour, they began to grow brighter and then focused into three rays of light, which shone all around him and immediately and with a growing sense of alarm, he felt very drowsy.

Go with them, a voice inside his head ordered and Chaz, his mind all befuddled, found his legs moving without his say so. In a trance like state, he walked over to the goblins who had now stopped the chanting and whose eyes were now back to 'normal.'

The loud thud of a heavy door closing jolted Chaz back to his senses. He was in a cell like room carved out of rock with no other opening than that of the door. A clump of plant-lights fixed in a wall crevice was just enough to see

183

by. A pile of rushes was thrown in one corner, obviously for the bed. A clay jar containing some stale water and another larger one, empty, completed the room's furnishing.

What the hell have I got myself into this time? Chaz wondered, as he lay down in his wet clothes.

***

The cell door creaked open and as Chaz blearily looked up, a one-eyed apparition appeared in the doorway. 'God, I wasn't dreaming,' he muttered to himself, thinking he must have dropped off for a while.

The goblin fixed its eye on Chaz and began to chant. As before, the eye changed colour and a ray of orange light enveloped Chaz for a moment before being turned off.

'Come,' ordered a voice inside his head. Chaz stood, a glazed expression on his face and followed the one-eyed goblin through a series of tunnels with a stiff-legged gait which made him sway like a drunk. He was totally unaware of his situation.

The tunnel ended in a large chamber in which several peasants were working. Using picks, they were hacking into the rock at the far end. Others were carrying the quarried rock to a wicker basket, which had been lowered through a hole in the top of the chamber by a vine-rope. All the peasants had the vacant, stupefying look of those controlled by the one-eyed goblins.

Chaz was led into the chamber and handed over to a goblin 'supervisor' or guard. *Take this pick and join the others*, the mental voice ordered. Stumbling over the rocky floor, pick in hand, Chaz joined the group hacking the rock face. Like an automaton, he swung his pick.

33

Bryden jumped off his horse and ran down to the river. He had seen that a swirling eddy of current had brought some of the stain towards the riverbank. Reaching down, Bryden scooped up a handful and examined it closely. He even tasted it, though he immediately spat it out. 'It's not blood, thank God,' he shouted in a relieved voice. 'Though it sure looks like it.'

Bolyar Chaydar nodded and looked back up the river and said, 'I think this has something to do with Chaz and we ought to backtrack to see where this stain is coming from.'

'Sounds right to me,' Bryden said as he remounted his horse. 'Let's go.'

Borislav was leading, threading his way through a thicket of trees and shrubs. A deep feeling of concern for Chaz his new friend, was urging him on. He suddenly reined in his horse. The stain in the river had gone. How could it disappear just like that?

The others caught up with Borislav. 'What's up?' asked Zltan. 'Why have you stopped?'

Borislav pointed dramatically. 'The stain. It has gone.'

'I'll go and see where it is,' said Zltan. 'It was visible not too far back so I won't be long and there's no point in all of us going, is there?'

The horses were feeding and the others were stretching their legs when Zltan came trotting back a short time later. 'I found the stain,' he called out. 'It's just the other side of these trees. We missed the break because of the thick undergrowth. There's another river, smaller than this one across the other side. The stain is coming from there.'

'Well done.' Bryden was pleased that they had picked up the trail so quickly. Now all they had to do was cross this blasted river.

The ripples of white water just up river from where he

was standing gave Bryden pause for thought. He noticed one or two rocks jutting out of the water too. Going over to the edge of the riverbank, he could see that a ridge of gravel was exposed on the far side. He looked down at the river by his feet. Yes, there was a gravel bed on this side too.

'Everyone. Listen up. I reckon this stretch of the river is fordable. Bolyar Chaydar, would you go first. I trust you to find a way for us to follow.'

'You're too kind, Bryyyden,' the Bolyar replied with a smile and quickly mounting his horse, urged it down the riverbank into the river.

Bryden was proved right. The water only reached up to the horse's shoulders and they all crossed safely with just wet legs up to the thighs.

Pressing on as quickly as they could proved more difficult than they realized. This smaller river ran down a narrow but steep valley and they soon had to dismount and lead the horses by hand but they could still see traces of the red stain, which they took as a hopeful sign.

It was soon dashed. The river suddenly widened into a large pool situated at the base of a cliff, which rose up to merge into a big hill. As they approached the pool, the stain was seen to be bubbling up from its depths.

Iskra gave squeal. 'Look! Look! A boat.'
At the foot of the cliff was a dugout canoe, beached on the edge of the pool.

'That proves it,' cried Borislav. 'At least he or the whatever,' he paused for a moment, 'Brought Chaz this far.'

No one said a word.

'Yes,' Bryden said a few moments later in a worried voice. But what did *'he'* do next? There's no way we can go any further unless we can breathe under water. I'm assuming it's an underground river coming out here. He pointed to the pool. 'So there must be underground caves in there as well.'

Splash!

'What the hell was that?'

Everyone looked up and saw a small rock falling from the top of the cliff.

'Somebody's up there,' Zltan shouted, his hand clutching the hilt of his sword.

'Bolyars, follow me.' Bolyar Chaydar drew his sword and ran towards a path leading to the top of the cliff. 'Bring the horses if you can, Bryyyden.'

Before Bryden could move or say anything, the three armed Bolyars were halfway up the cliff.

'Come on Iskra. I'll lead three. You look after the others. OK,' urged Bryden.

Having to take a longer trail because of the horses, it was quite a while before they reached the top of the cliff and then they had to go higher still, up the hill to where they could see Borislav waving to them.

Bryden could have made a million guesses as to what they would find there and he would still have lost.

As he and Iskra crested the hill they saw an unbelievable sight. Mounds and mounds of small rocks were surrounding some sort of hoist. A wooden triangle of poles was perched over a hole in the ground. A pulley hung from the top of the hoist over which a vine rope was strung. One end of the rope was attached to a simple windlass fixed between two trees with suitable forks. The other end went down the hole.

Three dejected looking peasants sat on the ground guarded by a sword in the hand Zltan. Bolyar Chaydar and Borislav were looking at a small body sprawled on its back, blood seeping from a deep wound in its side.

'My God!' cried Iskra in astonishment, 'It's only got a single eye.'

'What happened and who is this?' Bryden asked, pointing to the body.

Bolyar Chaydar wiped his bloody sword with a handful of grass and said, pointing to the peasants.

'When we got here, those three were working for that one-eyed Goblin. They were under some sort of spell. They weren't speaking and they looked dazed as though they were half asleep. It was weird.'

It took some time but eventually one of the peasants became lucid enough to tell them about an underground complex controlled by the Vodynislav and his one-eyed goblins. He captured passing peasants using the lower river, taking them to be his slaves. Then the one-eyed goblins used their powers to take over the minds of their captives, making them into docile workers.

'My God, what a set up!' Bryden exclaimed. 'But how do the peasants get into the underground caves. The way in is blocked by the underground river.'

'The Vodynislav blows something into their mouths which makes them unconscious and somehow keeps them alive when he takes them underwater,' explained the peasant.

Further questions revealed that there was only one hand of goblins, (*five,* thought Bryden) helping the Vodynislav.

'Make that…' Bolyar Chaydar held up four fingers, pointing his sword at the dead body lying some distance away, the open wound already crawling with flies.

They also learnt that there were four hands of captured peasants trapped underground at that moment. Plus Chaz.

'What I don't understand,' said Iskra, who had been listening intently to the story, 'Is if the way into the caves is blocked by the river, how did the people get up here?'

'Through this hole,' replied the peasant, pointing to the hoist. Apparently each day the Vodynislav would swim out to the river via the pool in the big cavern, carrying with him a coil of thin vine rope. He would come up here, throw down the thin vine rope which a goblin would tie to the end of the heavy working vine rope. It didn't take long to thread the working rope though the pulley and back down to the cave below. It was just a matter then of hoisting up the guard goblin and the peasants one at a time in the basket by a group in the cave. At night the work rope was pulled back down. No on could possibly escape.

Bryden called Bolyar Chaydar over and had a quiet word

with him. The Bolyar nodded.

'We think,' said Bryden, 'That to rescue Chaz and possibly the peasants as well, some of us will have to go down into the cave. In fact Bolyar Chaydar, Zltan and me will be that team. Borislav, I know you want to go down but your arm is still not fully healed. However, you will have a big job to do up here. The hoist must be protected and when the time comes you and these three men will have to pull us up from the cave but first you have to let us down.'

'What about me,' cried Iskra, 'I want to go down as well.'

'Out of the question,' answered Bryden and Bolyar Chaydar together.

Iskra turned away furiously, walking towards her horse, and grabbing a piece of bread, began to chew vigorously. At least it stopped her speaking her mind. They might have got a shock otherwise.

Bryden turned to Borislav. 'Once we are all down, bring the basket back up here. Then they can't use it.'

Borislav nodded and calling to the peasant who had helped them, his name Stoyan, showed him how to hang the basket over the hole once they had removed the remaining rocks. A few minutes later, with the help of the other peasants, they began to lower Bolyar Chaydar sword in hand, into the cave below.

34

The one-eyed goblin guard was confused. He had been waiting for the empty hoist basket to come back down for ages. The slaves, including Chaz, had been working non-stop, hacking at the chamber wall with their picks and the pile of loose rocks was now considerable.

The clatter of small stones hitting the floor and a cloud of dust drifting down from the hole in the top of the chamber meant that the hoist was on its way down. Relaxing somewhat but still puzzled by the delay, the goblin sent a mental command ordering the slaves to stop using their picks and to get ready to load the basket. To save time and catch up with the backlog, it would be quicker to use them all, he thought.

The basket was mid-way between the top of the chamber and the floor when the guard realized there was somebody standing in it. Sensing a threat, it began to chant.

Bolyar Chaydar, holding himself steady with one hand on the hoist rope, sword in the other, heard the chanting and leaning over the side of the basket saw a one-eyed goblin staring up at him, the single eye pulsating and as he watched, begin to change colour.

Fearing the worst, his head already feeing dizzy, the Bolyar threw his sword like a spear at the goblin. Glinting in the dim plant-light, it missed the head and body but pierced one of its feet. Squealing in pain it fell to the floor of the chamber, the chant gone, eye normal.

A big sigh echoed round the chamber. The slaves and Chaz lost the dazed expression and rose from their hunched posture and standing upright stared at the screaming goblin.

A small peasant, with one arm hanging limply by his side, obviously broken, was the first to react. As the basket carrying Bolyar Chaydar settled onto the floor, he clambered over the pile of loose rocks and stooping to pick one up, rushed over to the moaning goblin and smashed the rock into the eye.

The cry of agony broke the spell and as one, the peasants scrambled to the top of the pile and began to throw lumps of rock at the writhing, screeching goblin. The Bolyar just managed to grab his sword before it was buried alive under a mound of rocks.

Chaz stood transfixed on a pile of rocks as he witnessed the horror going on before him, not realizing the significance of what had happened. Then to his amazement, he saw Bolyar Chaydar and then the chamber for the first time as a fully conscious person. He also felt for the first time the pain in his hands, the palms rubbed raw. Turning round, he saw a row of picks lying at the base of the chamber wall.

'What the hell's going on?' he said to the Bolyar, grimacing in pain. 'Why am I in here?'

With a sudden jerk, the hoist basket began to move upwards. Bolyar Chaydar came over quickly and explained to Chaz how he had been abducted by the Vodynislav and put under the spell of the one-eyed goblins. He went on to say that Bryden and Zltan would be down as fast as they could work the hoist.

A warning cry from one of the peasants made the Bolyar turn round. Eight vacant-eyed peasants waving picks, lurched into the chamber. A one-eyed goblin keeping well back was clearly controlling them.

'Arm yourselves,' roared the Bolyar as he rushed forward to block the way to the hoist. If they lost the use of it they were doomed. Two of the released peasants grabbed a pick each and scrambled to join him as he jabbed at the nearest 'zombie–like' peasant.

Chaz, with an 'Oh my God,' picked up several small rocks and began to throw at them. The two hits he made didn't even make them flinch. He had to stop when the two peasants reached Bolyar Chaydar and got in the way.

The 'zombie' peasant lifted his pick high over his head and the Bolyar smiled as he thrust his sword deep into the belly. Blood spurted out of the wound as he withdrew his blade. The pick came down as though he hadn't been touched and missed the Bolyar by a hairs breadth.

'By the Saints,' cried Bolyar Chaydar as he jumped back. 'What do we have to do to kill them?'

With the help of the two peasants, the Bolyar at least stopped the advance of the 'zombies.' They were slow moving and had no tactical sense. (Or their controller hadn't). Instead of separating, (they had the numerical advantage after all) they kept together as a group. But they were immune to pain and kept pushing forward.

'Hold fast,' a shout came from behind and Zltan appeared at Bolyar Chaydar's elbow.

And about time too,' said a relieved Bolyar.

'Agh!' One of the peasants helping them, collapsed to the floor, a pick sticking out of his head and a 'zombie' leant forward to yank it out.

With a cry to wake the dead, Zltan swung his sword so hard, it decapitated the 'zombie' in one stroke. The headless corpse spraying gore everywhere fell to the floor.

'Aim for the head and eyes,' shouted Bolyar Chaydar, as he put his words into practice, jabbing his sword point into the face of the next 'zombie' who fell to the floor, sightless.

Two more of the released peasants carrying picks came up and now aware of the limitations of the slow moving 'zombies,' it became a slaughterhouse. The blind were quickly dispatched and those that had suffered head injuries soon joined their brethren.

The controlling goblin didn't wait around when the last 'zombie' peasant was killed. When the two Bolyars went to the passage to deal with him he had gone.

'Do you want any help?' Bryden asked, tongue-in-cheek, having just arrived.

Bolyar Chaydar shook his head and wiped his brow. 'By the Gods, that was close.' He turned to Zltan. 'I owe you one. You showed us the way to fight the spirit people.'

Zltan shook his head. 'It was a lucky blow. It could just

as easily have been you.'

'Sorry to but in,' interrupted Brydon, 'But we need to make sure those little bastards that are left and their master are finished off for good. Otherwise they could start up again and not be stopped by anyone.'

Bolyar Chaydar led the way through the passage. Chaz, following slowly behind the others felt sick as he passed the unfortunate dead peasants. They had had no choice in the matter. They were all part of an unscripted play. Anything could happen.

The passage dipped downwards. 'I reckon this leads to the underground river or maybe to the large pool Stoyan told us about,' Bryden said quietly before adding, 'Don't you think we ought to slow down a bit? Those little devils might be waiting round the next corner for all we know.'

Bolyar Chaydar held up a hand and they all stopped. 'I agree. We are too eager. More stealth would be better.'

'Before we go any further,' Bryden said, 'What if we come across any of the one-eyed wonders? How do we avoid being made into a 'zombie' ourselves?'

Before anyone else spoke, Bryden answered his own question. 'It will all depend on you Chaz.'

'What! Why the hell me? I'm just a kid. What do I know about killing a one-eyed git?'

'Steady, Chaz. Steady. It might not mean you killing anyone. I'm thinking of us making a diversion and all you have to do is throw a rock in their faces.'

'Oh, just like that. Throw a frigging rock …. You must be off your flaming rocker, Uncle.'

'Chaz, Chaz. Think about it. You can throw better than any one of us. Anyway, what are the alternatives? we might, some of us, get out using the hoist. But what if they get control of some of us before that. What then? We have to destroy the lot of them first before they get a chance to get us.'

Chaz felt dizzy. He hadn't eaten for ages. The sights he had just witnessed would haunt him forever, never mind the gaze of his uncle and the others staring, staring at him. *God it wasn't fair. Jeez, he never wanted to come to this bloody country in the first place, had he?*

Then he thought of the lost hours when he was under their control. They could have made him do anything they liked and he couldn't lift a finger to stop them. Just like those poor sods sent to kill us.

Taking a deep breath, Chaz looked at his Uncle. 'OK. I'll try.'

Brynden went over and gave him a big hug. 'That's all I want you to do, Chaz. Try.'

Taking extra care, they began to creep along until they met a side passage. Stopping just before it, Bolyar Chaydar whispered that he was going to rush across the gap.

Chaz, feeling as nervous as hell, stood by the corner, gripping the two cricket-ball sized rocks tightly in his hands. He nodded that he was ready, one arm half raised.

Bolyar Chaydar stood up and ran across the gap. A flash of fear speared through him as he caught a glimpse of a goblin in the corner of his eye.

Chanting at a rapid rate, two goblins suddenly appeared from the side passage, their eyes beginning to glow orange.

Range twenty metres, roughly the length of a cricket pitch, go for the bails. A two-man run out. Chaz was in a dream world. One. Two. He let fly. Two squeals of pain, then two squelchy, squishy sounds.

Chaz woke from his dream and saw Bolyar Chaydar and Zltan pulling their swords from the eye socket of the two goblins, who writhed and jerked for a moment and then were still.

Chaz began to shake and then turned to the nearest wall and retched. Bent over he had nothing to bring up and he heaved again, the taste of bile in his mouth the worst thing he had ever experienced.

A pair of strong arms grabbed hold of him. It was Bolyar Chadar. 'I believe that you have saved us all from a fate of unimaginable terror. We now have the time to get rid of that monster Vodynislav.'

Zltan looked over and smiled as he held up his sword in a salute to Chaz.

Bryden walked up to Chaz and asked quietly if he was alright. When he got a nod, he turned to the others. 'We need to keep the pressure on – sorry.' He looked at the Bolyars. 'I meant to say that we must keep going. The Vodynislav could be making his escape even now.'

Zltan took the lead, moving as fast as he dared but with caution in mind. Chaz, holding his aching stomach struggled along as best he could at the rear.

In the dim glow of the plant-lights, Zltan saw the end of the passage outlined by the even gloomier cavern. The sound of a struggle made him warn the others to stop.

Bryden came up to Zltan and crouching down on all fours, they made their way to the end of the passage and gasped in astonishment at the Vodynislav and a one-eyed goblin having an argument not twenty metres from their position.

The Vodynislav was trying to get free from the grip of the goblin whose arms were wrapped round one of his stunted legs. A cuff by one of the web-like hands to the goblin's head finally made it let go. Staggering back, the goblin began to chant and the eye began to change colour.

Snarling and hissing, red eyes flashing with anger, the Vodynislav bent down and grabbing hold of the goblin's head, twisted hard. The loud crack of a breaking bone and the stifled squeal of pain came at the same time and the goblin's lifeless body, dangling like a doll, was thrown contemptuously into the pool. Then, on his flipper-like feet, the Vodynislav moved unsteadily towards the edge of the pool.

'The bastard's going to escape,' cried Bryden in dismay.

'Not if I can help it,' shouted Bolyar Chaydar and he threw his sword just as the Vodynislav prepared to dive into the pool.

The blade pierced the left arm and with a howl of pain

the Vodynislav fell into the water and disappeared, just a swirl of red tainted water indicating the spot where he had fallen in.

'Back to the hoist,' Bryden called out in an urgent voice, 'We have to catch him.'

35

The sound of fighting came up through the hole in the top of the cavern and Iskra, careful not to get too close, held onto one of the hoist supports and tried to see what was happening. Bryden had been gone some time and they were stuck up there without any idea of what was going on.

'The answer is still no.' Borislav was adamant.

Iskra stamped a foot in frustration. 'But I want to help.'

'I know but you're not going down there. It's too dangerous. Besides you'll only get in the way.'

'God! You men. I …' Iskra stormed off angrily towards the horses. Making a snap decision, she leapt on the first one, which happened to be Bryden's and rode down the slope to the cliff edge overlooking the large pool formed by the underground river deep below her.

The silence was a wonderful change from all that shouting and cursing coming up from the chamber. Sliding off the horse she sat down, the reins still in her hands and looked down for a while, idly thinking about the strange position she was in, stuck back in time but not in her real world. Would they ever get out of it she wondered. They seemed to blunder on from one crisis to another.

A splashing noise broke her reverie and moving closer to the cliff edge, she looked over. A gasp came from her lips as she saw a monstrous figure struggling in the water.

A head covered with slimy algae was bobbing in the water. It turned to look at the sky and she saw a greenish face before it turned round. The scaly skin of the body broke surface, one arm stretched stiffly by its side, blood oozing from a wound which left a trail of red ripples as the other arm frantically tried to make a swimming stroke in the water. A pair of stubby legs with flipper feet churned up the water but the creature was only making slow progress towards a dugout canoe, which lay directly below where she was sitting.

'The boat! It's going for the boat,' Iskra cried out in alarm. 'How can I stop it?' Looking around she saw Bryden's horse had a small reed basket tied to the saddle. Pulling herself up by the reins she patted the horse and reached up to the saddle and retrieved it.

It contained two clay pot grenades and unbelievably, a gas lighter. Hands trembling, Iskra took them out and put them on the ground, keeping hold of the lighter.

A quick peep over the cliff edge showed that the creature was almost at the boat. Examining the grenades she saw the fuses sticking out. It jogged her memory. *Chaz had been really excited when he had told her about the experiments with the gunpowder. He had never seen anything like it. He had told her how careful his uncle had been when lighting one of the grenades, something about doing it quickly.*

Holding a grenade in her best throwing hand, Iskra went to the cliff edge and gingerly looked over. 'Oh my God! It's getting into the boat.' Flicking the lighter, she held it to the fuse and immediately threw the grenade. It wasn't lit she knew it. *Damn and blast*, she thought, as she watched the clay pot smash to pieces in the front part of the boat, black powder everywhere.

The creature stopped pushing his dugout into the water for a moment and looked up before straining once more with its good arm and shoulder. The dugout shuddered and began to move again.

Iskra picked up the last grenade. It was up to her. She just knew it. So she lit the fuse. What she didn't know was how long it would take before it would blow up.

Leaning forward just enough to see over the cliff edge Iskra saw the creature scrambling into the boat. *It's got to be now* and with all the strength she could muster threw the grenade down towards the boat.

It exploded a couple of metres above it. The creature, having just left the shore was paddling furiously with one webbed-hand when he was torn apart by scores of flying shards of pottery. Then a spark from the explosion ignited the black powder scattered in the bow of the dugout, which then burst into flames. The burning pyre moving slowly in a half circle and beached itself not too far from where it started.

'Iskra! Iskra! What the hell do you think you are doing?' Bryden, running down the slope shouted anxiously, 'What was that explosion?'

Iskra just smiled and handed him his lighter.

36

The reunion of the remaining peasants was heart warming to see. As the last one climbed out of the hoist basket, he was welcomed with a hug amongst much back-slapping and relieved laughter. The atmosphere was also tinged with sadness for those lost for no other reason than being in the wrong place at the wrong time. The hoist was then destroyed, so hopefully the caves would never be used again for such diabolical purposes.

A last wave to the peasants and Bolyar Chaydar urged his horse forward. 'We need food and shelter and the only place near enough is the Monastery of St Jeorge. If we make good time we will reach it before the mid-day Angel bell.'

So they followed him in single file along a different track, one more suitable for the horses, although the terrain was still a series of short steep hills with narrow rocky valleys between them.

The bell tolled high above them. They hadn't made good time and the monastery's mid-day Angel Bell had been ringing for some time.

Chaz looked down the small valley. The river they had just crossed flowed towards an isolated hill whose sheer cliff-like sides forced it to pass on either side. Perched on the very top of the hill was the monastery. A tiny tower poked above the simple thatched roofs of the huts arranged perilously around it. The toll of the Angel bell coming from it suddenly ceased. *Not a bad place to put a castle,* he thought.

A steep, winding dirt track led up to the monastery. Half way up it they had to dismount and lead the horses on foot. At the top the monastery walls rose four or five meters high with just the odd tiny shuttered window opening near the roof level. A set of stone steps jutted out of the wall, going high up to the main door. *One slip and you're a goner*, thought Chaz when he saw them.

A young novice monk, still with a full head of hair, suddenly appeared from a gate at the end of the wall and spoke to Bolyar Chaydar.

'Leave your horse with young Dimiter. He'll take them to the stables. Take anything warm with you. You'll need it. (Chaz was glad that Borislav had looked after his 'Epirus' anorak when he was abducted). We go up these steps and as you can see, keep to the right. It's a long drop to the bottom.'

The doorway led into a courtyard. A long thatched hut at the far end with a tiny tower attached was obviously the church. Another novice monk came out of one of several small huts aligned in a row along the wall by the door. A slightly bigger hut finished the row. The other two walls had rows of even smaller huts butted up against them.

'Do they keep rabbits,' Chaz whispered quietly to Iskra, grinning at his own poor joke.

'You know very well that they are the monk's cells.'

The novice monk allocated them three wayfarers huts. The three Bolyars grabbed the first one, Bryden and Chaz the next. Iskra had Hobson's choice.

Each hut had just about enough room for three travellers so the Bolyars were glad that they were good friends. At least the straw was fresh and within minutes the whole party had crashed out.

The evening Angel Bell jolted them awake and the smell of hot food soon stopped Chaz from moaning about the noise. The big hut was the food hall. Two wooden refectory tables filled most of the room. They were the only travellers so the novice monks served out the main meal of fish and vegetable soup right away, with a hunk of bread each and a wooden beaker of watered wine.

The lack of regular meals during the last few days was very apparent by the speed at which they ate and the novice server got plenty of grins when he came round again with the soup pot.

Afterwards, Bolyar Chaydar had a word with Bryden. He was concerned about where they were going. A sacred ritual was due to take place in the next day or so. He wasn't exactly sure when and it was possible that they might be in danger from the followers of the Firebird.

Firebird! Chaz froze. He stopped talking to Iskra and turned to listen.

'The followers go into a trance. Some say they go to the spirit world and become possessed,' said the Bolyar in hushed tones.

Chaz started to snigger and stopped. *After what he had witnessed during the past week or so, maybe they do*, he thought.

'I suggest, he continued, 'That we make an early start in the morning.'

Bryden agreed and as they left the food hall to go back to their huts, Chaz gave the novice monk a huge smile and took three hunks of bread from the basket.

The novice monk was too surprised to protest.

37

'Not again!' Chaz stuffed a finger in each ear. It didn't do much good. This time it was a peculiar tapping noise. It sounded like someone was clacking two pieces of wood together. Then the bell clanged deafeningly as though it was in the same room. It seemed as though he had only been asleep for minutes since the last ding-dong. Then there was the blasted chanting that followed it. That went on seemingly for ages. Unable to suffer in silence, he got up. The sun was just about visible. 'Jeez, what time is it? Talk about the crack of dawn,' he mumbled, irritatingly.

Bryden looked over at his nephew and smiled from his bed of straw. 'Early morning services, Chaz. One at around 2am our time, the other at sunrise, it's part of their ritual. There are several more during the day as well,' he added.

'God! How do they do it? Sorry, I suppose I'd better watch what I say round here, hadn't I?'

A last stretch and Bryden stood up. 'Yes. I suggest that you do. Come on. I have organized an early breakfast and we don't want to be late. The best stuff will be gone.'

'What?' The mention of food galvanized Chaz and he hurriedly put on his trainers.

He need not have bothered. More fish soup and bread, though he had the option of honey to spread. A beaker of watery wine added to his culinary pleasure.

Nobody spoke during breakfast. Bleary-eyed faces testified that Chaz was not the only one to be disturbed by the bells and the chanting monks.

The novice monk met them at the bottom of the stone steps below the main doorway, holding the horses' reins. Each mount had a small reed basket of food tied to the saddle. Bolyar Chaydor was entrusted with a skin of beer.

When they were all mounted, he led the way down hill but not before throwing a small silver coin to the novice monk. The sun would have failed to compete in the brilliance of his smile of gratitude.

The morning was well gone when a cloud of dust warned of an approaching group of travellers coming their way.

They turned out to be merchants leading a string of packhorses. Four Bolyars were acting as guards. One at the front of the column reined in his horse, spear pointing and stared warily at them. Then he smiled and called out, 'Bolyar Chaydar. Greetings from your servant, Desislav.'

Bolyar Chaydar laughed and spurred his horse forward to meet an old friend. 'Desislav! You old rascal. What news do you have?'

'Not good. The cult followers of the Nevinarstvo are having their ritual ceremony at the Cave of Bats. Many of them are bewitched with the leaf brew of the Henbayne and are causing much trouble in that area. I advise you to take care.'

Much perturbed by this news, he was glad that Desislav was able to provide him with a sword to replace the one he had lost in the caves of the Vodynislav.

It was a contemplative party that resumed their journey.

The next rest stop came soon. The constant up-down nature of the terrain was especially tiring for the horses. Bolyar Chaydar took Bryden away from the others and said, 'My friend, I'm beginning to worry about where we are going. I think we are not going to the Great Lake?'

Bryden swallowed and coughed. *Caught with your pants down*, he thought.

'Well, I … er... It's difficult to explain,' he began. 'I'm not really sure myself.'

He looked around and scuffed the grass with a foot in embarrassment. He didn't want to lie but the truth …

'It was our intention to make our way to the Great Lake but to be honest with you I wasn't sure what we were going to do once we got there. However, that chance meeting with your Bolyar friend who told us about the Neva . . . Nevi ..'

'Nevinarstvo,' offered Bolyar Chaydar.

'Yes! The Nevinarstvo. That made me think. I now believe that we need to get to the bat cave as soon as possible.'

'What! That's impossible. They could kill us all. Once under the influence of the evil brew of the Henbayne, they stop at nothing.'

'Maybe if we sort of blend in …'

'I don't understand. You Epirusians are not very clear at times.'

'Sorry, I meant to say, what if we pretended to be like them. The cult followers.'

'Ah! But I have heard that they wear a white robe as part of the ceremony.'

'I see,' said, Bryden, thinking hard. 'Let's travel on a bit further and see how things go.'

By late afternoon they had passed small groups of white clad followers, many of whom were staggering along in some sort of daze, chanting a kind of incoherent mantra in time to the erratic beat of several unsteady drummers.

Bryden had already had a word with Chaz and Iskra. He had to warn them that from now on it could become very dangerous. It was essential, he emphasized, to be ready for anything.

So when Bolyar Chaydar held up a hand, the signal to stop, nerves began to jangle. He waved to them to come nearer. 'A hand and one are in front of us. We need to get some white robes and I say we strike now. This part of the track is quiet enough. Zltan has checked the rear and no one is in sight. – Borislav.'

'I have them,' he said, as he passed round enough wooden cudgels for each of them, including Iskra.

'We don't need to kill. They're half dazed with the evil brew so a knock on the head should be enough,' went on Bolyar Chaydar.

Chaz looked over at Iskra who raised her eyebrows and nodded. *Jeez,* he thought, *If she's up for it, I'd look a right twerp if I said I couldn't do it.*

'We ride up and as we overtake them, pick one and jump

off your horse and hit hard. Behind the ear is the most effective place,' continued Bolyar Chaydar. 'Is that clear.'

Everyone nodded.

They rode round the bend of the tree-lined track and saw the group. A lone drummer was beating a pathetic rhythm and the rest were lurching along in single file, chanting a monotonous phrase over and over.

It nearly went to plan. Chaz jumped down off his horse and rushed at his victim, cudgel raised. At the moment of contact the woman turned her head. He tried his best to stop the blow but only half succeeded. She fell screaming to the ground, holding the back of her head.

Chaz froze and stood there looking down at the woman he had just struck, his cudgel held by his side. He began to tremble, when a figure rushed up and pushed him aside. A cudgel rose and fell and a crunching sound came to his ears. The screaming stopped.

Borislav stood upright and patted Chaz on his shoulder and walked away.

The full-length white linen cloaks, for that was what they had acquired, made things easier. They just put them over their existing clothes. The hood was a big plus. They left the unconscious bodies by the side of the track. At least Chaz hoped they were all unconscious. He kept his eyes averted as they rode past, just in case he saw a bloody head bashed in beyond all recognition.

Iskra suddenly called out, 'I think we're near the village of Rabisha. Remember that little hamlet?'

Chaz rubbed his knee.

'That blasted fart of a goblin. I'll shove that stool right up his arse if I meet him again.'

'It wasn't a goblin. It was a Schopanyn, a house-guardian,' Iskra added.

Chaz just shrugged. His memories of the little people were not good ones.

Soon afterwards, hidden in a small glade in the middle of a wood overlooking a river, they enjoyed as best they could the remains of the meal provided by the monastery that morning.

They had seen and passed more and more cult followers. Not many rode horses, just enough not to make them stand out as strangers. The stupefied state most of them were in allowed them to pass without any problems anyway. It also meant that they were going in the right direction.

Zltan and Borislav stretched out beneath a large tree, dozing and keeping half an eye on the hobbled horses whilst Iskra and Chaz sat across the glade talking quietly. Bryden and Bolyar Chaydar returned.

'Would you believe it,' Bryden called excitedly. 'Just up there is the Magara Caves. I'm positive it is. Would you and Chaz go and have a look but keep under cover. There are hundreds, er, lots and lots of cult followers.'

He stopped and glanced at the Bolyar.

Bolyar Chaydar was giving him one of those, '*not Epirusian,*' looks again.

Iskra and Chaz agreed and were soon peering through the bush they were hiding under on the edge of the wood. Sure enough, at the top of the slope was the rock face of the Magura Caves.

The rough track they had walked on days before lay some distance from where they were and scores of white robed cult followers were climbing up the hill, about to join the throng of chanting followers already sitting there in semi-circular rows.

As the latecomers arrived, they were offered drinks from wooden goblets filled by young maidens dressed in white tabards and carrying goatskins full of the leaf brew, Henbayne.

Then Chaz spotted something he thought unusual. A line of followers were carrying armfuls of small logs which were laid in what appeared to be a pit of some kind made on the nearest area of flat ground to the cave.

Iskra gave a hiss of alarm. 'They're building a fire pit,' she whispered.

'What the hell for? It's not that cold,' Chaz muttered in amazement.

Iskra gave him such a look. 'It's probably for the ceremony. Come on. Let's go and tell the others.'

As they turned to go, a loud sigh came from the crowd of followers. Two white clad figures, each wearing a startling bright golden feather attached to his forehead by a black band, came out of the cave. They carried between them, on a sort of stretcher, a reed cage containing the most brilliantly coloured bird Chaz had ever seen.

Then he gave gasp of disbelief. He had seen one like it before in the Magura Cave what seemed like ages ago. It was the spirit bird known as the Firebird. The same Firebird! It was impossible but it was there right in front of him. *Bloody hell.*

The glittering bird, eyes sparkling, hopped about inside the cage as it was carried to a small mound overlooking the fire pit on which a stone pedestal had been erected. As the cage was gently placed on the pedestal, a hush fell over the watching throng.

Then, from the cave came the sound of a drumbeat. Quietly at first, a steady rhythmic pulsating echo merged with the heart-beats of the faithful. As the speed of the beat increased, the crowd rose as one and began to sway in unison to the rhythm.

A flicker of movement at the cave entrance went unnoticed by the swaying crowd. Three naked Shamens covered in white chalk, with five golden feathers fixed to their foreheads by a black band had emerged. They stood still for a moment before slowly approaching the pedestal supporting the caged Firebird, with arms outstretched.

Fingertips touching, they began to chant. A roar came from the swaying throng and they too began to chant. The drum beat increased, faster and faster. Then stopped.

Silence.

Turning round, the Shamens flaunted their nakedness and hands held high, intoned in unison a deep nasal droning sound. It was a signal to sit. Without a murmur and only the rustle of robes to indicate movement, the throng sat down in their semi-circular rows.

Then the Shamens bowed to the crowd and with stiff–legged gait went back to the cave.

A flurry of activity on the far side of the cave entrance turned out to be the young maidens, each carrying a reed basket full of Henbayne infused cooked meat. They then proceeded to walk between the seated rows, handing out to the cult followers, an offering from the basket.

A second group of maidens followed with goatskins of the Henbayne leaf brew, making sure that everyone partook of it.

During the consumption of the offering, a hand of young boys, wearing loincloths and powdered with chalk dust, began to light strips of cloth ready soaked in pine resin which had been pressed between some of the logs that completely filled the fire pit.

Soon plumes of smoke began to drift over the area as the fire caught and the naked Shamens came out and stiff-legged, walked to stand in front of the Firebird where they were each presented with a wooden goblet of Henbayne leaf brew, which they promptly drank.

The Shamens quickly formed a circle and as their eyes glazed over, they began to intone the sacred words of the Nevinarstvo cult.

The drum began to beat a short, sharp rhythm.

As though a switch had been turned on, the front row of followers stood, throwing off their white robes. They were naked underneath and chanting in unison, shuffled in single file to the fire pit. Then the first one in the line began the fire dance, a series of arm-waving gestures, head bobbing and body swaying, all accompanied to the chanting and the beat of the drum. The line grew longer and louder as the followers danced around the fire pit, now blazing furiously, flames and sparks shooting high into the air.

Chaz tugged Iskra's sleeve. 'God! What a sight. No one

would believe me in a million years if I told them about this. Come on let's get the others.'

38

Bolyar Chaydar asked Zltan to check that the horses were hobbled securely. The last thing he wanted was to return and find out that they had gone.

Chaz then led the way in the gathering gloom of evening to the place from where he and Iskra had been watching the cult followers.

Following the smell of burning wood and the sound of chanting made it much easier for Chaz to find the bush he had used earlier that day. It was now practically dark but the dying flames of the fire pit highlighted the dancing figures, still chanting their way around the fire pit. Though the voices were sounding a little ragged, the dancers still seemed strong enough for many more circuits. *It must be an awfully strong drug,* he thought.

Bryden and Bolyar lay together side by side under the bush. *It was time to put his cards on the table,* thought Bryden. *And he wasn't looking forward to it either.*

'We have to take that bird into the caves,' he whispered to the Bolyar.

'What!' The Bolyar half sat up in amazement. 'Take the bird down. Are you mad, Byyyden? Look at that crowd. They would throw you into the fire and pile more wood on top.'

'I know. I know. But we have to do it. We have no choice.'

The Bolyar strained to see Bryden's face. A look would tell him if it was true but it was too dark.

Hell, thought Bryden, *How do you explain that you're from the future without sounding mad?*

Bryden patted his ally and friend. *Yes, friend,* he thought. *After all they had gone through during the last few days, he deserves that.*

'The truth. Bolyar Chaydar. I'll tell you the truth. We are

___

211

here because we broke a spell. It was an accident but we broke it, Chaz, Iskra and me. Look at our clothes, the way we speak. We understand each other but I often use strange words that we say are Epirusian but they are not. We did not want to lie to you and your friends Bolyar Chaydar but how could we explain our position without sounding mad. That is why we said we were from Epirus. To get back home we need to take the bird back into the caves. Whether we can make the spell work for us I don't know but we have this one chance. I hope the Great Bolyar Chaydar will help us.'

Bryden paused and wiped his brow. *God! He was sweating like a pig.*

Rolling over onto his side, the Bolyar could just make out the outline of Bryden. He wished he could see his face. However, he had led many, many men and found that the voice of a man telling the truth didn't waver and Bryyden's voice hadn't wavered. A maajik spell he could understand.

He made his decision.

'We have fought together and I have seen you help the unfortunate. I think you are an honest man Bryyyden. I will help you as will your friends Zltan and Borislav.'

On the other side of the bush Chaz gave Iskra a nudge and whispered, 'Did you hear that?' Even though he couldn't see her he sensed her nod.

The drumbeat changed to a slow intermittent thud and Bryden looked through the screen of leaves his bush was providing and saw that the dancers, bodies streaked with ash and sweat had withdrawn to one side of the fire pit.

Thud! Thud! Thud! The slow beat of the drum echoed in the air. Suddenly the Shamens broke the circle with a screeching cry. Arms held aloft they stood, waiting.

A droning wail came from the cave. Then a white clad figure with three golden feathers fixed to his forehead appeared, playing a gajda bagpipe.

Two chalk-dust covered boys on their hands and knees, carrying the sacred tupan (drum) made from wolf skin fixed

212

to a harness on their backs, came into view. The drummer's naked body, streaked with white and with four golden feathers fixed to his forehead, was holding a long double-headed stick, one end larger than the other. It was padded with a piece of cloth and he pounded out his slow hypnotic beat.

When they were in position on either side of the caged Firebird, facing the fire pit, the rhythm changed. A faster, more vibrant pulsating sound mingling with the eerie drone of the gajda bagpipes infected the Shamens. They began to writhe and shake, heads held back, eyes rolled up to show only white orbs. Froth dribbled down their chins. In this trance state, unintelligible sounds issued from grimacing mouths as they called upon the fire spirits

Then with uplifted arms, they walked into the fire pit, now a bed of red embers. A groan of ecstasy came from the watching followers and they began to clap and sway in time to the drumbeat and the wailing bagpipe.

The Shamens crossed the fire pit unscathed and were met by a group of maidens who wrapped each of them in a white robe and presented them with a goblet of Henbayne leaf brew to drink. Carrying the goblets with two hands held aloft, they went to pay homage to the caged Firebird.

Pipe and drum stopped.

The Shamen formed a circle and touching goblets, drank. Throwing the empty goblets aside, they dropped to their knees, arms outstretched, heads bowed.

The sacred drum spoke. Three slow beats and the gajda bagpipe began to play. The Shamen slowly stood and waited.

The sacred drum sounded again, faster, demanding action. The incessant beat became hypnotic and the Shamen began to dance, spinning, swaying bodies and heads twisting one way then the other, arms and legs gyrating. All the time the never-ending wail of the pipes droned on and on.

Dancing towards the fire pit the Shamens began to chant,

turning at the last moment to go around it. Pausing just long enough to throw off their white robes. The followers swaying and clapping to the frantic beat, linked up with the whirling Shamen. Soon the whole mass of the Firebird cult was involved in a frenzy of chanting and dancing round the fire pit.

'Come on,' whispered Bryden, though with all the row coming from the top of the hill he needn't have bothered. 'Now's our chance.'

39

Bolyar Chaydar crawled through the bushes, the others not too far behind and stopped. There just in front of him was the Firebird in its cage on top of the pedestal. The persistent beat of the drum and the wail of the bagpipe from either side of it were deafening at this close range. It had been agreed earlier that he would attempt the snatch. If successful they would all rush to the caves.

From behind the mound the Bolyar looked past the two sweating musicians to the fire pit. The Shamen and the Firebird cult were still chanting and dancing around it like the frenzied people they were. Crouching low, he crept forward and grabbing the Firebird's cage, ran unnoticed back to the bushes. He handed the cage over to Borislav.

The problem now was to enter the cave unseen. That meant passing the fire pit and the entire dancing cult. They had one good advantage, two if you counted the drugged state of the cult followers. Away from the fire pit it was dark. So keeping to the edge of the cliff face, which fortunately offered plenty of cover with the tall bushes growing along its base, they reached the cave entrance. Inside a handful of rushlights made it possible to see where they were going.

'Blast,' exclaimed an exasperated Bryden, 'I forgot about the lights.'

'Hang on.' Chaz stopped by several piles of stuff obviously brought by some of the cult followers. Beer skins, some empty and smelling strongly of Henbayne lay beside a couple of discarded white robes and some reed baskets, all empty except for one, which was full of rushlights.

'Well done Chaz.'

Then before Bryden could say anything else, the Firebird gave out an almighty cackle, then again and again. It was an echo but sounded just as loud.

'Jeez, shut the bugger up,' Chaz shouted as he felt a shiver of fear run up his spine. 'Those nutters will be here before you can say Jack Robinson.'

Borislav nodded and putting the cage down went over to the pile off discarded items and using his knife, cut a large piece of cloth from one of the robes, with which he covered the birdcage.

Bryden held up a hand. They heard nothing for a moment. The drumming and bagpipe had stopped. Then faint sounds of shouting and howls of rage could be heard.

'I suggest that we get down to the other caves as quickly we can. Iskra, grab one of those lit rushlights please and then lead the way. Chaz, bring that basket of rushes as well.'

The dark passage into the caves sloped down and began to narrow and twist before becoming even steeper and the stones and small rocks littering the floor made walking difficult. This was not helped by the fact that the smoking rushlight that Iskra was carrying was not giving out enough light for the ones at the back to see where they were going, so Bryden had two more lit. Progress became much faster.

Iskra stopped.

'What's the matter?' Bryden asked.

'The bat cave is just ahead. I thought I had better warn you.'

A groan came from behind Bryden. Borislav coughed and said, 'This place is not what I expected. Man to man I fear no one but here I can sense the spirits and they are not happy.'

He went on, 'Maybe it's because I've covered the birdcage to stop it making any noise. The bird can't see where we're taking it and it is afraid.' (A snigger, quickly smothered came from Chaz, helped by a big dig in the ribs from Iskra's elbow). Borislav pushed his way to the front where they could all see him and the white cloth covered birdcage he was carrying.

'Well,' said Bryden, 'I've heard of the sixth sense before

but I have never met anyone with it. One thing I do know is that Borislav is a man of honour and we should heed his words … Borislav.'

The cloth was removed in one swift movement and a sudden radiant light emanating from the cage immediately dazzled everyone for a few moments before the eyes adjusted to it.

'Jeez! I don't believe it,' cried Chaz in amazement. 'That's what I call cool.'

The Firebird hopped and chirruped, its eyes flashing like diamonds in the sun, adding to the spectacle.

'It's so, so beautiful,' Iskra said, her arms hugging herself tight in pure delight.

Borislav and Zltan just looked at each other and smiled as though sharing a wonderful secret.

It was Bolyar Chaydar who brought them down to earth. 'I think I can hear some of the cult followers. They can't be too far behind us.'

'Lead the way then,' Bryden said to Borislav. 'With your special light we will have no problems following you.'

'Don't forget the bats,' warned Iskra.

For some unknown reason the bats didn't stir. As they crossed the large chamber Chaz forced himself to look up. He had after all, got bad memories of this place and he saw hundreds, maybe thousands of sleeping bats hanging down from the roof of the cavern, clearly visible in the light emanating from the Firebird's cage. He nearly slipped as he tried to catch up with the others. *God,* he thought, *the blasted droppings. They're just the bloody same.*

There was a jam up ahead at the end of the passage and Chaz called out, 'What's the trouble?'

'Come and see,' replied Iskra.

It was the Hall of the Stalactites and Stalagmites. Borislav held up the firebird's cage and even its radiance failed to reach the far side of the huge cavern. The magnificent columns, some as thick as pillars, others like dangling ropes shimmered and shone as the calcified rock reflected the brilliant light of the Firebird.

A path of sorts zigzagged down to the floor some twenty metres below them but of course there was no handrail.

Borislav went first. He had the light. The rest went down slowly, some better than others. Chaz unsurprisingly, went last.

Both Bryden and Iskra felt strangely excited although they had not said anything to each other. What was before the new cave, was now only a few metres away. What would they see?

Of course there was no path as such in this time period so Iskra had to guess how far to go before turning to the side of the cavern. Winding in and out of the stalagmites with Borislav just behind her holding the radiant Firebird's cage up high, its light formed a series of shadows as they passed the bigger columns. One particular stalagmite, taller than a man but three times his girth, made Iskra stop when she reached it. 'This is one I remember. We turn here,' she said confidently.

It was just a matter of finding the side of the cavern and soon they were all examining it for the fissure that led to the cave they were seeking.

'What about this one?' Zltan said, pointing to a large crack.

This one looks promising, thought Bryden. *A couple of others proved to be nothing more than that. Cracks.*

'Can you bring the cage a little closer?' he asked.

Borislav obliged.

'Yes,' said Bryden, bending down a little. 'This fissure definitely goes deeper into the rock and it's just about wide enough for me to get through I would say.'

A shout from the other end of the cavern made everyone turn. 'The cult followers,' Chaz cried, 'We'll all be killed!'

'Stop it Chaz,' Bryden snapped. 'It's no time for talk like that. Pull yourself together.'

Chaz blushed. *What the hell made him say that?* He looked at Iskra but she looked away, embarrassed.

Borislav pushed the birdcage into Bryden's hands. 'You take this Bryyyden and make your maajik.'

Bolyar Chaydar nodded in agreement and said, 'We will protect you. Go.'

Bryden was overwhelmed but realized they had no choice.

Thinking quickly, he said, 'Chaz give those rushlights to Borislav. They are going to need them once we go with the bird. He turned to Bolyar Chaydar. 'A last favour my friend. Can you Bolyars block this crack with those, he pointed to the floor, which was scattered with assorted sized rocks. 'Just in case.'

The Bolyar nodded knowingly.

Then Iskra went to Bolyar Chaydar, pulling a small object out of her bag, her torch.

'A bit of Epirusian maajik for you. Push this here.' She showed him as the torch came on. 'Push again it goes out.' The Bolyars gasped in amazement. Then to her surprise Borislav and Zltan bent down and began to pick up some of the loose rocks.

Bolyar Chaydar smiled as he took the torch and said, 'We have plenty of maajik here too.'

Iskra aware of the lack of time, added quickly, 'The maajik will only last part of a day so use it carefully.'

More shouts came from the end of the cavern so Bryden gave each of the Bolyars a big hug of thanks before picking up the birdcage.

Not knowing what to do, Chaz shook hands and added a pat on the back for Borislav who responded by giving him a slap on his back. Chaz then stood back feeling quite emotional. Iskra stepped forward and gave each Bolyar a kiss on the cheek as tears formed and ran down her face.

'We have to go,' Bryden said quietly to Iskra and Chaz.

He turned to the Bolyars.

'Farewell my friends. May your spirits protect you,' he said, his voice cracking with emotion.

Then, 'God! I nearly forgot. The lights. He felt in one of

219

his pockets and pulled out his gas lighter.

'Zltan, another bit of Epirusian maajik for you. Pass me one of those rushlights please.'

Perplexed, Zltan picked up one of the rushes.

'Watch what I do, Zltan,' Bryden clicked and lit the lighter, then the rushlight, which he jammed into the rock face.

Zltan, smiling broadly took the lighter and clicked it. He nearly dropped it when it lit up. Still beaming he waved his hand about, the gas flame flickering.

'No, No,' Bryden said. 'Only light it for a moment or the maajik will not work.' *I wish I had more time to explain this,* he thought.

40

Bolyar Chaydar made his way back through the maze of stalagmites as best he could towards the cavern entrance. He had hoped that the maajik light given to him earlier by Iskra would make it easier for him.

However, when he tried to use it, he flinched at the brightness and dropped it. He tried to make it work again but the maajik had gone, *maybe because he wasn't an Epirusian.*

A flicker of rushlights being waved at the top of the zigzag path helped point the way. With one hand held out in front of him to avoid bumping into the smaller columns, he made slow progress. The bruised big toe proved it was not always a successful strategy.

Approaching the bottom of the zigzag path he stumbled over the body of a cult follower. The screeching cry that they had heard earlier was probably this one falling off it.

The waving lights at the top were sufficient for him to quietly and safely climb up but dim enough to keep him hidden from anyone looking down.

The cult drummer was still half-drugged. He was seeing double most of the time and his head was pounding with an incessant throbbing. With a clear head he might have even appreciated the beat. He had another look over the edge of the path. It was too dark to see anything anyway. Then he began to sway, the two rushlights spluttering in his hand. Two lights. He looked again and saw one. Shaking his head, he went back to the passage where the piper was leaning drunkenly against the wall, his rushlight ready to fall out of his unsteady hand at any moment.

Why was he here, the drummer wondered. He went to stand next to the piper, fixing his light into a crack in the wall, the long double-headed drumstick a welcome leaning post. A sound made him look up and he saw two fuzzy men holding swords coming towards him. 'Hey!' he shouted to the piper, as well as giving him a nudge, 'We're being attacked.'

A wicked gleam came into the piper's eyes as he straightened up. His other hand held a long bladed knife. Throwing down his rushlight he uttered a loud shriek and rushed at Bolyar Chaydar.

The shrieking madman leapt and the Bolyar calmly stepped aside and thrust his sword between the ribs. Eyes suddenly bulging, the piper gave a gurgling cry and a spout of blood shot out of his mouth. Dropping his knife, the piper grasped his chest, trying in vain to stop the blood which, oozing through his fingers dripped to the floor as he staggered two more steps before plunging over the edge of the path, twenty metres to the bottom, where he joined his fellow follower with a bone crunching thud.

The drummer hefted his double-ended stick. In the dim light it was difficult for him to choose which one of the two to attack first. Swinging his heavy stick he rushed forward to the other side of the Bolyar as though he was standing in that position.

Clever, thought the drummer. *A quick mover too.* He swung round and raised his large drumstick over his head and gave a gasp of pain. His left hamstring was cut. As his leg gave way and he collapsed to the floor, he saw a swordsman looking down at him. *Only one. Where has the other one got to?*

The naked drummer lay sprawled out on the floor, blood seeping from his wound. Taking a step forward, the Bolyar placed a foot on the drummer's groin and pressed down. A squeal of pain ended almost before it began as a sword thrust pierced the heart.

The sound of footsteps coming from behind made Bolyar Chaydar twirl round, sword at the ready. Borislav and Zltan came up to him from out of the darkness. Are there any more ready for a fight they asked him.

'Maybe,' replied Bolyar Chaydar, 'We'll find out soon enough. Did you finish the blocking alright?'

Zltan and Borislav nodded together and the three friends turned to go back into the passage that led to the way out, grabbing the rushlight on the way, swords out, just in case.

41

Chaz eased his way through the fissure and stumbled into the narrow passage right after Iskra. As he did so, he heard the ominous sound of rocks being placed in the opening behind him. One way or another they were now trapped. He tried not to think about it as he followed the others.

Thanks to the Firebird there was no problem in seeing where they were going. They came to the 'staircase' or irregular 'steps' in the narrow passage that made walking difficult, especially going down.

The small chamber was reached fairly quickly but as Bryden stooped to enter it he let out a gasp of astonishment. 'They're back,' he said in a shocked tone. 'I didn't expect this.'

Chaz crowded Iskra to get a better look. He saw that the back walls of the chamber had a similar series of cave-paintings as before. In fact he would swear that they were the same.

Bryden was sure that they had only been made recently. They were so pristine. He went over to check, first putting the Firebird's cage on the floor, its light illuminating the small chamber quite adequately, and found two small clay pots on top of the large boulder (which he remembered contained a mixture of red ochre). 'I say Iskra.' He held up one of the pots. 'Come and look at these. I reckon that this is the inner sanctum of the Firebird cult and the artist of these paintings went out to join the party. What do you think?'

Iskra moved round Chaz who was still blocking her way and had a closer look at the wall paintings and the clay pots. She sniffed one and nodded her head. 'It's got to be that Bryden. Nothing else makes sense. You were right all along. The Professor will not be happy at losing what he thought was a new collection of prehistoric cave paintings.'

'That's if we get back,' Chaz reminded them.

'Well, we need to get ready,' Bryden said, casually lifting up the birdcage and placing it on top of the large boulder, knocking the clay pots over. They rolled off, smashing to pieces on the floor.

'Oops, sorry about that.'

Maybe it was the change of position, whatever it was, the radiant firebird started to chirrup and hop about the cage.

Iskra looked at it for a moment and then said, 'I think it knows where it is.'

Chaz gave a loud laugh, 'How the hell do you know that. It's just a bird.'

'Its more than a bird, Chaz. It's a Firebird,' she said heatedly. It's a spirit bird.'

'Oh my God, don't start that again. Spirit bird, bloody hell. What next, spirit dogs. Heh. Heh.'

'Haven't you learned anything, Chaz? What about how we got here? What about the water sprite that healed your hand or the little house guardian? The man-vamps. Do you want me to go on?'

Chaz felt his face go red. *Who was he trying to fool? He was in denial and he knew it. There was no rational explanation. What was that saying he had read somewhere? Remove the possible and the impossible remains. God, he was going nuts.*

He looked over at the Firebird. It was here. It was real and it was maajikal, a spirit with magical powers. He'd witnessed it.

He groaned aloud, 'It's not fair,' he whispered, 'I'm not clever enough to understand all this,' and he began to sob, his shoulders shaking.

A pair of warm arms wrapped round him and held him tight. Iskra whispered into his ear, 'It's alright, Chaz, it's alright, Chaz. You've been through hell and back during the past few days. Think about how you helped those poor people in the fortress. You spent days doing that and you never complained. Remember how you learned how to ride a horse. You couldn't sit down properly for days, thinking no one would notice. I did and I thought how well you coped and don't forget how you helped to destroy the one-eyed goblins, all of those things.

You're a brave and considerate man, Chaz, but you aren't ready to admit it yet. Your jokes are just camouflage aren't they?'

Chaz sniffed and looked at her. 'Yes,' he mumbled and suddenly became aware that he liked being in her embrace. He felt her tremble before she gave him a quick kiss and let go of him.

Bryden had tried not to notice what was going on but of course it was impossible not to overhear what was said. A sudden rush of love for his nephew passed through his bones. *I should have tried to look after him better*, he thought. *God forgive me if he comes to any harm.*

A chirrup from the birdcage jerked him back to the present. The Firebird was hopping to and fro, stopping now and then to bite the cage bars.

'Bryden.'

He turned to Iskra, 'Yes.'

'I think it wants to get out.'

'You know, I think you're right.'

'Chaz, come over here please. We will have to do everything that happened in reverse. I mean exactly. Does that make sense to you two?'

Iskra and Chaz both nodded in agreement.

Then Iskra opened her bag, saying, 'I'd better get our feather out now before you release the bird.' She rummaged inside it for her clamshell glasses case.

'Thank God it's still here,' she said opening the case and taking out the little plastic bag containing the feather. 'What would have happened if we had lost it?'

'Don't even think about it,' Bryden replied anxiously. His nerves were beginning to jangle.

He gave a quick look round. 'Are you ready?' Bryden's voice cracked with the tension he was feeling. *God, would it work, or were they being bloody fools in believing in thirteenth century magic spells when in a moment or two, they watch a blasted so called magic bird walk or fly out of it's cage and nothing happens. They'd be up the Swanee River without the proverbial paddle.*

'Chaz. Up onto the boulder. Iskra, you hold onto a leg.'

Scrambling up, Chaz made sure not to knock the cage containing the agitated Firebird resting on the edge. The tiny feather was clenched in his right fist.

Bryden eased himself to one side of Iskra, who by now was holding onto Chaz's leg. He opened the cage door, immediately grabbing hold of Chaz round the waist as he did so.

The Firebird poked its head out of the door and twittered, then flew out of the cage and made one circuit around the chamber, fluttering like a giant firefly before flying up to the fold in the rock face and perching in it.

Immediately it landed, a halo of light surrounded the Firebird, its own radiance swallowed up by a dazzling array of iridescent, kaleidoscopic patterns of colour, which began to expand wider and wider.

'The feather Chaz! The feather!' The urgent cries of his Uncle got through to Chaz who had been unable to move, frozen by the dazzling, hypnotic effect of the shimmering light.

Squinting, eyes half closed, Chaz reached up with his right hand and pressed the tiny feather onto the Firebird's tail. The halo flashed a deep red and began to flicker and shimmer, then streams of dazzling light flowed down the rock face, turning into a cloud of glittering golden feathers, which enveloped them in a ghostly presence, whose ethereal essence embraced them for what seemed an eternity.

***

It was dark, quite cold and damp. Chaz rolled over onto his back. 'Is any one here,' he called nervously.

'My God is that you Chaz? Iskra are you alright?'

Bryden's excited voice echoed somewhat. *We must still be in the cave*, he thought.

'Just a minute Bryden, I think I have a book of matches in my bag,' Iskra replied. 'Yes, I'm ok.'

A match struck and they all looked at each other.

'Jeez, we made it,' shouted a much-relieved Chaz, as he took his hand out of a piece of sticky Barista. It must have been at least two weeks old. He looked up and saw the painted prominent tusks of the wild boar, higher still, in the fold of the rock face … the match went out.

***

The car park was empty except for one old taxi. 'Well I suppose beggars can't be choosers,' Bryden said cheerfully. 'Come on, let's get you to Belogradchik, Iskra,' and they walked over to the taxi.

A blackened and twisted toothed smile turned to greet them. 'Allo agin, I take you quic, yes.'

The face of Chaz had to be seen to be believed.

6334832R00128

Printed in Great Britain
by Amazon.co.uk, Ltd.,
Marston Gate.